GW00375151

TH_ _

The picture of Hitchin Market painted in 1840 by Samuel Lucas and now hanging in the Council Chamber of the North Herts District Council has inspired local author, Edgar Newman, to write *The Quack* a novel which features many of the seventy characters portrayed on its crowded canvas.

Prominent among these is 'Doctor' William Mansell who had spent his early years as a surgeon's mate aboard a man-of-war and as a medical officer to a whaling fleet before setting himself up as a doctor in Hitchin about 1820. He had no degree in medicine, no surgery and no pony and trap but he had got a tall hat and a professional frock coat. For a time he prospered and was very popular as an accoucheur or male midwife.

The novel is written around him and his life and times in the early part of the nineteenth century when poverty was prevalent, dirt and disease general and the practice of medicine primitive. Even duels, although prohibited by law, still occurred, stage coaches were occasionally stopped and robbed, murder was not uncommon and coiners plied their nefarious trade despite the frightful penalties imposed on those caught at it. The Mansell of this story, and it is a story, becomes involved with the town and country folk taking part in these misdeeds and in doing so meets up with, among others, Joseph Lister, the surgeon, Henry Bessemer, the inventor, and Henry Hawkins, the noted advocate and judge, all of whom lived for a time in Hitchin and became famous in later life.

THE QUACK

EDGAR NEWMAN

Castlemead
PUBLICATIONS

WARE

First published in 1990

CASTLEMEAD PUBLICATIONS
Swains Mill, 4A Crane Mead, Ware
Herts., SG12 9PY
Proprietors: Wards Publishing Services

ISBN 0 948555 27 0

© Edgar F. Newman

The cover photograph of Dr Mansell and title page painting by Samuel Lucas Senior 'Hitchin Market' c 1840, are reproduced by kind permission of Hitchin Museum

British Library Cataloguing in Publication Data
Newman, Edgar F. (Edgar Frank) *1913 –*
    The quack.
    I. Title
    823.914 [F]

    ISBN 0-948555-27-0

Phototypeset by Input Typesetting Ltd, London
Printed and Bound in Great Britain by
The Bath Press, Avon

For Patricia, my wife, with my love

*Without her encouragement this book
would never have been written*

Foreword

There is far more of fiction than of fact in this book. The old North Hertfordshire town of Hitchin does of course exist and Samuel Lucas, the Quaker brewer and artist, did paint in the early 1840s a large picture of its busy Tuesday market scene, but the happenings in and around the town as related in this novel are only fabrications and are certainly not part of the town's history.

The late Reginald Hine, solicitor and local historian of considerable repute, styled the Lucas painting as being an historical item of great value because, he writes, 'every one of the seventy figures on its crowded canvas is a studied portrait as Lucas's sketch books show.' It hung for many years on the wall above the halfway landing of the main staircase in the Hitchin Museum and it provided me with the idea for this book.

In the left foreground of the picture the quack doctor, William Mansell, is shown attending to a tumour on a girl's head. Behind him the town's sporting squire, Frederic Peter Delme-Radcliffe, is conversing with his brother, the rector of the nearby Holwell village. Gypsy Draper is centrally placed with his family and their donkey. John Hawkins, the town's formidable lawyer, is also there together with some others I have taken to people my pages. Not one of those portrayed on the canvas has been featured as a rogue. This, then Quakerish, town did not breed rascals and the scoundrels who do appear are quite definitely figments of my imagination.

Mansell, the Quack, was not, I earnestly believe, quite the drink-sodden charlatan of Hine's short study in his *Hitchin Worthies*. There was an elderly lady who, on the book's publication in 1932, sought out the author and threatened to belabour him with her umbrella for so maligning her grandfather. I too have reason for presenting Mansell in a different light from that shed upon him by Hine.

He was, so I have been told, my own grandfather's great grandfather!

Therefore to please myself in writing this novel I have endeavoured to make Mansell a much more acceptable forbear!

EDGAR NEWMAN

Hitchin

September 1989

Contents

PART TWO 1847

PART THREE 1857

Painting of Hitchin Market

Edward Clisby, the chemist and his man
Kefford, the fishmonger
Dr William Mansell and some patients
Croft, the herbalist
Gascoigne, the butcher with his stall on wheels
Margaret Lucas, a Quakeress
Gypsy Draper and his family with their donkey
Isaac Newton, painter and decorator
Dr Oswald Foster MRCS
John Ransom, Quaker farmer
William Lewin, another butcher
F. P. Delme-Radcliffe, the Squire
The Reverend Delme-Radcliffe, Rector of Holwell Village
Dr Niblock, the schoolmaster
William Lucas, Quaker farmer and brewer
Samuel Allen, a Quaker of the Peace Society
John Mayne?
John Hawkins, lawyer of Portmill Lane
J or CW Wilshere
Mrs John Hawkins and mother of Henry Hawkins
Mr and Mrs Mason, poulterers
Ann Lucas, another Quakeress
Mr Cherry from Pirton Village
Edward Burr, miller of Charlton Hamlet
Charles Kingsley, farmer
Thomas Hailey, farmer
John Whiting Quaker fellmonger
Mrs Baker
Joseph Lucas, Quaker
Richard Oakley J.P.
Jack French, the carrier
Betsy Beadle, the housekeeper
Jack, the huntsman
R. Hawkins, the barber

together with poultry dealers, pig dealers, cattle dealers and a shepherd

This list is based on the key to the the Market Place painting compiled by W. P. Flint and R. L. Hine

Some Hitchin Worthies
and Two Who Were Not Quite so Worthy

SAMUEL LUCAS (1805–1870)

This Quaker brewer of beer who painted prolifically and exhibited regularly at the Royal Academy lived in Tilehouse Street Hitchin.

FREDERICK PETER DELME-RADCLIFE (1804–1875)

The sporting squire of Hitchin who lived at the Priory near the town centre. He governed the town kindly but firmly and was much liked. He was a good shot, a great rider to hounds and an authority on horses and racing. He was the chairman of many of the town's Boards and Committees.

JOHN HAWKINS (1791–1877)

The bulky lawyer who obtained such absolute dominion in the town he became known as the 'King of Hitchin'. He established the Town Hall, a Market Company, a Corn Exchange, a School, a Savings Bank and a Benefit Society.

SIR HENRY HAWKINS (1817–1907)

Henry Hawkins, son of John Hawkins, was as a youth, notorious for the many pranks he played on his fellow townsfolk. After being 'exiled' by his father from Hitchin, Henry in time became a lawyer of high repute, eventually becoming a very famous judge.

SIR HENRY BESSEMER (1813–1889)

Henry Bessemer was born at Charlton, a hamlet on the southern side of Hitchin. There his father, an inventor, who had escaped from Paris and the Revolution, set up business in typeface cutting and foundry casting of type metal by a secret process. Because of this secrecy there is a legend still current in Charlton that the Bessemers were coiners and forgers. Henry himself also became an inventor and among many other things developed the process for converting cast iron into steel.

LORD LISTER (1827–1912)

Joseph Lister, who became renowned for promoting the value of anti-septic treatment in surgery, was, as a boy, at school in Hitchin, and lodged for a time with his cousins, the Lucases, at their home in Tilehouse Street.

WILLIAM RANSOM (1826–1914)

William Ransom, a manufacturing chemist, was born into a Quaker family at a farmhouse in Bancroft, Hitchin, on 18 January 1826. By 1851 he had become well known as the cultivator of herbs, a distiller of fragrant oils and as a fairly large scale producer of galenicals (medicines made from natural raw materials and herbs). He was at school in Hitchin with Joseph Lister and remained a lifelong friend of this great pioneer of antiseptic surgery.

GYPSY DRAPER (1797–1902)

Gypsy Draper, real name Frederick Draper, often encamped with his family and the family donkey, in the Tatmore Hill lanes to the south of Hitchin. He was an oft-times convicted poacher, a dubious horse dealer and a clever fiddler greatly in demand for dances in Hitchin except by the town's Quakers who thought his fiddling 'more dangerous than gunpowder!'

'DOCTOR' WILLIAM MANSELL

The year of Mansell's birth does not seem to be known and the date of his death is uncertain. Apparently he was born at Deptford and spent his early years as a surgeon's mate aboard a man-of-war. Then for a time he served as a doctor on whaling vessels which plied between England and Greenland. He is thought to have appeared in Hitchin in 1820, setting himself up as a doctor, although he had no degree in medicine, no surgery and no pony and trap. He did however own a tall hat and a professional frock coat. For some years he prospered and he was particularly popular as an accoucheur or male midwife. When he had delivered a child alive he charged five shillings, 25p in today's money, but if the child was dead he charged nothing.

THE QUACK

In his latter years it is alleged that Mansell took to drink and fell upon hard times. His tall hat and his black frock coat may have become shabby and green with age but in a photograph taken about 1855 and now in the Hitchin Museum, Mansell is seen sitting quite upright and facing the camera with an alert and penetrating gaze. He shows no signs of advanced alcoholism.

Part One

1840

1. Morning Surgery of a Quack at Large

It was the 29th day of April in the Year of our Lord 1840 and, being a Tuesday, it was market day in the pleasant and ancient North Hertfordshire town of Hitchin. Although the clock in the nearby sturdy tower of St Mary's Church showed it to be only a few minutes past the hour of nine the Market Square stalls were already thronged and busy. As it was a fine, albeit blustery, morning, more folk than usual had come in from the villages, hamlets and farms close girdling the town and Mansell, top hatted and frock coated and, by general acceptance rather than any medical qualification, known as Doctor Mansell, had set up his surgery close to Butcher Gascoigne's shop on wheels. He could see a busy and profitable morning ahead of him, because on market days most of his patients were from out of Hitchin itself, coming from the villages of Ickleford, Holwell and Pirton from the north of the town, from the Wymondleys, Great and Little to the east, from Gosmore, Charlton and St Ippollyts to the south and from Offley Village to the west.

A small queue was forming even as he set up a folding table and began laying out a selection of bottles of medicine and small pots of ointment taken from a shabby carpet-bag. To complete his display he brought out a polished wooden box decorated with mother-of-pearl and a shallow tin tray. This tray he filled with a pungent liquid poured from a flask. Finally, with a touch of showmanship, he took a surgical knife from the box, flourished it and dropped it in the tray.

Two boys, both about twelve years of age, standing to one side of the queue, watched these preparations with widely opened and curious eyes. One of the boys, Joseph Lister by name, was tall and thin, the other, Richard Howard, was stocky and well built. Both were neatly dressed in sober Quaker grey and both were, as Mansell knew, pupils at Isaac Brown's school situated at the junction of Bridge Street and the London Road, not far from where he himself had a cottage. They must, he felt

3

sure as he noticed them, be absent from the school that morning only with the stern Isaac's express permission and he wondered vaguely why that permission had been granted.

Richard Howard was pulling a face of disgust as he said 'I can smell that horrid tar-water stuff Aunt Lucas gives us, Joe, when she thinks we're out of sorts.'

Joseph Lister grinned. Mistress Lucas with whom the cousins lodged during term time had a penchant for dosing them with the obnoxious infusion at any sign of bowel irregularity. 'Thou do'st? 'Tis not surprising,' he said 'Aye, 'tis tar-water in that tray!'

'But why has he put the knife in it?'

At this point Mansell, who had overheard what was being said by the boys, looked up with his deep-set, brown and piercing eyes and barked out 'Why, Master Howard, Why? A good reason, boy. I want the knife to be clean if I need to use it this morning.'

'But why tar-water, Sir,' asked Lister.

'Because it's good for making knives specially clean and clean knives make a lot of difference when it comes to cutting into flesh. When I was surgeon's mate aboard *Vengeance* at Trafalgar we had to take off more than a dozen legs and nearly a dozen arms that day. Because of my surgeon's great belief in washing knives and wounds with tar-water there was little putrefying of the stumps and most of our patients lived. On other ships most of the sailors and soldiers who lost arms or legs died. I've never forgotten what Mr Harvey taught me. He was a wonderful surgeon and a very wise man.'

'I'm going to be a surgeon one day,' announced Lister solemnly at the conclusion of Mansell's declaration.

'You are?'

'Yes, Sir.'

'What? You a sawbones, lad?'

'Yes, A surgeon, Sir?'

'You think you've a stomach for it, do you, and you think you can stand the sight of blood?'

'I think so, Sir.'

'Perhaps you'll not be of the same mind when you get to medical school!'

'I shall, Sir, I know I shall. I've written and told my father what I want to do and he's coming down from London today to talk to Isaac Brown about my future and Richard's 'cos he's Richard's guardian, and he wants to see if we should stay on here in Hitchin or go to another Quaker school in Tottenham for more advanced studies.'

'Is Richard also planning to be a surgeon?'

Richard shook his head vigorously from side to side. 'Not me,' he said 'I'm going to be a lawyer, I am.'

Mansell chuckled 'So it's one for the law, is it, and one for the saw? But why are you here wasting my time and not at school?'

'We've been asked to meet my father off the London coach this morning,' said Lister, 'and we've got the whole morning off.'

'Then get about your business and leave me to mine. And, young Lister, if you ever do become a surgeon don't be afraid to use plenty of tar-water if you want live patients and not dead ones!'*

Somewhat reluctantly the two boys began wandering off in the direction of the coach terminal at the Swan Inn at the top end of the Market Square and Mansell turned to his queue of patients.

'Who's first?' he called.

'Me doctor, me!' piped a young voice. 'Me! I'm first!'

'Who is me?'

'Me, Doctor! But it ain't me I've come about. It's me gran.' The girl who had spoken was, so Mansell guessed, about the same age as young Lister. She also was quietly and neatly dressed and he could see under the warm, dark cloak she was wearing that she had a pretty pale blue dress trimmed with a darker blue ribbon which matched the ribbons on her close fitting straw bonnet. She was an attractive child in an elfin way but not a child he could recollect as having ever seen before.

'And who is this grandmother of yours?'

'Mrs Fostring, Doctor.'

'Of Ickleford?' he queried. 'Mrs Fostring who keeps the shop there?'

---

*In March 1865 Joseph Lister, then Professor of Surgery at Glasgow University, used carbolic acid (derived from coal tar) to control a case of hospital gangrene. In the following year he took it into regular use as an antiseptic.

'That's 'er. She said you'd mind 'er.'

'Yes! I know her! And now I know who you are, young woman. I helped to bring you into the world and gave you your first smack on the bottom!'

'That's when me ma died, weren't it?'

'It was!' Mansell remembered vividly the wild March night when he had battled through gale driven rain to be at the bedside of the young Ickleford girl giving difficult birth to an illegitimate baby conceived as the outcome of a vicious rape forced upon her by Simeon Radcliffe, the Squire of Hitchin's eighteen year old cousin, who had been a guest at the Priory where the victim was employed as a kitchen maid. The youth had seen the young servant in the stable yard, inveigled her into one of the horse-boxes and there, despite her screams, overpowered and raped her.

Squire Delme-Radcliffe, returning from his morning ride, had found the girl distressed and sobbing in the horsebox, and having heard her story stormed off in a rage, riding crop in hand, to seek out his cousin. He had found him in his bedroom sponging blood from the front of his breeches and quite unable to deny what the girl had said. His plea that the girl was only a serving wench further enraged the Squire, and the riding crop was put to savage use which left Simeon weeping.

Two months later the girl, then only fifteen, was found to be with child. On hearing this, Delme-Radcliffe instructed his solicitor, John Hawkins, to provide financial help for the girl until the child to be born reached the age of twelve and could then earn his, or her, own living.

When despite Mansell's efforts, the mother died in childbed, the baby, a girl, had been placed in the care of an aunt who lived in the East End of London and brought up by her within the sound of Bow Bells.

Mansell brought his mind sharply back to the present to say 'And I was also there when you were christened in Ickleford Church. You were named Amanda, weren't you?'

'Yes, Doctor, I'm 'Manda.'

'And now you're back with your grandmother?'

'Yes, Doctor. Me money stops soon and I've got to find a place for meself. Mr 'Awkins, the s'liciter, wot's bin seeing to me money is lookin' our fer me. Gran reckons 'e'll find somefink real good 'cos 'e knows many rich'uns round 'ere.'

'I hope he does, Amanda, and when you get a position I hope you'll be happy in it.' Mansell thought it unfortunate that the girl spoke so very badly and with such a pronounced cockney accent. It might well prejudice her chances with some possible employers. He hesitated for a moment and then asked 'What about this head of your grandmother's? You say it's bad. Bad in what sort of way, girl?'

'She says it aches proper 'orrible and she don't 'arf feel poorly.'

'How long has this been going on?'

Amanda thought for a while and then said 'More 'an a week, I reckon it could be.'

'Is she constipated?'

The girl's puzzled look was followed by 'Didyer say pated? Pated? Wot's that mean?'

Mansell's eyes twinkled. 'Doesn't she shit well?'

There was a grin from Amanda. 'That! No she don't! She ain't bin fer a fortnight. I knows 'cos I 'heard 'er tell in the shop ter old Mrs Norman.'

'Well that's probably the trouble. She was like this once before and I can give her something for it. Something stronger than I've got bottled here. I'll give you a note for Mr Clisby the chemist at the shop over there and he'll make the mixture up for you. When you get home tell your grandma to take two large spoonfuls straight away and what's left in the bottle two hours later if the first dose hasn't worked. And you'd also better tell her to keep close to the privy!'

'Cor! I'll tell 'er, Doctor!' Amanda was bubbling with laughter. 'I'll tell 'er all right. I reckon I can mind the shop if she's busy at the back! An' 'ow much 'ave I got ter give yer?'

Mansell gave her the prescription he had written and said 'Sixpence, please.'

'That all, Guv, I means Doctor?'

'That's all, Amanda. Mr Clisby will charge you another sixpence for the mixture.'

The girl, still smiling, reached into a pocket in her cloak and brought out a large purse. From this she slowly counted six pennies into his hand. 'Ta!' she said.

'Thank you, Amanda. I'm sure it will put matters to rights for your grandmother before the end of the day. Goodbye, my dear.'

'Ta, lots, Doctor.' Then to Mansell's astonishment she stretched upwards and kissed him on the cheek before turning to run towards the apothecary's. Halfway there she looked back to wave to him. That was her undoing. She stumbled and fell sprawling at the feet of three gentlemen standing in front of the steps up to the chemist's shop and engaged in earnest conversation.

One of the three, the most portly, bent down and helped her to rise and she found herself peering up into the smiling countenance of the lawyer she had recently been taken to see in his musty Portmill Lane office.

'What's all this, Amanda?' asked John Hawkins, not unkindly. 'Why all the hurry, young woman?'

'Sorry, Mister, sorry!'

'I should think so too! You nearly had Mr Delme-Radcliffe and me over, just then.'

Amanda turned her head sharply to look at the gentleman Hawkins was indicating. 'Im?' she queried. 'Is that 'im?'

'It is! Your benefactor for so many years!'

There was a gasped 'Gorblimey! Bloody 'ell!' There followed a moment of shocked silence before Amanda added contritely, 'I 'adn't oughter ter 'ave swore, 'ad I?'

'No! That you certainly shouldn't!' The third gentleman, the Reverend Arthur Delme-Radcliffe, brother to the Squire and Rector of the nearby village of Holwell, spoke sharply to the now abashed girl. 'It was most improper of you to use such language before your betters. You should be ashamed of yourself!'

The Squire however was smiling broadly as he looked more closely into the girl's face. He said 'So this is our Amanda, is it, Hawkins? And the time has come to find her a place?'

'It has, Sir, it has. Perhaps Mrs Delme-Radcliffe can find something for her at the Priory?'

'I think not, Hawkins. Not in view of her origin. It would be better if she went somewhere else.' Delme-Radcliffe turned to his brother. 'What about your wife, Arthur? You've room for her at that huge rectory of yours and she could help look after that growing brood you're fathering.'

The clergyman raised his hands in horror. 'Never! Never! Never! he declared emphatically. 'It would never do! The girl's language is appalling! So too, is her accent! I don't want my children to copy her and speak like that! It wouldn't do at all!'

During this outburst the Squire was intently surveying Amanda from head to foot. At the conclusion of his examination he rubbed his chin and said thoughtfully. 'Do y'know she's a nice looking little filly with good bones and you can see there's a deal of good Radcliffe blood in her. She's spirited too! I like it! We should be able to do something better for her than skivvying, Hawkins!'

It sounded at first to the lawyer that Delme-Radcliffe had in mind sending Amanda to a stud farm at Newmarket. The Squire was a horse racing fanatic and often rode in races himself.

'Do what with her, Sir?' he asked. 'What is it you think could be done?'

'What can we do, Hawkins? Do, man? What about sending her to school? A good school could do a lot for her. It could even turn her into a young lady! See if you can get her into that place in Bancroft. I've heard good reports of it. What's it called?'

'Mrs Bonnamy's Academy for the Daughters of Gentlemen. My own girls go there.'

'Do they, begad! Well I suppose she is the daughter of a so-called gentleman. Nobody can deny that. And when she is finished there, Arthur, you can have her as a governess. Now what about it?'

The clergyman primly pursed his lips before saying, 'We'll see about that when the time comes but I think you are wasting your time and your money, brother. I really do. Maybe the girl doesn't want to go to school. She may hate the idea!'

The Squire put his crop under Amanda's chin and raised her face so that he could look directly into her eyes to ask, 'What say you, girl? Do you not like the idea of going to school?'

Amanda, who had taken a sudden liking to this smiling gentleman in his smart riding clothes and highly polished boots, gently dodged away from the crop and said, with a hint of pride, 'I've bin ter school, I 'ave, Sir. I can read real good, I can. And I can do me letters and me sums!'

'Good, but this is a different kind of school. One where you will be taught to be a lady and to speak properly. Wouldn't you like to be a lady?'

Amanda gave an impish grin. 'Me? A lydy? A proper lydy? Cor! Not 'arf! Mister! Yes, please!'

'Then a lady you shall be, Amanda!' Delme-Radcliffe turned to the solicitor and said, 'Please arrange everything, Hawkins, and see that she has all the clothes she needs to be a boarder with this Mrs Bonnamy. And see that she has some pocket money too. I should think two shillings a week for the first year ought to be sufficient. What do you think, Amanda?'

'Two bob? Two bob every week?'

'Yes, my dear.'

'Blimey!' Amanda suddenly directed her attention to the Squire's brother who was shaking his head in disapproval of the whole matter and said fiercely, 'I'll show yer, I will! You see if I don't. I'll be a lydy all right. I'll be a real proper lydy, I will. I knows I will!'

Delme-Radcliffe chuckled at the clergyman's obvious discomfiture and said, 'Good for you, girl! Now get about your business, whatever it was, but watch where you are going in future. Remember young ladies walk and do not run in public places! Mr Hawkins will be sending for you as soon as he has completed the arrangements with Mrs Bonnamy and in the meantime you can tell your grandmother what we intend to do with you and where you will be going. Goodbye for now. I expect we shall meet again soon.'

Amanda stepped back with a smile on her face and gave a deep curtsy to the Squire before turning about and walking off with an exaggerated dignity towards the chemist's shop.

Mansell, having seen Amanda helped to her feet by an amused Hawkins, and apparently none the worse for her tumble, had resumed his consultations. Next to come forward for attention were a mother and youthful son from Charlton, a tiny hamlet on the south side of Delme-Radcliffe's great Priory Park. Both were well known to Mansell.

'What is it this time, Mrs Wingrave?' he asked. 'Another boil?'

'Yes, Doctor. On the back of his neck again. 'I've been bread poulticing it just the way you told me to the last time he had one.'

'Good! I hope they were really hot poultices.'

'Hot enough to make me holler!' declared the youth with feeling.

'Splendid! Now let me see how it is!' Mansell spun his patient round with a firm grip on his shoulder and surveyed the ugly, angry looking swelling with experienced eyes. 'Excellent!' he said. 'Couldn't be better! It's ripe and ready for the knife. I hope you brought some rag, Mrs Wingrave. We don't want too much of a mess on his collar when we open it up, do we? It's a nice coat he's wearing.'

'I've brought a piece of towelling, Doctor. I was sure you'd need something.'

The boy's eyes goggled when Mansell dipped into his tray and with something of a flourish brought out the dripping knife.

'Bend over, lad, and then stand still. I'm not going to hurt you – at least not much – and you, Mrs Wingrave, stand by to give me the towel quickly!'

Mansell made two quick strokes with the knife. There was a short sharp cry from his patient and, as the bloody pus began to ooze from the neat crosscut, there was a loud murmur of admiration from the onlookers at the speed and skill of the operation.

Whilst still controlling the flow with the towelling Mansell grinned and acknowledged the plaudits with a nod of his head. 'All over!' he announced with satisfaction after only a few moments. 'You can hold this pad in place now, young Charlie, and you can straighten yourself up.'

The youth did so with a look of relief on his face and Mansell returned his knife to the tar-water. Mrs Wingrave, smiling thankfully pressed a large coin into the Doctor's not unwilling palm saying, 'My husband sent this for you.'

Looking down at what she had given him Mansell saw it was a bright and shiny crown piece. 'Five shillings, Mrs Wingrave? That's generous of him. I'm much obliged to him,' he said but as the couple moved away Mansell had another quick look at the coin. It seemed genuine but coins from Charlton had long been suspect in Hitchin, ever since the time, in fact, when a gentleman named Anthony Bessemer had set up a type-making factory in the hamlet where metal had been cast by a suspiciously secret method. Charlie Wingrave, 'Old Charlie', and father of the boy on whom Mansell had just operated, had worked in the foundry right up to the time when the Bessemers hurriedly packed up and left for London in 1830. Following their departure Wingrave and a brother who had been in the bakery trade set up their own bakery business in the former factory buildings and flourished, so it would seem exceedingly well. The rumours of counterfeiting still persisted however and Mansell dropped the coin in his pocket with some misgivings before turning to his next patient.

By eleven o'clock the queue had dwindled to two – a widow and her daughter. The mother was one of his regular patients and had been coming to him for some months. She and the girl lived in Chapman's Yard, one of several noisome offshoots of Back Street which ran its stinking way by the eastern end of St Mary's Church and housed most of Hitchin's poorest inhabitants.

Mansell had been treating Mrs Deamer for consumption but there was little he could do for her; she needed what no doctor could provide – bed rest, good nourishing food and fresh, untainted air. Once again he handed her a bottle of his herbal cough mixture, well aware that it would do little to alleviate her coughing. She thanked him and then said, 'Will you please examine Susan's head, Doctor? I don't like the look of a hard growth which is forming there at the base of her skull.'

The woman had a pleasant, cultivated voice and Mansell was sure she was of gentle birth and upbringing but had fallen on hard and difficult times.

Susan had removed her bonnet and Mansell gently parted her dark, luxuriant hair to reveal a curious growth about two inches above the nape of her neck. He immediately pursed his lips and shook his head saying, 'I can do nothing here, Mrs Deamer. It's something which can only be dealt with in a hospital or Dr Hawkins's dispensary. She may have to lodge there for a day or two while the abscess drains.'

Mrs Deamer's eyes showed concern and Mansell added hastily, 'Don't worry about the cost. Hawkins won't charge you much, if anything at all. I will give you a note to take to him.'

Dr Frederick Hawkins, brother of the town's formidable lawyer, was disposed in a far more friendly manner to Mansell than any of the other medical practitioners in the town. In fact during the serious outbreak of cholera in the Back Street slums in 1833 he had employed Mansell as his assistant. A note from him would receive sympathetic consideration by Hawkins and he was sure that the matter would be dealt with promptly.

While he was writing this note Mrs Deamer opened her thin looking purse and stood waiting, looking rather uncomfortable, until he had finished. 'How much do I owe you?' she eventually asked. 'The usual shilling?'

Waving away the proffered coin Mansell said, 'Nothing today, my dear. Nothing at all.'

There was a blush and a look of relief on the woman's face as she took the note from Mansell and he guessed that she had been offering him her last shilling – how she made ends meet with her small earnings from her sewing and plaiting of straw was difficult to imagine. Today he could afford to be generous; it had been a profitable morning with eighteen paying patients and takings in excess of a guinea in addition to the dubious crown piece he had received from the Charlton bakery; it had also been a largely trouble-free morning surgery with no teeth requiring extraction. He disliked tooth pulling despite the fact he had the best reputation in the town for dentistry. No, it had been mainly coughs and colds left over from a nasty winter and a few skin troubles mostly brought about by failure to use sufficient soap and water. He was highly satisfied with the outcome of his morning session and with no one else requiring attention he considered it high time to close down his surgery before adjourning to the Swan Inn. He hoped to find convivial company there and enjoy a tankard or two of strong ale before returning home with his pockets still jingling.

However, before setting up the tankards, he had better, he thought, have a word with Gypsy Draper. He had noticed that pleasantly smiling rogue passing by with his family and their donkey some ten minutes before and he was sure that he also was making for the inn. It was more than likely he would have a few freshly snared rabbits in the donkey's panniers and Mansell knew his wife would be pleased if he took home one of these with him. Anne was a good cook and rabbit pie was one of her specialities.

By the time the clock of St Mary's had marked the half past the hour of eleven Mansell had repacked his carpet bag, closed down his table and set off for the inn.

2.   The London Coach

The great yard of the Swan Inn was a busy and extremely noisy place not only on market days but all other days of the week except the Sabbath. Not only did it contain ample stabling for the coach-horse changes but also several work places, shops and cottages for traders and craftsmen. There were among these a saddler, a basket maker, a tailor, a cobbler and, of course a blacksmith. It was close to the blacksmith's forge where Mansell eventually found Draper. The gypsy, an active man in his early forties, curly headed and handsome, was generally well liked in the town. Besides having for sale poached rabbits, and occasionally poached hares and pheasants, he was a fiddler of considerable skill and he and his fiddle were in much demand for wedding feasts and dances. Even Delme-Radcliffe, the town's chief magistrate, employed the known poacher to entertain his guests at the Priory once or twice during the year. However, to the town's Quakers Draper's wild music was, as one of them put it, 'almost as dangerous as gunpowder'. Draper had laughed on hearing this and from that time ever afterwards he played his violin loudly by the front door of Quaker Whiting's house in the market place, causing the distracted man to gather his children together and take them to the far end of his back garden, where they could not hear such Satanic strains.

It was while Mansell and the gypsy were concluding their bargaining for the largest of the three rabbits taken from the donkey's side panniers that they heard the first distant fanfare of a coaching horn, and it was only a minute or so later when the coach rattled under the high archway and into the cobblestoned yard.

Mansell, having dropped his purchased rabbit into the carpet-bag, looked to see who was alighting from the coach. The first to do so was a tall but round-shouldered man who, from the quiet sobriety of his attire, was one of the Quaker persuasion. He was greeted warmly by the two boys, Joseph Lister and his cousin

14

Richard Howard, and in turn each boy was kissed affectionately on his forehead. This little group was then joined by another grey-clad Quaker. This was Samuel Lucas, the artistic one among the town's industrious farming and brewing family. Together the two men and the two boys, chatting among themselves quite happily, moved off into the inn.

Next to alight from the interior of the coach was a rotundly bulky, red-faced gentleman in a bottle-green coat. He, once safely on the ground, then assisted down a thin, middle-aged woman who seemed to be some kind of servant, and a girl in her mid teens. The girl's red-rimmed eyes showed signs of recent and prolonged weeping. They too moved off into the inn but as they passed close to Mansell and the gypsy the man glared malevolently at Draper and muttered something which sounded like a curse.

Mansell looked at his companion, and asked when the trio was out of earshot, 'And what have you done to upset the master of Manley Court?'

The gypsy grinned and said, 'Nothing as far as I know, Doctor.'

'Nothing? Haven't you been poaching on his land?'

'Once or twice lately but I haven't been catched at it neither by Master Quint himself nor by that old bastard Thickpenny who runs the farm for him. Perhaps it's something to do with Nelson.'

'Nelson? Your eldest boy? What's he got to do with it?'

'He's working on the Court farm. Has been for about a year now.'

'Doing what? You gypsies don't generally take kindly to farm work!'

'Horses, Doctor, horses! He's looking after them. He's good with horses is young Nelson. Better even than me!'

'Do you really think he could be in trouble?' asked Mansell wondering if the boy had been thieving. Most gypsies were, in his opinion, born thieves and it was rumoured that Manley Court was a treasure-house of rare and valuable objects of eastern origin. These had been acquired, so it was said, by Quint in his seafaring days when, before settling down as a tea merchant in Mincing Lane and a landowner in Hertfordshire, he had been the owner and captain of a large schooner on a regular Shanghai run.

'Nelson in trouble? If you think he's been on the pinch that ain't likely, so forget it! He ain't that sort!'

But Mansell's attention had now been drawn to the three passengers who were clambering down from the top of the coach. Two of the men were, like himself, in their fifties. The third was a much younger man who was smartly, almost foppishly, dressed, carrying an elegant, silver-knobbed walking stick. This he dropped whilst he was descending so that it bounced and rolled under the coach. Draper ran forward to retrieve it but he was only rewarded with an ungracious grunt when he handed it to its owner.

'Young puppy!' thought Mansell as he heard one of the older pair say, 'Well, Radcliffe, we'll expect to see you later at the Sun if you intend to join us for a game or two this evening.'

Simeon Radcliffe nodded and smiled. 'Yes, I'll be there,' he said. 'They usually dine at five at the Priory and if my dear cousin does get over the shock of seeing me and invites me to the meal I fully expect to be with you by seven at the latest!'

'You'll be well breeched, I hope?'

'Well enough if our talk goes as I hope it will!'

With that Semeon, overnight bag in hand, disappeared under the archway and out into the Market Place. The two older men smiled with meaning at each other in such a way they reminded Mansell of birds of prey and he could guess where they next intended to strike. He then left the gypsy and entered the inn to make for the taproom. It was not particularly crowded, which was surprising for a market day. Four bluff, rosy-faced men, obviously farmers, occupied the table nearest the door. By one window sat the Manley Court trio whilst the Quaker group had gathered round the table by the other window to the room. One table still remained vacant but as Mansell neared this young Joseph Lister called out, 'Please Doctor, come and join us here! I want to introduce thee to my father.'

Joseph Lister's father stood up. He said, in a cordial manner, 'Yes, do please join us, Dr Mansell. It's thee I hear who's been encouraging my boy to take up surgery. Is that not so?'

'He needs little encouragement, Sir, but it's not the easiest of paths to follow. However, there's much satisfaction in saving lives with proper use of a knife.'

'I shall not be standing in his way. The lad shall have the best training I can find for him. Now sit down and join us, Doctor. May I order thee an ale?'

'Thank you. A strong ale if you please. Something special from Mr Lucas's own brewery of course!'

Samuel Lucas smiled and said, 'Not that I'm much concerned with brewery matters today. I've something else to occupy my mind.' He laid his hand on the closed sketchbook on the table. 'It's something much more to my liking although I must admit it's something of a challenge.'

There was a brief pause while the potman brought a trayful of tankards to the table, strong ale for the three men and small beer for the boys, with the score being settled by Mr Lister.

'A challenge, Mr Sam?' asked Mansell. 'What kind of challenge do you mean?'

'A commission from the town's Market Company. They've asked me to paint a picture of the Tuesday market in being and to include some of the town worthies. I've been making some preliminary sketches today.'

'May we look, please, Cousin Sam?' It was Joseph Lister who put the question and put it eagerly. 'Please!'

Samuel Lucas smiled, opened his book and slowly turned the leaves holding the pages so that all could see the drawings. Altogether there were about a dozen-and-a-half people portrayed. Most were easily recognised by Mansell and the boys. They included Dr Niblock, the master at the Free School in the town, Margaret Lucas, the Quakeress, John Ransome, a Quaker farmer, and a group containing the Squire, his reverend brother and Hawkins the solicitor. Also there was one drawing which showed Gypsy Draper and his family and, to Mansell's surprise, included a sketch of himself examining the head of the girl with the tumour.

'Am I to be included in this picture?' he asked.

'That's what I am intending,' replied the artist with another of his warm smiles. 'After all thou art one of the regular attenders at the market and the scene would not be complete without our popular man of medicine! When I've committed thee to the canvas thou must come to the studio and see thy portrait for thyself!'

''Why hasn't thou got our Ikey in thy book?' broke in Richard Howard.

'If, disrespectful youth, thou mean thy master, Isaac Brown, there is goodly reason for his not being there. He was not in the market this morning! I trust thou obtained proper leave of absence from the school and that he is not waiting thy return with his cane in hand!'

Mr Lister smiled as he looked fondly at the two boys. 'I do not think they will be in trouble, Sam. I wrote asking that they be released to meet the coach – and that reminds me that time is pressing. I have an appointment with Isaac Brown at noon and we had best leave here now and get on our way.'

After the Quaker group had broken up and left Mansell seated alone at the table, he ordered another tankard of strong ale and sat back to study Quint and his female companions with some interest. Several times in the past minutes he had seen them looking pointedly in his direction and he was certain he was the subject of their quiet-voiced, but animated, discussion. Then, quite suddenly, Quint and the girl Mansell had taken to be his daughter rose from their settle and quickly departed. The thin woman, and he was even more sure now that she was a servant, got to her feet and approached his table with a determined look on her face.

Mansell stood up.

'Doctor Mansell?'

'Yes, Madam. At your service.'

'Sit down, please.'

When they were both seated the woman asked, 'Do you know who I am, Doctor?'

'You were with Mr Quint and a girl I had assumed to be his daughter, and from the way Mr Quint was speaking to you I suspect that you are in his employ.'

'I am. I am his housekeeper. Formerly I was nursemaid to Felicity but on the death of Mr Quint's wife, just about three years ago, and before he bought the estate in Hitchin, he made me his housekeeper.'

The woman was softly spoken and had what seemed to be a slight north-country accent.

Mansell said, 'Is that so? It accounts then for my seeing you in the marketplace occasionally.'

'And I have seen you. One of the maids at Manley Court has spoken to me about you. I know your reputation.'

'You do? Well what is your name, Madam? Who is it that I am addressing?'

'My name is really of no consequence in this matter Doctor but you may address me as Mrs Lestrange.'

'And what is this matter?'

'A delicate one.'

'Medical?'

'Yes, but it is not one that I am fully at liberty to disclose.'

'Then I do not see how I can assist you very much.'

'Wait. I think you can.' Mrs Lestrange took a gold half sovereign from the reticule she carried and placed this on the table in front of Mansell. 'You would like to earn this and more?'

'Of course! I never mind receiving a handsome fee!'

'There is a good one to be earned if you come to Manley Court this evening and bring your surgical instruments with you. Mr Quint will then tell you what is required.'

'It is no major operation, I hope – something I am not qualified to do?'

'It is not beyond your skills or your practice, of that I am sure. You will come?'

'I will come. But at what hour may I ask?'

'About eight will do. Take the coin on the table as an earnest and please be discreet. Now and in the future!'

With that Mrs Lestrange quickly left the now thoughtful Mansell pocketing the coin. 'Discreet is it?' he said to himself. 'Discreet's the word is it? Yes, I can be discreet, Mr Quint. Very discreet. I think I already know what I've to be discreet about. Young women in tears and with thickening waistlines can only mean one thing but we shall see what there is to see when the time comes to see it.'

It was past one by the taproom clock, and another strong ale later, before Mansell left the Swan. He had settled the score not with Quint's half sovereign but with the over-bright crown piece from Charlton. It was probably a good one, but then just possibly it was a dud, and he thought himself better rid of it.

3. Simeon Calls and Stays

Delme-Radcliffe was seated in the library at the Priory when the baize-covered door was opened by a footman to admit his cousin Simeon. After the door had been closed again the Squire did not rise to his feet for his visitor nor did his voice hold any warmth of welcome when he spoke.

'What did you want here, Simeon? I forbade you this house twelve years ago!'

Simeon smiled weakly. He said, 'I've come to see you, cousin, to make my peace. Twelve years is a long time for us to be at odds over my youthful folly. It's a folly I've long since repented and been sorry about.'

'Sorry about?' Delme-Radcliffe's voice was sharp. 'Sorry, are you? By God you've need to be sorry! More than sorry! You were a damned scoundrel then and I've no reason to think that you're any better now!'

There was a pause and then the now red-faced Squire said, 'You don't know it I suppose, because no one will have told you, but the girl died. Died in childbed by reason of what you had done to her!'

Simeon's face went ashen. He clutched at the table near which he was standing.

'She's dead! She died?'

'Yes. She died. The child lived!' Delme-Radcliffe hesitated when he saw Simeon began to sway. 'Sit down, man!' he commanded. 'I'll get you a glass of spirits.'

After Simeon had swallowed the neat brandy he appeared recovered to some extent and asked somewhat tremulously, 'Where is the child? Is it a boy or a girl?'

'A girl.'

'Where is she? May I see her?'

'Her whereabouts are not for your knowing and you may not see her. So far as you are concerned she thinks her father is also dead. It is best she continues to think so. I've seen to it that she has been provided for so far in a modest way; now I am arranging to have her educated so that she can take a better place in the world and earn her living at something other than being just a servant girl. Since you've shown up I do not see why you should not contribute towards the cost of this from the Trust Fund – ' Delme-Radcliffe hesitated for a moment upon seeing the curious look which had passed across Simeon's still white face, ' – set up by your late father and administered by brother Arthur and myself.'

There was a nod of acceptance from Simeon at this proposal and when his cousin had finished speaking he said quietly, 'It's because of this Trust Fund I've come to see you, cousin. It has to be dissolved, I think next year when I'm thirty-one, doesn't it?'

'Under the terms of the Trust, yes.'

'And the capital realised has to be shared equally between my mother and myself?'

'That is correct.'

A short but uncomfortable silence followed. Then Simeon asked, 'Would it be possible for me to have a small advance now?'

'Have you a good reason for asking this?'

'Yes. I want to get married.'

'Want to get married or have you got to get wed? From something I read in the last letter I had from your mother I imagine it's the latter!'

'That's not true! I just wanted to get married but the allowance I get from the Trust isn't enough to set me up for it.'

'Who are you marrying? Has she money?'

'She's a widow. She's older than me and she's quite comfortably off.'

Delme-Radcliffe seemed thoughtful as he walked across to the window and stood to gaze out over the lawns, the small river and the rolling Priory Park beyond. Eventually he said, facing Simeon again, 'A marriage like that with a mature woman might settle you down. God knows she's welcome to you and I hope she knows what she is letting herself in for, but that's her business. How much do you want?'

'Only a thousand pounds, please!'

'That's no small amount!'

'You'll let me have it?'

'I'll consider it. Five hundred would be more reasonable but I must first discuss the matter with Arthur and our man of business, Hawkins. That will take two or three days to settle.' After another pause for thought the Squire added reluctantly. 'You may stay here if you wish, Simeon, but keep out of my sight. I will arrange a room for you and I'll arrange for you to have your meals in it. I'm certainly not having you to dine at my table with my family and my friends – ' here came a ringing of the bell to call the footman, 'and you can keep your bloody filthy hands off my servants this time otherwise you'll really rue the day you set foot in this house again!'

4. The Tea Merchant's Daughter

Anne Mansell did not serve a rabbit pie that evening but instead prepared a rabbit stew thick with vegetables and well flavoured with herbs. Her husband, having wiped the last of the gravy from his plate with a morsel of bread, said with satisfaction, 'That was good, my dear, very good. I doubt whether they dined better at the Priory tonight!'

Replying with that curiously half secret smile which always warmed Mansell's heart, Anne said, 'I don't suppose they did, William, I don't suppose they did. After all, it was, I suspect, one of the Squire's own rabbits we have just eaten and most of the vegetables certainly came from the Priory garden.'

'That means you saw our Mary today?'

The Mansells' daughter was married to John Timmins, who, although he was not yet thirty, had complete charge of the Radcliffes' huge kitchen garden. From time to time produce from this garden found its way into the Mansells' kitchen.

'Yes, I saw her. We went shopping together. We saw you in the market. You seemed busy.'

'I was. It has been a good day so far – '

'So far. Does that mean you've got to go out again tonight? I looked in your book today but I did not see you had any births booked this week.'

Mansell chuckled and shook his head. 'No, I haven't. It's something else and it could be more profitable!'

'Something else?' Anne gave him an enquiring look. Although he did practise some general and some herbal medicine it was as an *accoucheur* or male midwife that Mansell was best known in the town. For this service he was in much demand by the poor because he would deliver a child alive for as little as five shillings and charge nothing if the child was stillborn.

Anne pressed the point. 'Something else and more profitable? What is it, William?'

'A summons to Manley Court!'

'That large house along the road to Pirton?'

'Yes. Mr Quint requires my attendance!'

'Mr Quint, the new owner? I've heard it said that he's very wealthy. He's a tea merchant isn't he? And owns ships as well?'

'So I believe.'

'And the house, they say it is full of wonderful things.'

'That's what's rumoured, my dear, but I'll be able to tell you more when I return tonight.'

'Will you be late back?'

'I doubt it. I think I know what is required, not that I care much for the doing of it.'

Anne knew at once what he meant. 'The daughter? She's been foolish?'

'I rather think so.'

'Well, at least she'll be in safer hands with you than she would be with either of the Back Street hags we know about. They're butchers!'

With that Anne disappeared into the scullery with the dirty plates. Mansell, watching her go, thought how bright and well she was looking that evening. She still had almost the same trim figure he had admired twenty-five years earlier on meeting her for the first time. She was then employed at a tavern just off the wharfside at Wapping, and he had called in at this just after disembarking from the whaler in which he was serving as doctor to the small Greenland fleet. After making only one more voyage he had given up the sea to marry her and to take a post as a pharmacist's assistant. In 1820 they, together with their three small children, had moved to Hitchin. There, despite some early objections by the resident doctors, he had set up his peripatetic practice and prospered. Now the family had grown up. Mary, married to Timmins, had a son who was nearly four and Tom, their elder boy, was also wed. He and his wife Charlotte, with their little daughter, lived quite close to the Timminses in Tile-house Street and not far from the Priory. Dick, the younger boy, who was something of a ne'er-do-well in his father's eyes, worked and lived in at the Angel Inn near the Market Place.

Anne returned to break into his reverie on things past and present carrying a lighted lamp and asked 'At what time have you to be at Manley Court?'

'At eight.'

'Then you'd best get moving William. It's a fair step from here and it's not the brightest of evenings. It will be almost dark when you get there.'

Mansell glanced through the living room window. The gusty wind of the morning had strengthened considerably and was tossing the still bare branches of the trees across the road with an angry ferocity. A flurry of rain on the window panes made him wish that he had not to go out. When he did emerge from his house he was not wearing his top hat but a dark seaman's cap and he was well wrapped around in his ancient, but still serviceable, boat cloak.

With a stout stick in one hand and his carpet-bag in the other, he strode down the hill from his home and made for Manley Court.

There were few signs of life when he bypassed the town centre and began making the ascent of the largely Quaker-inhabited Tilehouse Street. A solitary horseman riding by at a weary plod acknowledged him with a wave of his whip before turning into the Priory entrance and there were some lights in the small cottages where the Timminses and Tom's family lived. Much higher up the hill two men, obviously much the worse for drink, staggered out of the Highlander Inn and reeled past him with some ribald greeting. Mansell was half tempted to tarry for a while at the inn. It was always a warm and pleasant place and since he had brought the inkeeper's wife safely through a very difficult birth some years earlier he was always specially welcome there. But he knew time was pressing and he did not intend to be late for his appointment with the impatient-looking Quint. Quint, he was sure, was not a man to cross unnecessarily.

Just beyond the Highlander the road forked left for the hatters' town of Luton and forked right for the village of Pirton. This right-hand road was known locally as 'the Manley Highway' and following this, still going uphill, Mansell eventually breasted the crest. There he paused for a moment to survey the rolling countryside beyond. Several times in the past years, on more pleasant evenings, he had stood at this point to watch the sun going down in red and gold glory behind the distant hills but now there was no setting sun to be seen, only a leaden coloured sky which seemed to grow darker with each passing minute.

With stinging rain suddenly beating cold upon his face he

stepped out resolutely in his descent to Manley Court which he could now see some half a mile ahead on the right-hand side of the road almost surrounded by tall elms. It was a small but attractive mansion when he reached it, one built of red brick mellowed by two centuries of summers and winters. The steps up to the front door were, however, most imposing; so too was the great iron knocker, shaped like a lion's head, on which he banged three times. These resounding knocks brought an almost immediate reply and the door was opened to reveal Mrs Lestrange and a spacious but dimly lit hall.

'Good,' she said quietly as she closed the door behind Mansell. 'You are in good time, Doctor, and that will please the master. Leave your cap and cloak on the settle here and I will see to it that they are dried before you return home.'

The room to which she led Mansell was, in contrast to the hall, brightly lit and he could see at once that it was nothing less than a repository of oriental treasures. There were great, curiously carved, chests against the walls, dragon-patterned silk screens, large pots and vases of various shapes and two life-sized wooden warriors clad in copper-coloured armour. Decorating the walls were grotesque masks, swords and shields and other weapons of eastern origin. A bronze figure of Buddha, about two feet in height, brooded in a candle-lit alcove and cast an eerie air of calm around it.

Quint, who was seated in a large carved chair by an ornately carved table, silently dismissed Mrs Lestrange with a gesture of his hand and then, with another gesture, indicated to Mansell that he should seat himself on the opposite side of the table.

After a prolonged pause during which the doctor was scrutinised closely by Quint's small, black boot-button eyes the tea merchant said in a rasping voice 'My daughter is carrying a child. She is not married and the child is not wanted. You will rid her of it.' There was another pause before he added, ' I understand you have a reputation for doing such things safely.'

'Safety depends on several things, Mr Quint.'

'And what, pray, are these, Doctor?'

'First, the stage of pregnancy. How far is it advanced?'

'She must have been put in the family way early in January.'

'She's four months gone then. That is no problem. I do not like to terminate pregnancies after five months. Now to the second thing. Is your daughter healthy and fit enough to have this rather unpleasant operation?'

'To the best of my knowledge she is in excellent health.'

'Good. Now – of major importance – is she co-operating willingly in this matter?'

Quint hesitated before replying and his answer, when it came, seemed qualified.

'Yes, she has been persuaded it will be in her best interests.'

Mansell, not quite satisfied with this, then asked, 'You are quite certain that she does not wish to marry the man and have the baby?'

There was an immediate showing of anger on Quint's florid face and he exclaimed emphatically, 'Marry him? Not bloody likely. I want a better match for her than a bloody nigger even though she does think she's in love with the young bugger!'

'You know who it is?'

'Yes, I know who it is all right. I made her tell me this morning. It's that sodding gypsy I employ in the stables and for odd jobs about the house.'

'Nelson Draper? Gypsy Draper's boy? He's no nigger! He's dark skinned like his father, but he's no nigger!'

'Nigger enough for me! The girl's been a little fool with him. Last Christmas when she was home here from boarding school in London she takes it into her head to teach him to read and write. Instead the bastard taught her something else while they were in the hay-loft together!'

'A sorry business.'

'A very sorry business, but I'm making bloody certain he won't do anything like it again in a hurry.'

'How, may I ask?'

'He won't be around to do it, and if he's not around she'll get over the infatuation and forget him. Now, do you really think she'll be all right with this operation of yours?'

'I'm as sure as I can be. There's a risk with all operations but I've never lost a patient yet under similar circumstances and I've no intention of losing one now. Nor should she be any the worse for it in the future when she does get married.'

'Good! That's what I wanted to hear!' Quint took a purse from his coat pocket and from this counted five sovereigns on to the table. Arranging these in a neat pile he said, 'These you will get for tonight's work if all goes well. In a month's time if my daughter has fully recovered there will be another five waiting for you. Will that suit you?'

'An excellent arrangement, Mr Quint. Now I must see the girl and I shall want Mrs Lestrange in attendance please.'

'That can be arranged.' Quint rose from his chair and went to one of the chests by the wall on which stood a large brass gong. He struck this only once but the resonant reverberating clangour must have been heard almost everywhere in the house. Mrs Lestrange was quickly at the door of the room.

'Yes, Mr Quint?'

'Take Doctor Mansell to Felicity please. You are to stay with him while he does what has to be done and you are to do exactly what he tells you to. Is that understood?'

'Yes, Mr Quint, I understand.' With that the housekeeper turned to go and Mansell, picking up his carpet-bag, rose to follow her into the hall.

He was led up a wide stone staircase to a gallery which gave access to the principal first floor bedrooms.

Mrs Lestrange whispered at the top of the stairs, 'You'll be gentle with her, Doctor. She's not much more than a child yet. She's only just sixteen, in fact.'

Mansell detained the housekeeper by a touch on her arm. 'Yes, I'll be gentle with her and see that she doesn't suffer much. But a word or two with you before we go into her room.'

'Yes, Doctor?'

'When did Felicity discover she was pregnant?'

'It was only a few days ago. Certain things hadn't happened when they should have done and she was being sick in the mornings. She's fairly innocent and didn't realise their significance but at a school such as she was at other girls notice things and one of them reported the matter to the head teacher. She questioned Felicity and her father was sent for at once.'

'Thank you for telling me, Mrs Lestrange. It's better I know the background in these matters. Now take me to her please.'

When they entered the bedroom, which was dimly lit, Felicity, exhausted by her bouts of weeping, was in an uneasy sleep.

'You rouse her, Mrs Lestrange,' instructed Mansell looking down kindly on the white, tearstained, childlike face. 'It's best she wakes up to see your familiar face above her rather than mine.'

But tears sprang again when Felicity awakened and saw the doctor. But Mansell spoke to her softly and after a few moments the sobbing ceased.

'You know why I am here, Felicity?'

There was an almost inaudible, 'Yes, I know but please don't hurt me too much. Please.'

'I will try not to, my dear and it will soon all be over and you'll have nothing then to worry about.'

'Is there anything you want, Doctor?' asked Mrs Lestrange as Mansell began unpacking his bag.

'Yes. Hot water in a basin with some soap so that I can wash my hands, plenty of towels and an empty bucket. Also a good light.'

When the housekeeper had left to get the things required Mansell filled his tin tray with the sweet-smiling dilution of tar-water and, out of sight of the girl, took from his instrument box a long steel knitting needle and dropped this into the solution. It was while he was removing his frock coat and rolling up his shirt sleeves that Felicity called him to the bedside.

'Doctor, please, Doctor!'

'Yes, my dear?'

'I want you to help me please. It's Nelson. I know what they've done to him and I think I know what they are going to do.'

'Nelson Draper, the lad who got you into this trouble?'

'Yes, Doctor, but please don't blame him. I made him do it. I wanted him to and I still want him that way.'

'What have they done to him? And who has been doing it?'

'My father and that horrid Thickpenny and his sons. They've been thrashing Nelson with a horsewhip. I heard them doing it in the yard. Mrs Lestrange thinks he's been badly hurt.'

'Has he, by God! Where is he now?'

It wasn't Felicity who answered the question but Mrs Lestrange entering the room with the basin of hot water. She said, 'He's tied up and shut up in one of the horseboxes in readiness for the morning.'

'And then what? They can't keep him tied up for ever.'

'They don't intend to. At daybreak they will be hiding him in a cart and taking him off to the London docks. One of Mr Quint's ships is loading up there ready to sail to Shanghai at the end of the week. The gypsy will be put aboard her.'

'And he'll never come back!' wailed Felicity. 'I know he won't! They'll leave him there.'

'Then we must do something about it. We can't have that happen. His father is a friend of mine.'

'But what can we do?' asked Mrs Lestrange. 'If we free him they'll get after him – perhaps for stealing or something. Then if he gets caught and put up before the magistrates it's sure to be transportation. The Thickpennys will lie and say they found some of the master's valuables in the loft where he sleeps. They'll swear to anything if the master pays them enough.'

'That's something we must chance but if we do set him free we must get him right away from Hitchin. But first we must free him. Is the door to the horsebox locked or just bolted from the outside?'

'Just bolted, I think, from what I heard Thickpenny saying.'

'That makes things a lot easier but let us deal with one matter at a time. I'm sure we'll think of something when we've finished here. Have you got the bucket and towels I asked for, Mrs Lestrange?'

'Outside the door, Doctor, together with a good light. I'll bring them in.'

Just over an hour and a half later Felicity lay back in bed drowsy from the two opium pills which Mansell had given her. She was well padded and comfortable and the bucket, with its grisly contents covered up, was waiting for disposal by the door.

Mansell, completely satisfied that all had gone well with the girl, was washing his hands again. 'Now to the boy, Mrs Lestrange,' he said, 'we must attend to him to but avoid possible trouble for you or Felicity or even me we must make it look as though he made his escape without anyone's assistance.'

'How are we going to do that?'

'I shall take my leave now of Mr Quint and tell him all is well with his daughter who is now in a drugged sleep and will not wake until well into the morning. I shall also tell him you are sleeping in a chair in her room and will be watching over her all night. That should clear both of you from suspicion.'

'Then?'

'I'll leave here and go for help. I've a friend not so far from here who'll assist us and I don't doubt will keep the boy in hiding until we can make arrangements to get him out of the district and harm's way.'

'You'll be coming back?'

'I'll be back at midnight and meet you by the front door. I'll have this friend and you can then take us to the stables and show us where Nelson is being kept.'

'Then?'

'You return to the house, I hope before you're missed, and you leave us to get Nelson away.'

'Do you need money?'

'It would be of help.'

'I will bring some, probably about twenty pounds.'

'That should be ample.' Mansell having dried his hands was repacking his bag. 'Now I'll thank you to take me down to Mr Quint.'

The tea merchant was again sitting at the carved table when Mansell re-entered the room of treasures and curiosities.

'Well?' he asked, looking up from an exquisitely shaped jade and emerald necklace he was holding in his hands. 'What have you to report?'

'Success! Complete success! There is no longer a problem. I have given your daughter something to make her sleep through the night but just as a safeguard and to comfort her should she wake up Mrs Lestrange will stay by her bedside. In a few days the girl will be fully recovered.'

'Excellent!' Quint held out the necklace for Mansell to see. 'I shall then give her this. It was her mother's and I know she would like to have it.'

Putting the necklace down on the table the tea merchant rose from his chair and went to a sideboard. He came back with a dark bottle and two glasses. 'Now join me in a rum,' he said. 'You've earned a drink and I dare suppose that as a Navy man at one time you've a liking for that particular tipple?'

'I have and a tot now will keep out the cold until I get home and into my bed.'

The two men toasted each other solemnly and then Quint pushed the five sovereigns across the table towards Mansell who picked them up and put them in his pocket.

'Thank you,' he said. 'I shall be back about this time tomorrow evening to see that all is well with your daughter and if necessary give her another sleeping pill. Perhaps I shall see you then, Mr Quint?'

'Maybe you will, maybe you won't, Doctor. I'm off to London by the early morning coach and may not be back tomorrow. I've some shipping business to attend to at the docks.' Then Quint added with a vicious significance which was not lost on Mansell, 'It's a very special lading! One I must see to personally!'

Bidding the tea merchant good night Mansell left the room secretly smiling to himself to find Mrs Lestrange waiting by the outer door holding his stick and a now dry cap and cloak.

'Midnight,' she murmured as she let him out of the house.

'Yes, midnight it will be,' he replied softly.

5.   The Rescuing of Darkie Draper

The wind had dropped considerably and the rain had almost ceased by the time Mansell left Mrs Lestrange at the top of the front steps to Manley Court. At the parting she had pressed a fairly heavy purse into his hand saying, 'Here's the twenty pounds in case of need. Felicity will let me have it back tomorrow. She's never kept short of money and I know she'll approve of what we're doing.'

A quarter of an hour later when Mansell reached the door of the Highlander Inn he was far from pleased on hearing an outburst of raucous laughter from within. He had hoped as it was late and such a foul night what customers had been about had already made for their homes and the comforts of their beds. On opening the door and entering the taproom he saw three men seated at a table close to the fireplace in which a log fire was dying down to red embers and grey ash as though it was trying to encourage departures from its vicinity.

The innkeeper, Ralph Ashton, was standing by the table and it was obvious from the tray in his hand that he had just served the trio with more drink. His rubicand face however was showing little pleasure as the eldest of the drinkers threw a half sovereign on the table so that it rolled and dropped to the stone-flagged floor and then spun for a moment before settling down near one of the younger men's boots. It was stamped upon immediately.

'If the lady's on top it's mine!' claimed the youth. 'If it's not, you can have it, landlord, and give father the change!'

The father, a bulky stocky man with fair muttonchop whiskers fringing a weatherbeaten face, roughly kicked his son's boot from the coin saying, 'Stop your bloody fooling, Silas, and drink up, though God knows you've had a skinful already!' Then, much to Mansell's relief he added, 'We'd best be off right away. It's nigh on eleven and you two have an early start in the morning.'

Beyond giving Mansell a cursory glance in which there was

no recognition the three men ignored the doctor as he sat himself down at another table and gave themselves over to tossing off the contents of their tankards in long gulps and swallows. Eventually, with belchings and a loud breaking of wind from one of them which brought gusts of mirth from them all, they made for the door. There they seemed to burst out on to the road. Immediately there followed the awful sounds of violent vomiting.

The innkeeper with a look of disgust on his face hurriedly closed the door and then turned his attention to Mansell. 'Sorry about that, William, more than sorry,' he said. 'Those bloody Thickpennys, I'm never sorry to see the back end of them!'

'The Thickpennys? From the Manley Court farm?'

'That's them, the sods! The father's been made bailiff there. The elder son's a shepherd and the other one's supposed to be the gamekeeper. I'm thankful they don't come here often. They usually make for the Swan with Two Necks down the hill where the alewife is no better than she should be and doesn't mind a hand up her skirts. My Sue won't have that kind of thing here and they know what they'd get from me if they tried it on!' After this outburst Ashton asked, 'And what brings you out so late on a night like this? A childbed?'

'No. Not tonight. But it's something I want to talk over with you.'

'Then let me get you something to drink. What will you have?'

'Rum! And I hope you will be joining me.'

'Thank you, I will.' The innkeeper disappeared to come back moments later with a bottle and two small mugs. With the mugs filled the two men moved closer to the remnants of the fire and Ashton asked 'And what is it you want to talk to me about?'

'The Thickpennys and Manley Court!'

'Good God! I wonder if it's got anything to do with what I overheard them talking about earlier. Some gypsy they caught this afternoon and have been beating up?'

'It has – quite a lot to do with it. But it's not just any gypsy but Draper's eldest boy. They've got him shut up there.'

'Young Nelson? The one everybody calls Darkie?'

'That's the lad.'

'I thought he worked at Manley Court? Has he been after the rabbits or the birds or the sheep?'

'It's not that kind of poaching – although he has been tickling trout in a peculiar stream!'

'Meaning?'

Mansell took a sip of the rum. He said, 'He's put Quint's daughter in the family way. And, so it seems, with her willing co-operation!'

'But I doubt if he's sixteen yet!'

'That may be so, Ralph, but he certainly did a good job and I've just come away from the Court after putting matters to right. There'll be no baby now but that's not the end of the business. If we don't get young Nelson away tonight the Thickpennys have been ordered to cart him off to London tomorrow where he's to be shipped off to Shanghai in one of Quint's square riggers and may never come back.'

'Gypsy Draper wouldn't like that! Nelson's the apple of his eye. Always has been, always will be. He reckons the lad has a rare gift for horses. He's supposed to be able to talk to them so they understand every word he whispers in their ears.'

'So I've heard say, Ralph, but he won't be talking to many more horses if they get him on that boat for China.'

'Then we must do something quickly!'

'You'll be willing to help me?'

'Aye! Ready and willing. But what can we do to get him away from where he is?'

Mansell then told the innkeeper what he had arranged with Mrs Lestrange and asked, 'If we can get him out can you hide him up here for a few days until I make some arrangements with his father to get him well out of the district?'

'That's no problem, William. I've a good dry loft above an outhouse in the yard and my Sue will be able to feed him. She'll be glad to help if it means putting one across the Thickpennys!'

'Good! And what about a cart for tonight in case he's been so badly hurt he can't walk far?'

'I've a handcart that ought to do.'

'Splendid. Let's have another drink!'

Mansell and the innkeeper set off for Manley Court at a quarter to midnight watched by Susan Ashton who had been fully informed of what had been happening and what it was proposed doing. The cart with its wheel axles well oiled still made some clatter on the road but, as Ashton said, it was unlikely that the

Thickpennys would hear anything that night other than their own drunken snoring. Mrs Lestrange who was expecting someone to arrive did hear the slight noise they made when they turned into the driveway to the Court and was waiting by the foot of the front door steps when they arrived. She was carrying a dark lantern with the slide only open the merest fraction so that it could be seen she was there.

'Leave the cart here and follow me,' she murmured and with that led them off to the stable yard at the back of the house.

'You're sure the Thickpennys have left no one on guard?' asked Mansell.

'I think not. It was some time ago when I heard them in the yard but from what I heard of their voices I'm certain they all moved off together after they'd made a quick check in the horsebox. I expect they're asleep in their cottage down the lane by now.'

'Good! Which box is the boy in? We don't want to disturb any horses.'

'You won't. All the horses are boxed on the other side of the yard. The boy's in the first box this side.'

'Good! Now you'd best be off and leave the rest to us. Can you spare the lamp? We may need it. I'll return it when I come tomorrow night.'

'No need, Doctor, we've several. One won't be missed.' There was a swish of skirts as Mrs Lestrange turned and melted into the blackness of a night with no moon or stars.

Moments later the doctor and the innkeeper found Nelson. He was curled up on loose straw at the back of the horsebox and when they held the light over him they could see that he was bound at wrists and ankles with thin cords. He was also gagged with a dirty neckerchief. His eyes were wide open with fear as he peered up at the two men hovering over him.

'Don't be frightened, Nelson,' said Mansell softly. 'We're friends. We've come to get you out of here.' Then before releasing the gag he warned, 'Don't say anything. We'll answer all your questions when you're safely away.'

Nelson nodded his understanding and while Mansell was unknotting the tightly tied neckerchief the innkeeper was cutting the cords at wrists and ankles.

'God!' Ashton exclaimed when, on turning Nelson to his side he discovered the boy's torn shirt and bloodied back.

'Look at what the bastards have done to him!'

Mansell made a hurried examination. 'Hell!' he said 'The sooner we get him somewhere where I can do something about it the better. The sods have marked him for life!'

Together Mansell and the innkeeper carefully raised Nelson to his feet. 'Do you think you can walk a little way, Nelson?' asked Mansell. 'Just a few yards. Then we'll put you in the cart we've brought. It won't be a comfortable ride but it won't take us long to get you to a place where you'll be looked after.'

But the boy collapsed on them and he was quite unconscious when they lifted him gently and carried him to the cart.

*   *   *

Two hours later, on recovering consciousness, Nelson found himself not in the loft of an outhouse but in a bed within the Highlander Inn itself. This had been at the insistence of Susan Ashton.

'I'll not have him out there in the state he's in,' she said. 'We've a bed and he shall have it. He needs looking after properly.'

Between them they had stripped off Nelson's bloodstained rags and washed him all over gently but thoroughly and Mansell treated the lad's badly striped back and buttocks with a cool, soothing ointment. Finally they had put him to bed wrapped in an old soft sheet.

But the coming back to consciousness had brought the realisation of pain to Nelson and he had groaned as he opened his eyes to see Mansell and Susan Ashton bending over him. He recognised the doctor at once. 'Doctor Mansell!' he cried out. 'It is Doctor Mansell, isn't it?'

'It is.'

'Where am I?'

'You're somewhere quite safe, Nelson, and don't worry. You won't be hurt again.'

The lad's eyes showed gratitude. 'And I won't be put on a ship?'

'No. No ship. You were told that, were you? Were you also told why you were beaten up and were to be sent abroad?'

Nelson nodded. 'Yes. Old Thickpenny said I'd fathered a baby on Miss Felicity. Had I?'

'You had, you young rascal!'

This brought something of a grin from Nelson which revealed his white and even teeth. Mansell realised then what a good looking youngster he was. It was not surprising the girl had been first attracted to him, then been swept off her feet and finally swept right into the straw!

Then came a look of concern on Nelson's face. 'Is she all right?' he asked. 'She hasn't been beaten, has she?'

'No, she's not been beaten nor is she likely to be, but there's no baby now. I've taken that away from her.'

'And she is all right?'

'She soon will be. Now enough talking for the present. I'm going to give you some pills which will send you off to sleep for a long time. When you do wake up you'll be feeling a lot better – '

'And I shall be bringing you something to eat,' put in Susan Ashton as she bent over the bed and kissed Nelson on his forehead almost as though he was her own child.

It was nearly three in the morning when Mansell wearily clambered into bed. Careful as he was he disturbed Anne into wakefulness and being inquisitive about the happenings of the night. When with a yawn, he concluded his tale of events she asked, 'And what are you going to do now, William?'

'Do now, my love, do now?' He yawned again. 'All I'm going to do now is to blow out the candle and go to sleep!'

He blew and the room was filled with a velvety darkness.

6. One Queen Too Many

About the same time that Mansell was blowing out his candle a drama with some far-reaching consequences was taking place near the centre of the town in a private room at the Sun Inn. There, in an atmosphere reeking with cigar smoke and brandy fumes, five men were seated around a baize-topped table strewn with glasses and playing cards. Only two of the men were in no way befuddled with drink. One was a Major Bostock, late, so he said, of the Twelfth of Foot and known because of his nose as Beaky Bostock, and the other was Captain George Hill, also, again so he claimed, of the same distinguished regiment. Their evening, which had gone well into the night and then into the early hours of the morning, had been given over not to the pleasures of a hand or two of cards but to the serious business of rooking as much money as they could from – as they saw them – three simpletons, who had been blandished into playing with them. The sovereigns and IOUs in front of Bostock and Hill indicated how successful they had been in their efforts.

The two self-styled gentlemen farmers who had been caught in the web had thrown in their hands early in the last round; so too had Captain Hill, leaving only Major Bostock and Simeon Radcliffe facing each other across the table, cards in hand. There was a look of triumph in Simeon's eyes as he laid his cards face uppermost on the table to show a full house made up with a trio of Queens and a pair of Kings.

'Beat that, Major!' he cried. 'Beat that if you can!' He reached out to gather in the substantial pile of coins in the centre of the table but was stopped by Bostock shouting loudly, 'Hold it! Hold hard! That's mine! Not yours!'

Slowly and deliberately a hand of three aces and two queens was put down. Simeon stared with disbelief, first at the cards just laid out and then at his own hand. 'It can't be!' he almost screamed. 'That's impossible. That makes five Queens! There are only four in a pack. You must be cheating!'

A deathly silence followed in which the two farmers sat up shaken out of their stupor and Major Bostock and Captain Hill rose angrily to their feet.

Bostock said in an icy voice, 'What did you say, Radcliffe? What did you say?'

'I said you were cheating! You're a bloody cheat!'

'A cheat, am I?' The Major's blue eyes were flashing dangerously. 'You called me a cheat, did you?'

'I did!'

'You heard him, Hill?'

'Yes, I heard him. I distinctly heard him!'

'And you?' Bostock was looking down at the two farmers. 'Did you hear him call me a cheat?'

Both men nodded affirmatives. Then in a cold fury Bostock turned on Simeon. 'You have accused me of cheating, Sir. I can see there is one Queen too many on the table but there may be some good reason for that. There may be an explanation. We have been playing with two packs of cards this evening and there may have been a mix-up – '

'You cheated! There's been no mix-up!' Simeon had pushed back his chair and was also on his feet. 'You've been cheating since we sat down to play, Bostock. We've been fools to play with you. I'll not be paying up on those notes I've given you. I'll make damn sure of that. I'll see you hanged first!'

Bostock's face broke into a menacing, thin-lipped smile. 'Do you think you'll get away with that, you young fool? Well, I'll not be called a cheat by an ignorant pup and then robbed of my money. You've given me paper for the best part of two hundred and fifty pounds tonight and one way or another I'll have payment in full or my name's not Bostock. I'm calling you out, Sir. I'm calling you out!'

The phrase took a moment or two to register with Simeon and then he gasped, 'A duel? You mean a duel?'

'I do, Sir. I do! That's exactly what I mean! Name your second, Sir. Captain Hill will act for me, won't you, Hill?'

'Of course, certainly of course.' Hill then looked straight and hard at Simeon and asked, 'Who am I to call on, Radcliffe, to arrange matters on your behalf? Who am I to call on this morning and where do I find him?'

Simeon hesitated but only for a brief moment. A thought

struck him forcibly. Duelling had been made illegal in recent years and although occasionally duels did take place a duel was regarded by the magistrates as a breach of the peace. Warned in advance of such a possibility they would stop the event happening. If he named his cousin Delme-Radcliffe as his second no duel could take place as Hill would be informing the chief of Hitchin's magistrates of a likely breach of the peace. There was relief in his voice when he said, 'I name Mr Delme-Radcliffe as my second. You will find him at Hitchin Priory and I will tell him that you will be calling upon him in the morning.'

With that Simeon turned quickly on his heel and with what dignity he could muster stalked out of the room. He was followed almost immediately by the two farmers both of whom seemed more than a little dazed by the course events had suddenly taken. They were obviously anxious not to be further involved.

Left by themselves Hill asked Bostock, 'What went wrong, Harry?'

'I slipped myself the wrong bloody card! That's what went wrong. It was the fourth ace I intended to drop not that Queen. There was a lot in the pot and I intended to have it. The damned thing must have got caught in my sleeve!'

'Well the damage is done now! You've landed us in a duel and we may have lost out on these IOUs!'

'I doubt it on both counts, George.' Bostock was filling two glasses from the brandy bottle and the two men resumed their seats at the table. 'That young clown is much too yellow to face up to a loaded pistol and the Radcliffes will settle up as far as the money is concerned. This Delme-Radcliffe won't want the Radcliffe name bandied around the clubs and one of them spoken of as being a bilker. When you approach Delme-Radcliffe in the morning see if you can reach a settlement. Say I'll be satisfied with a written apology and a hundred guineas for the bills.'

'You will?'

'Yes. We've had a good evening. We must have taken fifty or sixty pounds from those farmers and had the contents of Radcliffe's own purse. There must have been twenty in that!'

'Twenty-two to be exact! Yes, if I can get another hundred out of him we'll have done well enough and we can get on our way. I've taken no great liking to Hitchin. It's no place for us as I can see damn few pickings here with most of the money hereabouts in the hands of the bloody Quakers. We'll not get any of them to a card table, that I'll warrant!'

'I agree. We'll pack our bags and get back to London and the lights and the ladies! There are plenty of other young fools there who'll be eager enough to part with their money!'

A few minutes later, after the brandy glasses had been emptied, the two men picked up two lighted candlesticks and made for their bedchamber. Both were soon asleep. Simeon Radcliffe in his high-ceilinged room at the nearby Priory was tossing and turning on his bed. For him sleep did not come easily that night.

7. The Day After the Night Before

Next morning, despite his tiring night, Mansell was out and about well before nine o'clock. First he proceeded to the Swan Inn yard where he was able to hire for the day from the blacksmith a pony and trap. He then set out to find Nelson Draper's father. With the pony's hooves clip-clopping merrily he took the road at the back of the Priory which would lead first to the hamlet of Charlton and from there into the complexity of lanes south of Hitchin which necklaced the Tatmore Hills. Somewhere among these lanes and hills he fully expected to find the gypsies' encampment as most of the land in this area was not owned by the Quakers – 'the bloody Quakers', as Draper called them – but by the much more gypsy-tolerant Delme-Radcliffe.

But his very thorough and widespread search revealed no signs of Draper, nor of his family or their forlorn-looking donkey. They seemed to have disappeared overnight from the face of the earth and the few farm workers Mansell saw and was able to question had shaken their heads and denied any knowledge of Draper's whereabouts. 'Must have gone on one of his walkabouts' was the only suggestion made, with the added rider by one farmer 'Good job too! He's poached this area almost out of rabbits in the last month or two!'

The rough unpleasant weather of the evening before had given place to a bright spring-like morning and Mansell on his return journey into Hitchin gave himself over to the pleasure of the ride and the joy of feeling the sunshine falling warmly on his hands and on a head from which he had removed his tall professional hat. He was disappointed, in a way, that he had been unable to find Draper and with him solve the problem of getting Nelson safely out of the district, but he had a feeling that a solution would, sooner rather than later, present itself. For the moment it was perhaps a good thing not to move the lad from where he was in good, kindly hands recovering from his ordeal. He was at least fairly safe from pursuit by Quint and the Thickpennys and the possibility of facing up to some trumped-up charge.

After he had handed back the pony and trap to the blacksmith Mansell made for his daughter's home in Tilehouse Street. It was his grandson Daniel's fourth birthday and he had a golden present for him in his pocket. Mary, the proud mother of this sturdy infant, greeted her father warmly and immediately offered him refreshment in the form of bread and cheese and beer. This offer was quickly accepted as Mansell's appetite had been much sharpened by his jaunt into the countryside and he was ready for something to eat and ale to quench his thirst.

After the meal he sat Daniel upon his knee and showed him a half-sovereign, holding it in the palm of his hand.

'Do you know what this is, Daniel?'

The wide-eyed Daniel said, 'Yes, Grandpa. It's money!'

'And what do you do with money?'

'Buy things, Grandpa.'

'And what will you buy with this if I give it to you for your birthday? It is your birthday, isn't it?'

'Yes, me four today.'

'You haven't told me what you are going to buy.'

'A horse. I shall buy a horse!'

'I don't think it's enough money to buy a real horse, Daniel, but how about a wooden one? One on wheels which you can ride?'

The child thought for a moment and then nodded his head. 'Yes, Grandpa, a wooden horse.' He reached out his hand to take the money but Mansell, instead of giving it to him clenched the coin into his fist and held this high over the boy's head. Almost immediately he lowered his hand and held it open. It was empty. As Daniel's face began to crumple with disappointment and tears seemed imminent Mansell quickly raised and lowered his fist again. Then when he opened his hand two half-sovereigns lay revealed in his palm.

Daniel's eyes goggled as he took the money,. A sunny smile appeared. 'You do that 'gain, Grandpa. Me like!'

Mary, who was standing by, was laughing. 'He can't Daniel' she said. 'He never could! That's an old trick of your Grandpa's. It's one he used to play on me when I was a little girl. Now stop teasing him, father, but you shouldn't have been so generous.

and Daniel, you say thank you and give your grandfather a big kiss.'

It was while kisses were being wetly exchanged that the door was suddenly opened and John Timmins, Mary's husband, appeared. It was Mansell he addressed.

'Thank goodness you're here!' he said somewhat breathlessly. I've been sent to find you. The Squire wants to see you as soon as possible. He says it's urgent!'

'How did you know I was here?'

'I didn't! I came here first because I thought Mary might know where I was most likely to find you today.'

'Well you've been lucky and found me quickly. I will go back with you immediately. You don't know what it's about I suppose?'

John said he had no idea of what was afoot. All he knew was that Mr Delme-Radcliffe wanted to see Mansell and no matter what the doctor was doing he was to drop it and come at once to the Priory. John then led the way at a run to a side door at the house and Mansell was admitted and taken without delay to the library and shown in.

Delme-Radcliffe and a tall, very thin gentleman who Mansell recognised immediately as the lonely rider who had turned into the Priory the previous evening, were seated close together at a table near a window. Open before them was a baized-lined mahogany case in which reposed two long-barrelled pistols, a powder flask, flints and a ball mould together with half a dozen balls.

The Squire pointed to a chair. 'Sit yourself down, Mansell. This gentleman and I have a very delicate matter to discuss with you. Let me introduce you to each other. Arthur, this is Mansell, the local doctor I was telling you about. He's someone we can trust to be careful in what he says. Mansell, this is Sir Arthur Hutchinson, my racing advisor and friend who is a bloodstock breeder with a stud farm at Royston.'

There was a polite exchange between the doctor and the baronet, a politeness which blossomed into warmth when Sir Arthur's face was lightened by a pleasant, lop-sided smile.

Delme-Radcliffe continued with a question. 'You will remember my cousin Simeon, Mansell? You've reason to, I know.'

'I do. I thought I saw him at the Swan yesterday alighting from the London coach but I wasn't sure at the time.'

'That was him! And a bloody fine mess he's made of things since he arrived!' Delme-Radcliffe then related what Simeon had blurted out to him early that morning about the happenings at the Sun during the night.

'And I take it that his story was confirmed,' said Mansell, 'by this Captain Hill when he called on you this morning?'

'It was. More or less. Hill produced Simeon's IOUs and said they amounted to two hundred and forty pounds and then had the cheek to offer, on behalf of Bostock, to call off the duel and settle for a single hundred and a written apology!'

'You didn't agree to such an arrangement?'

'Not bloody likely! I told him the duel would have to be fought and we wouldn't pay out a penny on those notes whatever the outcome from the exchange of shots.'

Mansell was astonished. 'But a duel!' he exclaimed. 'That's illegal these days and you're a magistrate!'

Both the Squire and the baronet laughed. 'True,' said Delme-Radcliffe. 'True enough, but we're arranging one. I intend teaching Simeon a lesson that he'll not forget in a hurry. I shall second him and Sir Arthur has agreed to act as director of ceremonies. You, I hope, will be the surgeon present. Hill's agreed to all this. I've told him you've had more experience with gunshot wounds than the rest of the Hitchin doctors put together.'

'Is Simeon prepared to fight?'

'Yes – reluctantly, very reluctantly – but he's got no choice if he wants any money from the Trust Fund I administer on his behalf. And he's desperate for money at the moment.'

'When is the duel to take place? Today?'

'No. Tomorrow morning at eight, on the rose garden lawn at the side of the house. But as soon as we've got the two of them in position and ready to shoot I shall step in as a magistrate and put a stop to the affair. There'll be no exchange of fire but it should have gone far enough by then to really frighten Simeon. Don't you agree?'

Mansell laughed. 'Yes,' he said, 'it probably will but it could even go one stage further if you wanted it to!'

Delme-Radcliffe and Sir Arthur both looked at Mansell with amused curiosity written plainly upon their faces.

'How? In what way?' asked Sir Arthur.

Mansell explained what he had in mind and when the resultant laughter had died down Delme-Radcliffe raised a query. 'You're sure you can do it without anyone noticing what you've done?'

There was a quick demonstration of his skill by Mansell with two balls taken from the pistol case. 'Satisfied?' he asked as he returned the balls to their rack.

'Well satisfied!' exclaimed Sir Arthur. 'I'll be damned if I saw how you did that under my nose and got away with it! By Gad, Sir, if all goes to plan tomorrow morning I'll be able to dine out on the story for the remainder of the year!'

Before taking his leave Mansell picked up the ball mould from the case and, with a smile for his fellow conspirators, dropped this in the pocket of his frock coat.

* * *

The two men who sat sipping their brandies in a room at the Sun Inn were far from pleased with the course taken by the events of the morning.

'I'm still of the opinion,' ventured Major Bostock, 'that the buggers will come up with a last minute settlement.'

'I'm not so sure,' said Hill, shaking his head. 'That Delme-Radcliffe is nobody's fool. He's a shrewd man and he seems to have some reason for not settling.' There was a pause before the Captain went on, 'Supposing no settlement is reached, will you continue with the challenge?'

'Yes, George, I shall!'

'You won't kill him, will you?'

'No. I don't want a murder charge hanging over my head for a whipper-snapper like him and have to fly the country. No, I shan't kill him but I'll certainly wing the sod and give that doctor a chance to earn a fee. I take it they're a good pair of pistols that are being provided? You checked them?'

'I did! They are a pair of Mantons.'

'Mantons? Good! Then whatever the outcome, settlement or pistols, we'll have no problem in the morning!'

8.   Evening Round

Mansell spent the afternoon restocking his carpet-bag and the kitchen was full of peculiar smells as he mixed and bottled a variety of potions and made up a large pot of soothing ointment in readiness for his call later in the day on Darkie Draper at the Highlander Inn. He also busied himself with pestle and mortar making a paste for pills. After supper, when Anne had put an excellent pork pie upon the table, he lit the cigar Delme-Radcliffe had given him that morning and for a brief time, while he smoked this, he sat back feeling at peace with the world.

But at seven o'clock, with the cigar reduced to fine grey ash and a damp stub to be tossed into the fire, he reluctantly rose to his feet and prepared to set off on his evening round.

First he made for the Highlander Inn. There he found the gypsy lad sitting up in bed and seemingly much improved although his back, when examined, was still raw in places.

'Do you know where your father is likely to be at the moment?' asked Mansell as he gently applied the ointment he had made up that afternoon. 'I've searched the Tatmore Hill lanes today but I can find no traces of him and the rest of your family. They seem to have vanished. Do you have any idea as to where they might be?'

'Baldock,' suggested Nelson. 'Baldock's likely. They sometimes go there this time of year and join up with Uncle Joe's lot. There's good poaching there! And chickens! And eggs! Uncle Joe's got a special shirt for egg gathering. Like a quilt it is, with rows of little pockets for the eggs.'

Mansell thought for a moment. 'Baldock?' he queried. Baldock was a small town about six miles from Hitchin at most. He could of course hire the pony and trap again and perhaps even take Nelson with him. 'Where in Baldock can they be found?'

'They can't, not unless they want to be. They don't usually want to be found when they're that way!'

'Could you find them?'

'Maybe I could. Maybe I couldn't.'

'Could you try?'

'Yes, I could try.'

'Good! In a few days when you are well enough to travel we'll hide you under some blankets in a pony trap and go and look for them.'

The innkeeper's wife, who was assisting Mansell, said firmly, 'You're not to hurry things, Doctor. Nelson's safe enough here for the time being and he's no trouble. No, you let him stay for a while.'

Before he left for Manley Court, however, Mansell insisted on Susan Ashton accepting some of the money placed at his disposal by Mrs Lestrange. 'Too much!' she protested as he pressed the coins into her hand. 'Far too much!'

At Manley Court he was admitted by a finger-to-lip Mrs Lestrange. 'We'll talk when we're upstairs,' she murmured.

Felicity, when they reached her room, was sitting in a chair by a small, cheerfully burning fire. She was still in her night attire over which was a bright blue dressing robe. Her hair had been neatly done and ribboned and she smiled quite happily when she saw Mansell.

'Feeling better! he asked.

'Lots better! I can't really believe anything has happened!'

'Oh! It's happened all right. You have had no trouble today? You slept well last night?'

It was Mrs Lestrange who answered his questions.

'Yes, she had a good night's sleep and things seem to have settled down very nicely.'

'Except with father and those Thickpennys!' put in Felicity. 'Mrs Lestrange has told me how you managed to get Nelson away. Is he all right? Is he safe now? Have you seen him today?'

Mansell chuckled at the spate of questions the girl had flung at him. He said, 'Nelson's doing fine, thank you, Felicity. His back is beginning to heal, he's in good hands and he was quite safe when I saw him a little while ago. But I'll not be telling you where he is. The fewer people who know that the better. Even you might let something slip, my dear, or be forced into telling someone.'

'Yes, I understand.' There was a momentary hesitation before

Felicity added shyly, 'When you see him next time will you tell him – tell him I still love him.'

Mansell nodded and smiled. 'I will, but don't you think it would be best for you both if you tried to forget each other?'

'No! Never!' Felicity's eyes were flashing fiercely. 'Never! Never! Never! One day I shall marry him! Then we shall have lots of babies. You'll see!'

Mrs Lestrange was smiling and Mansell gave a subdued laugh. 'We shall see, shall we? Well, if you do, my dear, we'll wish you every happiness, and as for the babies – well I'll be only too pleased to deliver them for you!'

'And I'll help you to bring them up,' said Mrs Lestrange, 'but enough of that for now, Doctor. What more is there to be done for your patient now? Anything?'

'Very little, almost nothing that I can do. The rest is up to you and Felicity. She needs to take things quietly for the next few days. She needs some small but really nourishing meals and that's about all.' Mansell took a pill from a box in his bag. 'Give her this tonight with a warm drink and she'll sleep the clock round again but I shan't come to see her tomorrow, in fact I don't intend looking in for another week unless you send for me. And I'm certain you won't need to do that.'

When he had put the pill box back into the carpetbag Mansell asked, 'And when did they discover that Nelson was missing?'

'Early this morning,' answered Mrs Lestrange. 'It was just before six o'clock when I heard the hullabaloo in the stable yard. The Thickpennys couldn't believe their eyes when they saw the horsebox was empty. Each was blaming the other for not bolting the door properly or for not seeing that Nelson's bonds were still tightly tied.'

'What did Mr Quint have to say when he was told?'

'He said quite a lot! Most of it is unrepeatable! He thinks that Nelson's father must have heard something about the matter and broken in here last night to rescue him. He was livid with rage!'

'Not a good thing for a man of his age and complexion! He might have had an apoplexy. Is he calmer now?'

'Still simmering but I do not think he intends to pursue the matter. It would still be as well, I think, for Nelson to disappear for a while. A long while!'

Rubbing his chin thoughtfully Mansell said, 'Then we shall have to see what can be arranged for the lad.' Turning to Felicity he asked, 'And what about you, young lady? What's going to happen to you? Are you going back to school when you are better?'

'Yes, Doctor. But not the one in London. They won't have me again. No, I'm being sent to Mrs Bonnamy's Academy in Hitchin.'

'Good! That's a capital idea. I'm sure you'll be happy there. Mrs Bonnamy is an old friend of mine, I know her well. But she's quite strict, Felicity, very strict, and you won't be able to get into mischief there! She's a real dragon when it comes to young men and her young ladies!'

'A worse dragon than Mrs Lestrange?' Felicity was squeezing the housekeeper's hand with affection as she asked the question.

'Worse? Far, far worse, I should think!' Mansell smiled and turned to leave the room but he paused at the door as Felicity called out, 'You won't forget, will you Doctor? You won't forget what I asked? You'll tell him when you see him?'

'No, my dear, I won't forget. I'll tell him!'

Preceded by Mrs Lestrange the doctor descended the stairs. On reaching the hall they made straight for the front door. They had agreed that for Mansell to call on Quint that night would serve no useful purpose.

9. Pistols for Two – Coffee for Three

May Day dawned a little misty and rather chill but long before the sky above Hitchin's Windmill Hill was suffused with pale pinkish light the town's mayers were about the streets. These mayers, largely from the grimy alleys and yards of Back Street, had set out about three in the morning to visit most of the larger and more respectable houses in the town, to affix branches of blossoming may to front doors where no offence had been given by the servants during the year, or, where offence had been given to or taken by one or more of the mayers, bunches of nettles. After four o'clock the mayers had started their day of frolicking, singing and dancing in groups in various parts of the town.

One such group, made up of people raggedly clad or decked out in tawdry finery, complete with musicians, vociferously greeted Mansell as he approached the junction of Sun Street and Bridge Street, where a Maypole had been erected for revelry later in the day. Their shouts followed him as, pursued by a face-blackened man brandishing a broom and a bonneted woman with a large ladle, he hurriedly turned into the Priory entrance gates. He then escaped their attention only by flinging down in the road a handful of small coins which they stopped to pick up.

Thankful for his escape, Mansell looked up to where Delme-Radcliffe and Sir Arthur Hutchinson were waiting for him at the top of the steps leading to the main door of the house. Both men were laughing heartily at his flight from the mayers; chokingly the Squire said, 'Gad, Mansell! You're lucky to be out of that in one piece. Mad Moll and her husband seem to be capable of anything this morning. He's been sweeping road dust over everyone who has passed him without leaving a copper or two in the road!'

With greetings exchanged Delme-Radcliffe led the way through the house and out to the rose garden. There on the lawn, a long table had been set up and covered by a white cloth. This was flanked by two chairs.

'As you requested, Mansell. I trust it's to your liking?'

'It is Squire, it is. It's exactly what I had in mind' replied Mansell. 'I see Sir Arthur has brought the case of satisfaction pistols and if he will kindly place this centrally on the table I will then arrange the rest of the display.'

From his carpet-bag the doctor first produced his box of surgical instruments and then he set out a horrifying array of forceps, scalpels, knives, pincers, clamps and strap tourniquets. He next took from the bag rolls of bandages and some pads for dressing wounds. Lastly he set out his shallow tin tray and filled this with the tar-water solution.

Delme-Radcliffe regarded the decked-out table with a smile twitching at the corner of his mouth. 'Damme Doctor!' he said, 'If that little lot doesn't scare Simeon the bugger's got more guts than I've given him credit for – what say you, Arthur?'

Sir Arthur grinned. 'From what I've seen of that fellow I'm sure it will almost frighten him out of his wits but I hope it won't frighten him too much. If it does he may not toe the line this morning!'

At that moment a footman appeared, bringing with him Major Bostock and Captain Hill. After introductions had been effected and the table regarded with some puzzlement by the newcomers, Hill took Delme-Radcliffe to one side and said, 'I see you're expecting bloodshed this morning?'

'It's a possibility of course. I expect your man is a good shot and not likely to miss. I can't say the same about my fellow. I doubt if he's ever handled a pistol.'

'Then wouldn't it be better to settle the matter on the lines we offered?'

'I've been given no instructions to agree to that. I think as things stand we must proceed and let the duel take place.'

Hill shook his head. 'Well, so be it. But where is your fellow? I just heard your clock over the stables strike eight and he hasn't shown yet. He's going to, isn't he?'

'That clock is fast by five minutes. We keep it that way so we're not late for church!' Delme-Radcliffe then pointed to the side door of the house, 'And there is my man. I can also see that Sir Arthur is signalling everyone to join him.'

The white-faced, stary-eyed Simeon drew close to the table and looked at it with horror. There was a frantic appeal in his manner as he turned to Delme-Radcliffe but the Squire only slowly shook his head. The appeal was being dismissed.Sir Arthur, when the principals and their seconds had gathered around him, said, 'This affair of honour on which you both seem to be set can now proceed but before it does I shall ask each of the contenders in turn whether or not he is prepared to accept some other form of settlement. You, Major Bostock, what say you?'

'I will only accept an apology and the payment of the money owed in full. Nothing less!'

'And you, Mr Radcliffe? Are you prepared to apologise and redeem your IOUs?'

The refusal when it came from Simeon was just a tremulous, 'No. I can't!'

'Then' said Sir Arthur, 'I shall proceed with the loading of the pistols.' He nodded to Captain Hill, 'I'm asking you, Sir, to select two balls from the rack in the case. Please examine them carefully for equality of weight and size. When you are satisfied place them both in the tray which Dr Mansell is holding out in readiness.'

Hill looked somewhat nonplussed but did as requested and dropped the balls into the liquid. 'Why wet them?' he asked.

Mansell answered him. 'It's a precaution,' he said. 'Just a precaution. A clean ball makes for a clean wound. A wound which should heal quickly.'

'You've no objections, Hill, have you?' Sir Arthur enquired.

Hill shrugged his shoulders. 'None, but I've never known this sort of thing done before. Carry on, Sir, carry on!'

The baronet then began to load the pistols with considerable care, taking the balls from Mansell, who appeared to be drying each in turn on a white linen cloth. When the weapons had been loaded they were laid side by side on the table uncocked. Sir Arthur then asked, 'Is everyone satisfied that the pistols have been fairly and properly loaded?'

There were muttered affirmatives from the principals and seconds.

'Good! Now, Major Bostock and Mr Radcliffe, I suggest that you remove your coats and hats and place these on the chairs.

The duel will take place in shirt-sleeves. A coat is not easy to remove from a wounded man.'

Again Hill showed signs of demurring on his principal's behalf but when he saw that Bostock was already divesting himself quite willingly and that Delme-Radcliffe had already slipped Simeon's coat from his shoulders he shrugged and let the protestation drop.

Sir Arthur said, 'Right. Excellent. Now pick up your weapons. Mr Radcliffe, who has been challenged, has the first choice.'

Simeon fumbled in lifting the pistol of his choice and Sir Arthur spoke to him sharply. 'Take care, Sir! I know the pistols are not cocked but mishaps can happen if they are not handled carefully. And, both of you, please move to the centre of the lawn. Take up your positions back to back over the tape which the doctor has just put down.'

When the two men were in position Sir Arthur ordered 'Cock your weapons gentlemen. I shall now start counting from one up to ten. At each count you will each take one pace forward. At the count of ten, after the pace has been taken, you will about-turn and fire and you must fire immediately. There must be no deliberate taking of aim. You understand?'

Bostock and Simeon nodded.

'Good! One!'

The first pace was taken by each man.

'Two! Three! Four! Five!' The counting was slow and clearly called out.

'Six! Seven! Eight! Nine!'

The sounds of the morning seemed to Simeon to have disappeared suddenly. No birds sang and the singing and shouting of the distant mayers died away to nothing. He looked up to the grey, cloud-covered sky. It hung above him without any sign of mercy. His lips began to tremble.

'TEN!'

The tenth pace was taken by each duellist. Both turned. Both fired. Half a dozen birds flew up from the rose bushes. Simeon dropped his pistol to clutch at his midriff where a dark stain had appeared. Then he sank slowly to his knees before collapsing face downwards on the turf. He was moaning slightly but Mansell did not hasten to his side. Instead, while the attention of the others on their feet was focused on the stricken Simeon, the doctor was surreptitiously engaged in another matter. What had to be done had to be done very quickly but when it was done he walked over to where Simeon lay writhing, as though in agony, with Delme-Radcliffe and Sir Arthur bending over him and Bostock and Hill standing close by looking most concerned.

In a loud voice Mansell said, 'Get up, Simeon, Get up! Get up at once! You're not hurt!'

The moaning gave way to a whining, 'I am! I am! I've been hit in the stomach! I'll die! I'll die!'

'Oh no you won't – '

'Do something! Do something! Do something quick!'

'Nothing for me to do! You've only been struck by a ball made of pill paste and boot blacking! It's stained your shirt and you may have a small bruise on your belly but you'll live!'

Sir Arthur and Delme-Radcliffe were both laughing as they roughly hauled Simeon to his feet but Major Bostock's face was red with anger. So too was Hill's.

'You've made a fool of me!' declared the Major.

'And me!' said Hill. Then turning to the doctor he added, 'You must have switched those balls!'

'He did!' put in Delme-Radcliffe. 'He did! You don't think Sir Arthur and I would let a real duel go forward under our noses, do you? We're both magistrates and know the law and must uphold it! You two scoundrels should be almighty thankful we've no need to hand you over to the constables. That also applies to you, Simeon!'

But Simeon was no longer there. He had picked up his coat and hat and was shambling off towards the house.

Bostock was confronting Delme-Radcliffe with a wild and menacing look. 'You called me scoundrel, Sir! I'll not have it, Sir! As one gentleman to another, you'll retract those words!'

'Gentleman? You a gentleman?' said Sir Arthur. 'You're no gentleman. Neither is Hill. You can no longer either of you claim the right to be called a gentleman. You forfeited that right six months ago!'

Bostock and Hill stared dumbfounded at the baronet, who continued, 'Early this year I was a guest in the Regimental Mess of the Twelfth of Foot at the Bury St Edmunds barracks. There was talk then of two officers who had disgraced the regiment by being caught cardsharping. They had been forced to resign their commissions. No names were mentioned but one had been a major, the other a captain. I have no doubt you two are the men concerned.'

Bostock glared at him but made no attempt to refute the statement. He then turned to Delme-Radcliffe to say, 'You've not heard the last of this matter. That cousin of yours owes me money. I hold his IOUs and I'll damned well claim every penny – '

'Debts incurred whilst playing with proven cheats?'

'No proof of cheating exists in respect of the games where those debts were incurred! He'll pay! And if he refuses I'll set some debt collectors on him who have their own ways of making people pay up!'

Having uttered this threat Bostock picked up his coat and hat and, followed closely by Hill, stalked towards the gate of the rose garden. Both were grim-faced. Neither looked back as they turned the corner of the house.

* * *

As soon as Mansell had repacked his carpetbag and Delme-Radcliffe had put the pistols back in their case the three conspirators made their way into the Priory and through to the library. There coffee was served and cigars were lit. After a while Sir Arthur, who was relaxing comfortably in a padded armchair, said, 'Do you really think those villains will press for the payment of Simeon's notes of hand? Some of those London debt collectors can handle people very roughly.'

'Well you've no need to worry about Simeon,' said Mansell, standing up so that he could delve deeply into the right-hand pocket of his frock coat.

'What do you mean?' asked Delme-Radcliffe.

Mansell grinned broadly as he produced some pieces of paper. These he put on the table and then weighted them down with two pistol balls.

'The notes? You got hold of the notes?' Both Delme-Radcliffe and Sir Arthur registered astonishment.

'Yes! Simeon's notes. And without them Bostock has no proof of any debt!'

'But how the Devil did you get hold of the bloody things?' queried the baronet.

'I picked the pockets of the coat on the chair!'

'Good God! I saw nothing of that. When on earth did you do it?'

'When you were all looking at Simeon stretched out on the lawn thinking he'd been shot! I guessed the IOUs would be in one of Bostock's pockets. Fortunately they were in the first pocket I rifled!'

'Well I'll be damned!' exclaimed Delme-Radcliffe. 'You've certainly earned your fee today! I had in mind three guineas but seeing what you've done ten would be more like it. Simeon can pay that out of his next allowance from the Trust. Now I'm going to send for the fellow and he can personally thank you and give you the money.'

A footman was summoned and sent off with an order to bring Mr Simeon to the library immediately, but within a few minutes the man was back in the room unaccompanied.

'Well? Where is he?' asked the Squire.

'He won't come, Sir. He's locked himself in his room, Sir!'

'Has he, indeed? We'll see about that! Follow me, man!' An angry Delme-Radcliffe stormed out of the room with the footman hard upon his heels.

It was while Mansell and Sir Arthur were left waiting that an idea occurred to the doctor. 'Sir Arthur,' he said, 'Could you find a place in your establishment for a youngster who is good with horses? When I say good I mean really good.'

'I might. Is he a patient of yours?'

'Yes, in a way. He's a good strong lad but at the moment the air of Hitchin doesn't suit him!'

'And you think the Royston air would be beneficial?'

'Yes, I do. He's done nothing dishonest, let me assure you of that, but it would be better if he left the district. I think you would find him more than a little useful at your stud farm.'

'Then on your recommendation I'll give him a chance. When can I expect to see him?'

'He'll be fit to travel by the middle of next week.'

'Then tell him to report to me at Laurel Lodge next Wednesday afternoon. What is his name?'

'Draper, Nelson Draper.'

The baronet nodded and made a note in his diary. Mansell, much relieved at this solving of the gypsy lad's problem, was thanking Sir Arthur when Delme-Radcliffe re-appeared. There was a broad smile on his face. 'It's not that he won't come,' he said, 'It's more like he can't come! He's no breeches!'

'Why not?' asked Sir Arthur.

The Squire began to laugh. 'Why not?' he spluttered. 'Why not? Because our laundry woman has got 'em and they're in the wash. Simeon was so bloody scared at the sight of Bostock's pistol pointing at him he bloody well shit himself!'

With that Delme-Radcliffe screwed up the promissory notes into a tight ball and moments later they were turning to thin black ashes in the library fireplace.

10. Chapman's Yard

A mostly tempestuous May had given way to a gloriously sunny
June and the hot weather had continued into July so that quite
early in this seventh month of the year the cornfields on the
gently rolling hills around Hitchin were almost ripe enough to
harvest. But a drought had settled on the land. In the countryside
the streams had been reduced to scarcely tinkling trickles and
the dusty leaves hung listless on the trees and hedgerows. The
town itself had also been hard hit. There, many of its wells had
run dry and the River Hiz, which normally carried away the
sewage of the Back Street slums, was so shallow and sluggish it
was failing in its noisome task. The stench from its partly exposed
bed hung heavily on the warm air and even pervaded the Market
Place, the Churchyard and the High Street.

Doctor Mansell trudging his Wednesday round had planned
that his last call of the morning should be on the consumption-
ridden Mrs Deamer in Chapman's Yard. This crowded offshoot
of Back Street consisted of seventeen small houses, had more
than a hundred inhabitants and was served by only two privies
where the excrement dropped directly into the river. As the
doctor turned under the archway into the yard with its central
gulley into which chamber pots and slop pails were constantly
being emptied the harsh ammoniac smell of stale urine assailed
his nostrils and even his strong stomach almost turned at the
thought of pursuing his visit. However he pressed on and as he
passed the white-aproned women who stood with their clusters
of ragged, pallid-faced children in the open doorways of their
homes he acknowledged their lacklustre greetings with a smile
and a cheerful wave of his stick. Most of them had been patients
of his at some time or other and he had helped to bring into this
wretched corner of the world many of the children who now
stared at him with wonder in their fly-tormented eyes.

Halfway down the yard his pathway was blocked by an
immense woman with feet firmly planted apart on the ground

and arms akimbo. She said fiercely, 'So yer've come at last, 'ave yer? About time too! I sent fer yer two hours back! Where yer bin?'

An aroused Mrs Bongers, Big Lil as she was known in the yard she ruled with her mighty fists, was twenty towering stones of flesh not to be lightly brushed aside and Mansell came to an abrupt halt. He said mildly, 'I've had no message. No one has told me I was wanted here urgently.'

The erupted mountain subsided. There was a muttered, 'Then it's that bloody boy of mine. Couldn't find yer, I suppose, an 'e's gone off an 'id 'isself 'cos 'e daren't come back an tell me. I'll give 'im something when I get 'old of 'im!'

'Is it a childbed? Something before its time?'

Mrs Bongers shook her head and said quietly, 'No, nothing like that, Doctor. It's Mrs Deamer. She's proper poorly. Right bad. That cough of 'ers is racking 'er cruel and she's coughing up blood quite a bit.'

'I was on my way to see her, Lil. That's why I've come. Not that I can do much. She's gone too far and there's nothing any doctor can do. There's no cure and she can't last long. The end will come soon.'

'Then make it easy fer 'er.' Lil was looking at him significantly. 'I've 'eard say yer've eased others – '

Mansell cut her short by raising his hand and saying, 'Enough of that talk, Lil, just take me to her. I'll do what I can. I promise you that.'

The big woman turned quickly and made for the doorway of the end cottage in the yard. Mansell in pursuit followed to find as he entered the door that she was partway up the narrow stairs to the bedroom. Regarding the huge, black-skirted bottom with some little amusement he wondered how Lil's diminutive husband had managed to clamber on her belly so often to beget the seventeen children she had produced and each one produced, so it was said, without a whimper. Having kids was easy, she had once told him. 'No wors'an 'aving a bloody good shit!'

All but two of that seventeen had survived the vicissitudes of being born and raised in Chapman's Yard but how Lil had achieved this was, in Mansell's opinion, something of a miracle. He knew that her highly skilled husband had long been the best paid workman at the tannery in Bancroft but it must have been an almost impossible task to feed and clothe the growing brood on even the good money he was bringing home each week. Now three of her sons were working with their father and two of her girls were in service in the town the situation for Lil must be very much easier.

Mansell followed Lil into the bedroom at the top of the stairs. Although this contained only a bed, a table and a chair, with a curtained alcove for clothes, the pictures on the wall and the vase of flowers on the window-ledge gave the clean and neatly kept chamber an air of gentility.

The white-faced occupant of the bed was awake and although obviously distressed in her breathing she made an effort to smile as she murmured, 'It is good of you to come, Doctor. Very good of you.'

Mansell bent over her and gently raised the emaciated hand clutching a pink-stained rag. There was a slight trace of blood on the thin, almost colourless lips, and he looked closely at this as he lowered the hand to the sheet.

'You've been coughing rather a lot, I see,' he said. 'We must do something about it, mustn't we?'

There was a faintly spoken, 'I hope you can, Doctor, I hope you can. I am so tired. So very very tired. The coughing does not let me sleep and it disturbs Susan every night. She needs her sleep now she is working.'

Following the operation on the ugly tumour on her head and a short convalescence, the surgeon, Doctor Hawkins, had found employment for Susan in the household of Samuel Lucas, the painter.

'She is at the Lucases' now?' Mansell asked.

'Yes. She will not be home until just after seven this evening. Until then Mrs Bongers will look in on me from time to time. She is very kind to us. I do not know how we should manage without her.'

'Yes. Mrs Bongers is a good neighbour and I know she is very worried about you.'

'Aye, I am that, Doctor. Can't yer give 'er something a bit stronger than the cough mixture she's got? 'Ark at 'er now!'

Mrs Deamer had broken into a prolonged bout of coughing which was shaking her frail body and bringing a new froth of blood to her lips. Lil picked up the rag which had been dropped in the spasm and, with care, wiped the blood away.

After delving deeply into his carpetbag Mansell brought out a tiny bottle containing a bright green liquid. He looked at Lil significantly as he asked her to get him a half-cupful of hot water. 'Really hot,' he insisted. 'I want to make up a potion for her.'

'Will it stop the coughing, Doctor?'

Mansell nodded. 'It will, Lil, it will.' Again he was conveying something with his look in her direction.

'Then I'd best get the kettle on. It'll take me a minute or two. Fire ain't lit.'

'I can wait.' With this Mansell seated himself close to the table and watched the bulk of Lil disappearing down the stairs. When he turned back to his patient he was astonished to see her trying to reach out to the table drawer.

'Can I get something for you?' he asked.

'My purse. In the drawer. I would like to pay you.'

'That can wait surely, until you are feeling better?'

'I would rather pay you now. I may not get better, in fact I do not think I have long to live, and I would like to be certain you had been paid for all your kindness to Susan and myself. I have money now. My sister sent me some two days ago.'

'Your sister?'

'Yes, my sister Ada. I had written to my father asking for his forgiveness and help but it was my sister who replied to my letter. My father died in April – ' Another spasm of coughing interrupted Mrs Deamer's explanation and it was several moments before she was able to continue with, ' – and although he had not entirely forgiven me for the wrong I had done and he had left most of his estate to Ada there was a bequest to me of five thousand pounds. His executors have been trying to find me.'

'But how had you wronged him?'

'How, Doctor? It was to do with Ada. I eloped with the man to whom she was engaged to be married. After we went off together she became very ill and nearly died of a broken heart.' Mrs Deamer's voice almost faded away but she went on, 'Father was very angry. Ada had always been his favourite.'

'Has she forgiven you?'

'No! And she never will even though she is now aware how badly my husband treated me. He was evil and he was cruel and he was a drunkard. He died from drink only a few weeks after Susan was born and he left us almost destitute.'

'But Ada has sent you money, you say?'

'Yes. She wrote in her letter that she had no wish that we should starve while the lawyers were settling our father's estate. But that is all. She wants nothing further to do with Susan and myself. Nothing!'

The effort of so much talking had obviously exhausted the sick woman and she seemed to have sunk back even deeper into the pillows. Mansell was relieved to see Lil re-appearing at the stairhead with a cup from which a wisp of steam was rising. She placed the cup in front of him and asked, 'Is that what yer wanted?'

Mansell thanked her and then uncorking the bottle of green liquid carefully allowed six drops to fall into the water. A slight, indefinable smell hung for a moment on the air. Looking towards Lil he said 'Let her drink this when it's cool enough.'

'All of it?'

'Yes. All of it. It's not unpleasant to take.'

Mrs Deamer was murmuring something and Mansell leaned over her to catch what she was saying. His words to her were reassuring. 'Yes, my dear. It'll help you to sleep for a long, long time.'

Mrs Deamer looked at him gratefully and then she said, and her voice was clearer, 'Now, Mrs Bongers, please get my purse and give the doctor three sovereigns.'

The big woman did as asked and Mansell picked up his bag. Rising he said, 'If I'm needed I'll come at once.'

He was followed by Big Lil down the stairs. As they emerged into the yard she touched his arm. 'Where shall we find yer if we do want yer?' she asked rather anxiously.

Mansell told her where he proposed being later in the day and Lil looked relieved. 'That's close enough,' she said 'but I'll only send if I 'as to. Now I'll get back to 'er an' give 'er that drink.'

11. The Viewing of a Picture

That afternoon Mansell, in a newly sponged and well pressed frock coat, accompanied by Anne, resplendent in a new bright blue gown and a refurbished bonnet, attended the invitation viewing of pictures by Samuel Lucas being exhibited in the Dacre Room at the Town Hall in Brand Street. It was something of a special occasion for the better class folk of Hitchin and everyone who was anyone in the town or the immediately surrounding countryside was expected to attend. Some sixty pictures had been hung on the walls of the room. These were mostly watercolours of local scenes but pride of place had been given to the large oil painting, just recently completed, of Hitchin Market commissioned by the market company.

A noisily chattering crowd had already gathered around this by the time the Mansells entered the room and among this crowd were several who were depicted on the canvas. Close by stood a somewhat embarrassed Samuel Lucas shyly accepting compliments on his work. By his side was the Squire.

Mansell was greeted by Delme-Radcliffe with a warm, 'Ah, Doctor, come to see yourself in paint, have you? A damn good portrait too, I'd say. Damned good! A real likeness, don't you agree, Mrs Mansell?'

'Yes,' agreed Anne, 'It really is just like him but altogether it's a wonderful picture. I'm sure I'll be able to recognise nearly all the people in it. I think Mr Lucas has painted them splendidly.'

The painter raised a deprecating hand. 'Thank you Mrs Mansell, you are kind, too kind. But everyone has been kind. Even Gypsy Draper.'

'So he's seen himself, has he?' asked Mansell.

'Seen himself? Yes, he's seen the picture,' replied Delme-Radcliffe with a grin. 'I made sure he was invited but I drew the line at his wife and children and the donkey, although Lucas has put them all in with him. He's here now and I've asked him to entertain us shortly with his fiddle.'

Samuel Lucas said somewhat wryly, 'Was that kind of thee, Sir, seeing that so many of my Quaker brethren are present this afternoon. Thou knowest what most of them think of his music!'

'Hm!' exploded John Whiting, the fellmonger, who was standing next to Mansell. 'Music? Devil tunes! Satan's music! I'll not have it! We'll not listen to it! We'll not stay!' Gripping his wife firmly by the arm he swept her through the assembly and out through the door. Several other grimly disapproving Quakers also withdrew.

Delme-Radcliffe shrugged his shoulders and smiling broadly moved off to join his reverend brother and his lady who were seated with Mrs Delme-Radcliffe at the far end of the room at tables at which teas were being served by maids from the Priory and from Samuel Lucas's home in Tilehouse Street. Among these Mansell noticed Susan Deamer in a sober grey dress, small white apron and a neat white cap. She was circling the Squire's table when she heard the exchange of words between the brothers. The clergyman was obviously not amused. 'I'm surprised at you,' he said. 'Shocked, in fact!'

'Shocked, Arthur? Shocked at what? My upsetting of a few over-pious Quakers?'

'They were your guests. But it's not only that, it's the invitations you've issued, the peculiar people you've got here today. Fancy asking that wretched gypsy to come. You know he smells! And those tradesmen and shopkeepers coming to mix with their betters. You've even asked that charlatan Mansell. There he is over there with his dressed-up wife pretending she's a lady!'

Susan was tempted to pour tea into the speaker's lap. She thought a lot of Doctor Mansell. He had been very kind to her and her mother. She managed to slop some tea into the Rector's cup and saucer to earn a frosty glare in return for doing so. The Squire chuckled at the show of clerical spleen. He said, 'Mansell? A charlatan? He's nothing of the kind. He may not have qualified through the usual channels but he's as good, if not better than most of the bloodletters in this town. He and Hawkins are the only two I trust. Neither will suck you dry with their damned leeches. As for the tradesmen you seem to be objecting to they're all in Lucas's picture and that in my opinion gives them every right to be here!'

The Reverend Arthur remained silent, staring malevolently

first at the puddle in his saucer and then at Susan's back as she moved off to another table. Petulantly he pushed the offending crockery to one side and grim-faced resumed his gloomy silence.

Meanwhile Mansell and his wife had been joined in front of the picture by the chemist Edward Clisby and his lady. With Samuel Lucas's assistance they were able to identify the few in the painting that they had so far been unable to recognise.

'And that one talking to Mrs Baker? The one mostly back towards us?' asked Clisby.

'That's Tom the shepherd. From Manley Court farm. You don't often see him in the market, mostly it's one of those wretched Thickpennys who come but Tom is a character I felt I couldn't leave out.'

'And this one?' queried Anne Mansell pointing to a small figure at the back of the painted crowd.

'That? I don't know his name but he's one of the cattle dealers who attend fairly regularly. He comes from Baldock.'

'I can even see my assistant peering from the doorway of my shop,' said Clisby. 'You've certainly captured his likeness Mr Lucas. I must tell him to come and see it for himself when the exhibition opens to the public.'

Ten minutes later, not long after the Mansells had moved on to examine the watercolours, Gypsy Draper, fiddle in hand, stepped up on to the platform which had been erected in the centre of the room. Smiling down on the assembled company he cut a fine and handsome figure in his patchwork waistcoat of many colours. He struck up with a merry jig, that set many feet tapping and then provided a selection of pleasant, homely country airs, all well known to his audience. Only towards the end of his half-hour recital did he fill the hall with the sound of the wild barbaric gypsy tunes so hated by Whiting and his friends. It was noisily wanton music, conjuring up vivid pictures of colourfully dressed, laughing gypsies dancing in the leaping lights of camp fires, with the womens' skirts whirling upwards to wickedly reveal bare brown limbs. For a few moments those who were listening entranced were whisked away in their thoughts to some forested country beyond the seas and the mountains.

Most of those present applauded enthusiastically as the music came to an abrupt end and the gypsy, with fiddle in one hand

and bow in the other, acknowledged the applause with bows in all directions before lightly stepping down from the side of the platform nearest to the Mansells.

He murmured in a low voice, 'I've something to tell you, Doctor.'

'You have? Well come and join us for a cup of tea.' Mansell led the way to a vacant table.

'Aye, I could do with a cup. Fiddling's dry work!'

Nothing more was said until after Susan had poured their tea and had moved out of earshot. The gypsy then said, 'It's Nelson. I saw him last Monday.'

'Here? Here in Hitchin?'

'No! No, I went to Royston to sell a pony and called in at the stud farm to see him.'

'So he got there safely?'

'Yes. No trouble. You know how I told you how I got him to Baldock hidden in a haycart, well after I'd dropped him he got another lift to just outside Royston on a wagon going that way and he soon found the stud farm. Sir Arthur, so he says, was expecting him and took him on straight away.'

'Wasn't he questioned?'

'About why he was running away from Hitchin?'

'Yes. He told him about Quint and the Thickpennys and the girl he'd put in the family way but all Sir Arthur did was laugh.'

'Hm! It sounds all right but has the boy settled down?'

'Settled down? I'll way he has. He's properly landed on his feet. Some really good horses to look after, a warm loft to sleep in with two other lads and they all get well fed in the kitchen. He's doing right well, thanks to you, Doctor.'

'Good! I'm glad that business has ended satisfactorily.'

The gypsy looked uncomfortable. 'I don't reckon it is finished proper,' he said. 'In fact I know it aren't.'

'What do you mean? Not finished?'

'That girl. He wants to see her again. He might even risk coming back for a visit if he thought he could meet up with her.'

'That wouldn't be wise. If Quint or the Thickpennys caught him he might well find himself again in danger of being shipped off to China.'

'I told him that. He says he won't try anything yet but he wants you to give her a message.'

'What kind of message? And why me?'

'He thinks you could do it safer than me. Old Quint or that Mrs Lestrange might think things if they catched me talking to her.'

'What's the message?'

'This.' Draper felt in a waistcoat pocket and brought out a folded paper.

'Nelson can write?' asked Mansell.

'A bit. The Quint girl taught him a bit of reading and writing and he's sharp is Nelson. Soon picks things up.'

Mansell opened the paper. A childish, crudely printed two lines read –

'I STILL LOVE YOU.
WILL COME BACK SOON. NELSON.'

Mansell showed the note to Anne who smiled and said, 'Well done, Nelson. It's all spelled correctly too!'

Draper grinned. 'He was helped,' he said with a chuckle.

'Who by?' asked Anne who was curious.

'Her Ladyship! So he said. She seems to have taken to him and has been helping him with his words and showing him things.'

'Has she indeed!' exclaimed Mansell with a laugh, not altogether surprised that the good-looking gypsy boy had made another kind of conquest. 'Well I don't suppose he'll get her into trouble though I'm surprised at her aiding and abetting him.'

The hall was emptying rapidly and soon after the gypsy had left them Mansell and his wife decided to leave. As they were walking over to say farewell to the Squire and Samuel Lucas there was a sudden but orderly influx of girls and young women headed by a lady in a smart black dress and a small highly fashionable bonnet discreetly decorated by a white bow.

'It's Mrs Bonnamy!' exclaimed Mansell, 'And the young ladies of her academy. They're latecomers.'

'Late at my request,' said Samuel Lucas. 'They're my occasional pupils and I wanted the hall fairly clear before I conducted them around the pictures.' He hastened away towards Mrs Bonnamy as Anne nudged her husband and asked,

'Isn't that Felicity Quint at the back with Amanda Fostring – the Radcliffe child?'

'So it is.'

'Are you going to give her that note?'

'If I get the chance when she is by herself.'

The opportunity came almost immediately when, instead of making towards the platform on to which Mrs Bonnamy and Samuel Lucas were stepping, Felicity made directly for Mansell.

'Have you heard anything?' she asked eagerly. 'Anything about Nelson?'

'I have!'

'Is he safe?'

'Quite safe. He's well and he's happy in the work that he's doing.'

'Where is he?'

'Not far away. He's at Royston. His father saw him there on Monday. He brought this back for you.' Mansell slipped the note into the girl's hand and the girl, sheltering behind Anne Mansell, opened it surreptitiously and read its short content. She was blushing when she asked, 'Do you know what it says, Doctor?'

'I do and I strongly advise you to burn it and forget it. No good can come of it. You know that, Felicity, no good at all.'

'But it will! I know it will! I shall marry him one day! You see if I don't! The girls voice had risen sufficiently enough to attract the attention of Mrs Bonnamy who called out a reprimand from the platform, 'Quiet, Felicity, quiet. Keep your voice down please. Now all of you, pay attention to what Mr Lucas has to say.'

Whilst Samuel Lucas was addressing the girls Mansell and his wife withdrew from the hall but as they descended the steps into Brand Street a small boy ran up and blocked their way. 'Doctor! 'Ere Doctor!' The boy was still panting from his running. 'Ma wants yer, wants yer quick. She said I'd find yer 'ere.'

'Ma?' Then Mansell recognised the urchin. 'Mrs Bongers is your ma, isn't she? And you're Bartholomew, aren't you?' All of Big Lil's children, at the insistence of their chapel-going father, had biblical names.

'Aye, Doctor. I'm Bart. But yer've gotter come quick.'

'What's happened?'

'Dunno. She didn't say but I reckon it's ter do with Mrs Deamer. She was coming out of 'er 'ouse when she called me.'

Turning to Anne, Mansell said gravely, 'If it is what I think it is, my dear, it will be best if you go back into the hall and see Sam Lucas. I expect he knows that Susan's mother is very ill so just ask him if she can leave at once. Don't bring her to Chapman's Yard though. Taker her home to our place. She will, I'm sure, have to spend the night with us.'

Anne nodded and went back up the steps. Mansell with the boy running beside him made for Back Street. Big Lil greeted him from the top of the stairs as he entered the house in the yard with a grim, 'She's gorn, Doctor, she's gorn!'

Brushing her aside as he entered the bedroom Mansell realised that haste was of little avail. If Lil meant that Mrs Deamer was dead, such would be the case. She would have seen death come many times to Chapman's Yard and would know when the cold fingers had touched again. It took no more than a cursory inspection to confirm the assertion which had been made. Mrs Deamer's eyes were closed and her face composed. There was even the hint of a smile on her lips but the spark of life was out.

Mansell glanced at the cup on the table. It was still as he had left it. He looked at Lil and said, 'You didn't give it to her?'

'I tried to but she wouldn't 'ave it. She told me she wouldn't 'ave it until she's done what she'd got ter do.'

'What was that?'

'Write in 'er bible.'

'Write in her bible? Was she able to?'

'It weren't easy for 'er but she did it. She made me get Mrs Brown from next door to be in the room while she wrote. Then when she'd finished she made us put crosses under what she'd wrote.'

'And then?'

'She looked at us in a strange kind of way and lay 'erself back and went ter sleep.'

'To sleep?'

'Yes, ter sleep! It were sleep. I know it were. She were breathin' quiet like and she weren't coughing at all, so we just left 'er. I reckoned I'd come back later and give 'er that stuff ter drink. I came back about twenty minutes ago and she'd gorn. She weren't breathing no more.'

'Where is the bible now?'

'Under 'er piller where we put it.'

Mansell felt under the pillow and brought out a small bible.
Opening this he saw, written on the flyleaf in spidery, shaky
writing obviously done with much effort –

> I leave everything to my daughter
> Susan Helen Deamer. I name Doctor
> William Mansell as my executor and
> as guardian to Susan until she
> is of age
>
> Helen Deamer
>
> Witnessed by Mrs Bongers and Mrs Brown.
> These are their marks   X   X

When he had finished reading this to himself Mansell asked,
'Do you know what this is, Lil?'

'No, Doctor. I can't read an' she didn't tell us what it were.'

'It's her will. It makes me responsible for seeing that she is
properly buried and that Susan gets money left by her grandfather. She is also put into my care until she is twenty-one.'

Big Lil seemed relieved. 'I'd 'ave looked after 'er,' she said.
'Yer know that. One more mouth with my lot wouldn't 'ave
made that much difference an' she's earning anyway.'

'You are a good woman, Lil,' said Mansell as he drew the sheet
over the dead woman's face. 'I don't doubt you'd have stood by
the girl. Now Mrs Mansell and I will try to do our best for her
and her mother can rest in peace. As things are now Susan will
not have to go to an aunt who does not want her. We shall
regard her as one of our own.'

Lil had picked up the cup from the table. 'What about this?'
she asked.

Mansell took the cup from her and looked down from the
open window of the bedroom into the yard. It was clear below
and he held out the cup and tipped out its contents. Then
without saying anything he returned the cup to Lil.

It was nearly seven o'clock before Mansell reached home and
was able to sit down to his evening meal. He had seen John
Jeeves, the undertaker, about the funeral arrangements and also
had a meeting with Hawkins in his Portmill Lane office. He had

been assured that the bible will was valid and the lawyer had agreed to write to Susan's aunt and also to take up the matter of the inheritance. As to the girl herself, she, according to Anne, had taken the news of her mother's death tearfully but she had been given a mild sedative and put to bed upstairs in a borrowed nightgown.

There was no doubt in Mansell's mind in respect of Susan's immediate future. Hawkins had supported his view that the money she had been left would, if properly invested, yield sufficient interest to pay for her schooling at Mrs Bonnamy's. In the morning he intended to call on that formidable lady.

12.   The Queen of Diamonds

It was not, however, until the afternoon that Mansell was free to visit Mrs Bonnamy. Three calls, one of which had been a sad and profitless stillbirth had kept him fully occupied throughout the sweltering morning, and when he eventually reached the elegantly fronted residence in Bancroft which housed the Academy for the Daughters of Gentlemen he was overwarm and not in the most amiable frame of mind. Having given a series of resounding raps on the highly polished knocker he waited somewhat impatiently for the door to be opened. Whilst doing so his appraising eyes surveyed this broad main thoroughfare of Hitchin and again it struck him as being a curious street of contrasts. On both sides it was bounded mainly by gracious, some even porticoed, houses yet it contained a tanyard, some farm buildings, the noisome Bridewell and a row of almshouses. It even curved its way close by the town's gasworks. Mansell sniffed. Borne on the warm almost still air, he could smell the distinctive odours of the tanyard and the gasworks but they were not, to his mind, offensive enough to cause concern and he knew if he could have afforded to have done so he too would have set up his home and a surgery in this street among the other doctors in the town.

The door was opened, after what seemed to be an excessive time, by a very small and very young-looking maid. She recognised him immediately, gave him a demure curtsy and said, 'Please come in, Doctor. Madam will be expecting you. She is in the garden.'

'Expecting me? Why should she be expecting me? Is she not well?'

'Oh dear! I thought she must have sent for you. It's her ankle. She's hurt her ankle!'

'How did she do that?'

'She fell off a platform yesterday afternoon. Now she's sitting with her foot up on a chair.

74

'Then you had better take me to her straight away.'

The girl escorted him through the house and out into a large, pleasant garden of sweeping lawns, bright flowerbeds and shady trees. Seated beneath a huge and ancient apple tree was Mrs Bonnamy, with her right foot resting on a cushioned stool. Seated near to her were her twin sons, Peter and Paul, presumably at home on Long Vacation from their Cambridge college.

Their mother greeted Mansell with a surprised, 'William? I do not recall summoning you. What are you doing here?' There were strong traces of her French background in her accented speech. 'It was only a little mishap. Tomorrow perhaps the swelling will have gone down and I shall be able to walk properly again.'

'I'll be the judge of that, Madeline, when I see what damage has been done. I know that you did not send for me and it is not on a medical matter on which I wished to consult you but I insist that you let me see your foot. It was a pity that you did not call me out when you had the accident, I might have saved you some distress.'

'La! William! I will not be scolded. It is nothing. It is a trifle, but I admit is painful and inconvenient.' Mrs Bonnamy winced as she turned and looked up at her tall good-looking sons who had risen from their chairs. 'Paul, Peter, after you have greeted the doctor properly you may leave us. They have grown, have they not, William, since you last saw them?'

'Yes. They have certainly grown taller but they seem also to have grown even more alike. I do not know which is which.' Mansell took one outstretched hand with a querying, 'Peter?'

There was a musical chuckle from Mrs Bonnamy. 'Wrong! That's Paul!' The two youths were smiling broadly and their smiles made them seem completely identical.

After a short exchange during which Mansell learned a little of their progress at university where they were both reading law the withdrawal took place but not before each of the twins had kissed the hand Madeline had held out for the purpose. At this display of respect and affection for their mother Mansell smiled to himself. 'French, they're all three of them more French than English,' he thought, and then his mind went back to when, heavily pregnant, Madeline Bonnamy had arrived in Hitchin. That must have been nearly twenty years ago and he himself had not been long in the town. Then a month before she had given birth to the twins with his assistance, she had purchased the mansion in Bancroft complete with its furnishings and fittings. There had been much gossip at the time. Mrs Bonnamy's wealth, her good looks and her French mannerisms had set tongues wagging furiously, particularly as there were no signs of a husband. However Mathilde, the maid she had brought with her and who spoke only fractured English, eventually revealed to one of the tradesmen that Madame had been recently bereaved and what she was carrying would be born posthumously. She also made it plain that her mistress was an *aristocrat*, the daughter of a *comte* who had fled from France soon after her *grand-père's* head had fallen to *la guillotine*. It was, as she had murmured, '*Triste, très désolant.*'

Gossip had turned to sympathy overnight, and soon after the birth of the boys when Mrs Bonnamy set up her Academy there was no shortage of applicants for places for their daughters from the better-off people in Hitchin. The education promised would be excellent. The two assistant teachers she had engaged were well experienced, so she had said, and the pupils would be thoroughly taught all the things they should know for the proper management of a home. There would be lessons in fine needlework, drawing and music, as well as a good grounding in reading, writing and simple arithmetic. Another thing, so it was whispered, every girl before leaving would be made aware of certain facts.

Mrs Bonnamy broke into his reverie. 'Thoughts, William? Thoughts. A penny for them!'

'Your pardon, Madeline, your pardon. I was thinking of the days when the boys were very young – '

'And we, William, were also a lot younger too!' A skirt was discreetly raised to reveal a stockingless leg and foot. 'You see?'

Mansell bent over to make a close inspection. 'Yes, I see,' he said and shook his head. 'It is not good.'

The foot and ankle were blue with bruising and very badly swollen but a gentle probing with his fingers revealed no broken or misplaced bones.

'You've applied cold compresses, I hope?'

'I have. Several times.'

'Good! They will have helped. Now I will dress the ankle with witch hazel. It will help ease the pain a little but not do much to hasten your recovery. Nature will have to take its course!'

She watched him with a slight smile on her face as he busied himself with a bandage and the bottle of cool astringent liquid which he had taken from his bag. When he had secured the bandage firmly in place she asked, 'And how long shall I be incapacitated?'

'At least a week.'

She made a face at him. 'A week? That is very inconvenient, William. I am due to go to London on Monday. I have booked a place on the early morning coach.'

'You cannot go.'

'But I must!'

'What is so important? Is it so important you cannot send one of the boys?'

'Yes! It needs an older head. Peter and Paul are going through a madcap stage. Because they are so alike it is easy for them to play pranks on people and then confuse everyone as to who to blame. I could not trust either of them. Certainly not both of them together.'

'I suppose you know which is which?'

'Not always until they speak. Paul is inclined to stutter. But no it would be very unwise in the matter of the business I have in mind.' Madeline Bonnamy was looking intently at Mansell. After a moment she added, 'But I could trust you with it.'

'Trust me with what?'

'I will show you, William. Let me summon Mathilde.'

Mrs Bonnamy picked up and then rang the bell she had taken from the table. Almost immediately Mathilde, now over seventy with a much lined face, appeared at the door of the house. When she reached her mistress's side she nodded at Mansell and then broke into quick voluble French. Mansell was able to gather it was a complaint about the small maid being slow in answering the door to *le docteur*. With a few placatory words from Mrs Bonnamy she calmed down and asked what was wanted of her.

Madeline Bonnamy took a large key from the chatelaine around her waist. This she handed to Mathilde, giving her instructions, so it seemed, about an iron box. Mathilde turned to peer at Mansell and then nodded, a smile revealing some gappy broken teeth. She muttered something as she moved away towards the house which sounded like '*Très bon*'

'I gather from that,' said Mansell, 'that she approves of what you intend doing.'

'Yes, she likes you. She always has done. She will return shortly with what I have asked her to get from the safe in my bedroom and she will also order young Emily to bring us some cool drinks. Let me tell you this while we are waiting. I am requiring you to go to London in my place for two reasons, William. The first is to escort Felicity Quint to her father's house and place of business in Mincing Lane. The girl is to stay there with him until September. Secondly, and of more importance as far as I am concerned, you will be taking something I wish you to sell on my behalf. Something of considerable value. I need the money to extend this house by adding two more dormitories. There is a constant demand for more places here but it is a demand I cannot meet at the moment.'

'Drat! I came here hoping that you would take one more immediately.' Mansell briefly outlined his involvement with Susan Deamer.

'How old did you say she was?'

'About fourteen but rather small for her age.'

'Hm! It may just be possible. She might be able to share a room with Amanda Fostring and Felicity Quint and it is also probable that Felicity may not be with us much longer.'

'Why not?'

'Her father is anxious to marry her off as soon as possible. He wants her safely out of the way of that gypsy boy. That is why she is to join him in London where he intends her to meet some eligible young men in the tea trade. Yes. I will take your Susan. If your wife will come and see me I will tell her what the girl will require in the way of clothes. As you know I do insist on uniform dressing.'

As Mrs Bonnamy concluded what she was saying Mathilde returned carrying a blue, soft leather bag secured by a drawstring. After placing this on the table she withdrew. Mrs Bonnamy loosened the string and took from the bag a square of black velvet and spread this out on the table. She then tipped on to this the remaining contents of the bag. Mansell gasped on seeing the cascade of glittering stones.

'Diamonds?'

'Yes, William. Diamonds. Diamonds of good quality. My lover was a diamond merchant who was convinced it was safer to have his money invested in diamonds than it was to have it in a bank.'

'Your lover, Madeline? Not your husband?'

'La! I was never married! He was but his wife was a beetch!' There was a trill of laughter from Madeline before she went on with, 'You are shocked, my William, you are shocked! I can see it in your face!'

'But the twins?'

'His of course! They know they are bastards but they do not care! But it is all our little secret, William. Ours and Mathilde's and the boys'! Their father was a good man and he left us well provided for when he gave me these diamonds on his deathbed.'

'Now you are selling some?'

'Yes. I have sold a few before but there are plenty left. I shall never want, nor will his sons. But now to business. I am going to select four for you to take to London on Monday. I will tell you where to go and how much I expect from their sale. For this service I shall pay you twenty guineas.'

'You are generous, Madeline, very generous. You are sure you can trust me?'

Mrs Bonnamy smiled. 'Of course,' she said and then carefully picked out four medium-sized stones. These she set to the side of the velvet square. The remaining diamonds were returned to the bag. Then she said, 'I shall expect you to be offered between seven hundred and fifty and eight hundred pounds. Maybe a little more than eight hundred if Solly is feeling generous!'

'Solly?' Mansell asked, watching her fold the four diamonds into a small package and taking it from her, 'Where do I find him?'

'You will find Solomon Abram at the corner where Hatton Gardens join St Cross Street.'

'A Jew?'

'An honest man! The brother of my lover and when you tell him who has sent you he will offer you a fair price.'

'Will he pay me in gold or by a bank draft?'

'It will be a bank draft.'

'That will be safer than gold.'

'Much. There will be no trouble in discounting it here at Sharples Bank in Cock Street.'

Somewhat relieved at the thought that he would not be responsible for carrying gold to that value through the streets of London Mansell pushed the package of diamonds into a concealed pocket on the inside of his frock coat. Scarcely had he done so when the small maid arrived with the cool drinks. Mansell supped his thankfully and then enquired about Peter and Paul's activities now they were home for the Summer break. Mrs Bonnamy's face clouded over. 'Mostly up to mischief, I'm afraid, William. They're keeping bad company and are much too friendly with Henry Hawkins, the lawyer's son. You must know what a trouble maker he is. Even worse, those three have now been joined by young Everett.'

'The haberdasher's boy? Another wild one!'

'A thoroughly bad influence. The ringleader of course is Hawkins. Can you imagine what he got up to last week?'

'Tied some more knockers together in Cock Street or put more snares across the doorways of you Bancroft folk? I'm aware that he got into trouble a few months ago for sending false obituaries to the local paper. Has he done that again?'

'No, it's been a new jape. He played it on Miss Mizen who lives next door to the Hawkins family in Portmill Lane.'

'I know her and don't care much for her. She's a very stuffy body.'

'Then perhaps you know that this is the season for her annual tea party. Being one of old Hawkins's clients young Henry knows her writing well. So what does he do? The wretch copies her handwriting and forges twelve invitations which he sends out to her friends in the town. When the day he had chosen arrived these great ladies tried to gain entrance to Miss Mizen's home. The poor maid answering the door was greatly upset and had hysterics and Miss Mizen, so I'm told, fainted and had to be put to bed!'

'Has young Henry got away with it?'

'So far, yes, but his father suspects him of being involved. Miss Mizen has seen John Hawkins and asked him to investigate the matter and he has promised to do so but proof will be hard to find.'

'But you know who was responsible. How?'

'Paul let something slip last Sunday when we were coming out of church and saw Miss Mizen talking to the vicar. I made him tell me the whole story.'

'But the twins were not directly involved?'

'No. They knew what was going to happen and watched what was happening from the doorway of the mill further up the road. They thought it highly amusing.'

Mansell who had no great liking for Miss Mizen, was inclined to concur with Peter and Paul, but keeping a straight face said, 'Well, I hope they'll have more sense than trying to outdo young Henry!'

Madeline Bonnamy nodded her head in agreement and held out her hand as Mansell rose to leave her. Mansell did what was expected of him and kissed it.

He was highly conscious as he was walking up the shaded side of Bancroft of the small and valuable package in his pocket and he was thankful that Hitchin was a quiet town and free from footpads. But the streets of London were a different matter. It might be well worthwhile, he decided, to carry a pistol with him. He was sure Delme-Radcliffe would lend him one.

13. Knaves in a Pack

The four riders, young and boisterously noisy, clattered into the ale-house yard, dismounted, tethered their horses and then scampered for the bar room door left open to the warm evening air. The Red Lion at Preston, a small hamlet only an easy three-mile ride from Hitchin, normally attracted few customers and had proved itself an ideal place for Henry Hawkins and his three cronies to meet and gloat over past triumphs and to discuss their plans for further mischief. On this occasion the place was deserted except for the beady-eyed ale-wife. She, without an order being given, immediately brought to the table at which they had seated themselves, a tray with four brimming tankards of mild ale.

'That's quick service!' exclaimed Hawkins. 'You must have known we were coming.'

'Saw you and heard you crossing the green,' said the woman with an ugly lopsided smile. 'I heard you all right and as you've been here twice before I knew what you'd be wanting.'

It was Paul Bonnamy who settled the score by tossing a shilling on to the tray as the woman moved away. Then addressing Mark Everett he stuttered, 'You c-c-can p-p-pay for the next r-r-round. It's your t-t-turn!'

'B-B-Balls!' Everett mimicked the stutterer. 'It's not m-m-my t-t-turn, it's Henry's!'

'Quiet, you two!' It was Peter Bonnamy intervening. 'I'll be paying! Henry's out of money. His father's cut off his allowance again.'

'Why? Has he found out about you and the Mizen affair?'

'No, Mark. He's not.' Henry answered. 'The old besom has brought him in two of the letters of invitation and asked him to make enquiries but as I wasn't fool enough to write them on the kind of paper we use in the office they won't get him far and he won't prove anything that way.'

'But he still suspects you?'

'Yes! He damn well does! He's threatened to throw me out if I don't mend my ways. He will too!'

'So you'll be lying low for a time?' It was Peter who put the question.

'I'll bloody well have to! If we're going to have any more fun it'll have to be one of you three responsible with me well in the background!'

After a moment of silence Mark Everett, in a low conspiratorial voice, came out with, 'I've got an idea.' In answer to their whispered 'What?' he said, 'I'll play ghost.'

'Ghost?' Hawkins did not sound impressed. 'It's been done before. Did it myself one winter evening last year when the moon was up. Did it in Priory Park. Borrowed my father's nightshirt and cap and took a sheet off my bed.'

'Did it work?'

'Not very well, Peter. Not enough people passing along the Charlton Road at that time of night to make it worth while. You were going to say, Mark?'

'But this would be in Tilehouse Street. We could get the Quakers up there out of their beds and make 'em quake properly. Everybody knows Tilehouse Street is supposed to be haunted.'

'I d-d-didn't. B-b-by what?'

'A headless Cavalier!'

'Tell us more,' demanded Peter Bonnamy.

'You know Highdown?'

'The place along the Hexton Road? The Delme-Radcliffe Dower House?'

'That's it! My father says that during the Civil War a small group of Royalists had a skirmish near Hitchin with some Round-head soldiers and were chased off to Highdown. Their officer was captured hiding in a tree and was hacked to death. Now they say his ghost rides into Hitchin from time to time and goes into the Priory and he passes through Tilehouse Street.'

'That's got possibilities,' said Hawkins. 'It's something worth working on. I thought you were going to suggest the ghost of that highwayman ancestor of yours who got hanged at Tyburn.* Didn't you say once that you'd got some of his things stored in your attic?'

---

*John Everett, a notorious highwayman, was born in Hitchin in 1660 and hanged in 1730.

'Yes. His hat, his cloak and a pair of pistols.'

'I'd like to b-b-borrow them!'

'You, Paul?' Henry Hawkins was looking closely at Paul Bonnamy. 'Have you a fancy for playing ghost as well?'

'N-n-not a ghost. A h-h-highwayman! I want to hold up the London c-c-coach on Monday!'

'You're mad!' exclaimed his brother.'Highway robbery is a hanging matter. You can't do that!'

'S-s-shan't rob anybody. J-j-just g-g-give 'em a scare and g-g-give a rose to someone on the c-c-coach.'

Enlightenment flooded across Peter's face. 'Felicity Quint! It's Felicity Quint. You've been mooning about her for days. Ever since we got home. You know she's going to be on the coach on Monday morning. You heard mother talking to Mathilde about it!'

'Gone romantic, has he, Paul?' said Henry Hawkins. 'Got a fancy for this Felicity, has he?' I reckon what he's suggesting is a bit risky but it's something we could get away with if we plan it right.' Then he added, 'And provide him with a good alibi in case anything went wrong.'

'What sort of alibi?' asked Mark Everett.

Hawkins grinned. They're look alikes, aren't they, him and Peter? They've confused people before, haven't they? There's only one thing that'd give the game away. That's Paul's stutter but we can get round that, in fact we can make use of it.'

'How?' asked Mark Everett.

'Peter plays Paul when he comes into your shop at the time the coach is going to be held up and buys a hat. He's got to stutter then just like Paul would do. Then, when he's bought it, he goes out and comes back after five minutes and asks to buy a hat similar to the one his brother has just bought! This time he doesn't stutter!'

'Brilliant! Brilliant!' acclaimed Mark Everett. 'Do I come into this myself?'

'Yes. Somehow make sure that your father does the serving and also that he notices the time. If anything should go wrong and Paul needs the alibi your father is a churchwarden and everybody will believe him!'

Peter called for more ale and after it had been served the four conspirators continued in discussing the details of the plan for the hold-up – where it was to be, the time it would take place and how it was to be done with the least risk of Paul being caught out.

'It's foolproof!' was the verdict of Mark Everett as the discussion drew to a close.

'It'd better be!' said Henry with a grin. 'We don't want our Paul hanged, do we? Nor transported for life! Your mother wouldn't like it, would she, Paul?'

'I w-w-wouldn't be too p-p-pleased myself. B-B-But what about M-M-Mark's C-C-Cavalier idea? S-S-Shouldn't we talk about that n-n-now?'

Henry Hawkins pulled out his watch and frowned as he peered at it. 'Sorry, Mark,' he said, 'but it's just gone nine o'clock. It's getting late and we'd better be on our way home. Let's just leave your ghost in peace until after Monday. He's been waiting a long time and he can wait for a day or two longer!'

It was still light when they went out to their horses, mounted and rode off. The ale-wife, to whom they had bidden farewell and tipped with a third shilling, watched them go with speculative eyes. There had only been two other customers that evening and although she had been able to watch the four deliberating for most of the time they had done so mostly in low voices and she had scarcely heard a word of what was being said. But there was one thing of which she was sure. They were up to no good!

14. London Bound

Walking through the misted streets on his way to embark on the London coach Mansell was thankful that the long heatwave had broken over the weekend and he was not to be faced with a hot, dusty journey and a stifling night in a noisy city hostelry. The break had come with the first spattering of rain when Susan, he, Anne and Big Lil had been standing by the graveside as Helen Deamer was laid to rest in St Mary's churchyard on Saturday afternoon. Soon the spatterings had given way to a thundery deluge which resulted in the Hiz overflowing into Bridge Street and Sun Street where, despite frantic efforts by householders and shopkeepers with boards and sandbags, many premises had been badly flooded. But one good thing – the downpour had washed away the filth from the privies lining the river and even Back Street and its slum yards were less evil-smelling for a while.

It was an active scene which greeted Mansell as he entered the yard at the Swan Inn. There the Kershaw Flyer, its gaily painted coachwork dimmed by the moisture in the air, was waiting in readiness for departure with whistling ostlers giving finishing touches to the four sturdy chestnuts stamping and tossing in their anxiety to be off. Under the archway to the yard a florid-faced coachman, long whip in hand, and with a sardonic smile on his lips, greeted the passengers as they arrived, but his guard was paying attention to no one except a giggling maidservant he had cornered in a doorway. Several of those who were intending to travel and had heavy baggage to stow away were pardonably annoyed by this indifference to their need for assistance and stood glaring at the guard's back with looks which should have shrivelled the man in his boots.

Felicity Quint, accompanied by a grumbling Mathilde, was there and ready to join the coach when Mansell arrived. She was, to his mind, as pretty as a picture, her light summer cloak open over a flowered muslin dress and her pixie-like face framed by a beribboned straw bonnet. Apparently taking nothing but a small wickerwork basket, she seemed to be quite happy about the journey ahead and greeted him with a warm smile and a kiss on his cheek.

At five minutes to eight the coachman clambered up on to his seat. The guard who had eventually supervised the stowing of the baggage called for everyone to take their places and clutching at his long copper coaching horn took his own place on the step at the back of the coach. Having taken Felicity by one hand Mansell assisted her to a window seat inside the vehicle where she would be making the journey with her back to the horses. When she was settled with her wickerwork basket by her feet he seated himself centrally opposite to her and began to take stock of his fellow passengers.

Seated on his left was George Barker, a meek little man almost devoid of chin, someone for whom he had a great deal of sympathy. The reason for this sympathy glared down her nose from the seat facing her spouse. Mrs Barker, whose grandfather had been a bishop and whose own genteel upbringing as the elder daughter of a dean had been in a cathedral close, persistently made sure that everyone in Hitchin was made aware of her elevated station of origin. Her frequent progresses round the streets and shops were almost royal in nature, requiring not only deference but adulation from those she met or who served her.

How she had come to marry the quiet, homely George and then come to live in a modest house in Tilehouse Street continued to invite much speculation in Hitchin. Rumour had it, and it was thought in this matter rumour had truth in it, that she had married for money but that what money had been left to George by his banker father had been lost almost in its entirety by the failure of the bank in 1821 soon after the will had been proved. But it seemed that with what money remained the Barkers had planned to move to Hitchin. Their very arrival in the town had been legendary: on their coach, as it had drawn to the end of its journey in the Swan yard, Mrs Barker had given birth to a daughter. Mansell, being on the spot, had assisted with the premature delivery brought about by the joltings of a rutted road, and to his mind Mrs Barker still owed him five shillings, but he had never been regarded by the embarrassed lady with anything other than loathing.

She eyed him frostily now when he enquired after the girl, responding with, 'She is well enough, Mansell, quite well enough,' but George, despite a sour look from his wife said, 'We are going to London to see her, Doctor, and hope that she will be returning with us. We've been offered a better teaching post for her at Mrs Bonnamy's – ' The growing intensity of the look from his wife finally took effect and George lapsed into silence.

The other occupants of the interior seats were a bulky, rosy-faced woman and an even bulkier, even more red-faced husband. Both nodded and smiled in a friendly way at Mansell.

'Your pardon, Sir,' said the man. 'There's rather a lot of me I'm afraid. I'll try not to bear down on you when we round the corners but you'll have to forgive me if I do. The name's Bellamy by the way, Major Bellamy retired, and that of course is Mrs Bellamy next to your daughter.'

Mansell, conscious of the pistol he was carrying in his right-hand pocket being pressed into his side by his overweight neighbour, eased himself away, smiled and corrected the Major.

'Not my daughter, Sir, just a young lady put in my charge for safe delivery in London.'

'A pleasant duty, Sir, a pleasant duty, I'm sure. She's a pretty gal, right pretty. And did I hear you addressed just now as a doctor?'

'I am known locally, Sir, as Doctor Mansell. I am at your service, Major.'

'Hm! Good! Not that I've a deal of belief in doctors. Fresh air, Sir, a good sleep each night, a good table and, begging the ladies' pardon, regular bowels, and you don't need a doctor!'

'If you have such things, Sir, you are indeed a fortunate man.'

'I am, and I know it! Fortunate in war, Doctor – I served with Wellington at Waterloo with never a scratch, and fortunate in peace – I have a nice little estate to manage at Shillington, I have good hunting in the season and some excellent shooting on which I pride myself – ' here Bellamy paused and placed his hand on his wife's knee, ' – and I've the best of ladies about the house. What more could a man want, Doctor, what more?'

'Little indeed!'

Suddenly there was a shout from the coachman of, 'Mind yourselves, mind yourselves!' followed by a blast by the guard on his horn, as at precisely eight o'clock the coach lumbered under the archway and out into the Market Square.

Felicity waved farewell to Mathilde through the open window and received a grudging wave in return. Mansell settled himself down as best he could in his cramped seat and resigned himself to what he expected would not be an over-comfortable journey. Looking out to the left as the coach moved slowly across the square he could see the shopkeepers and their assistants taking down and removing the shutters from their windows. He saw that the Everetts, father and son, had almost completed their task; the haberdashery, next to the Red Cow Inn was already open for the day. 'Hats', he thought. 'Now I could do with a new hat.' He promised himself that out of Mrs Bonnamy's handsome fee he would buy himself one on his return to Hitchin.

Someone else with new hats in mind was watching the departure of the coach from the pavement not far from the Everetts' shop. 'Off to time!' Peter Bonnamy was saying to himself with satisfaction. 'Right on the dot! The bloody dot!'

Allowing, as they had done in their planning, that the coach would be travelling at its usual average of twelve miles in the hour, it should reach the Royal Oak along the London Road in about twenty-five minutes time. In about a quarter of an hour he would begin the process of establishing Paul's alibi by making the first purchase.

* * *

It was a heavy pull for the horses up the Hitchin Hill cutting and on to the London Road, but having breasted the hill they settled down into a steady trot and the passengers, both inside and out, relaxed as best they could on their seats. Twice, however, Mansell felt in the top inside pocket of his frock coat to assure himself the tiny package of diamonds was there and safe. Then he felt for the small double-barrelled pistol which Delme-Radcliffe had loaned him. 'Easy to load, easy to use and deadly accurate up to thirty paces!' the Squire had said, and then he had added, 'But I don't for a moment see you having to fire it, Mansell, there's been no trouble on that road for years!'

Mansell was hopeful that surmise would prove to be right.

Then, in the comparative quiet, the rattling bars, slapping traces, clinking pole chains and hissing wheels merged into a kind of lullaby, and Mansell allowed his chin to drop on to his chest as he went off into an uneasy sleep.

15.   Stand and Deliver!

The cloaked rider with kerchief-masked face below a tricorn hat
sat uneasily on his horse at the edge of a small roadside spinney
some two hundred yards to the south of the Royal Oak Inn. He
nervously fingered the butt of one of the two pistols holstered at
his saddlebow. It felt cold and clammy to his touch. The thick
white mist which shrouded the spinney and the London road
made conditions ideal for what the rider was planning to do but
he had come to realise in the past few minutes there was a
rashness in the matter and if things went wrong the consequences might be serious. So far, however, all had gone well for
Paul Bonnamy. He had dressed for the part in an old ruined
chapel at the top of the hill behind him, and when the charade
was over he intended to return there to resume his normal garb
before returning to Hitchin through side roads and lanes rather
than by the main road. His passage, he hoped, would be
unnoticed.

Looking upwards into the mist he saw the sun was beginning
to break through and that visibility would be improving rapidly.
Fumbling under his cloak he brought out his watch. In another
four or five minutes, he calculated, the coach should be coming
round the bend and be within hailing distance. He hoped the
mist would linger long enough for his purpose and enable him
to get away safely. In those minutes of waiting he screwed up
his courage again and listened intently. Then, somewhat muffled
by the mist, he heard the sound of a coach horn. It would be the
guard making the landlord of the Royal Oak aware of the passing
of the coach.

A flick of his reins set his horse in motion to take up station
well to the middle of the road. Having committed himself to
action the butterflies in his stomach ceased fluttering and the
two pistols he had taken from their holsters were rock steady in
his hands.

It was a frightening moment for the driver of the coach, down to a crawl for rounding the awkward bend in the road, when he got his first view of the menacing horseman blocking the road ahead.

At the loud cry of, 'STAND AND D-D-DELIVER!' the coach was brought to an abrupt halt with a juddering of brakes and a jerk which nearly unseated the passengers. Dropping his reins the driver quickly raised his hands above his head as he saw one of the pistols was directed at his midriff.

'Don't shoot, Mister! Don't shoot!' he shouted. 'We don't want no shooting, does we?'

Paul made no reply to this plea but his silence seemed all the more threatening as he indicated with the pistol that the coach driver should get down from his box and stand by his horses. While this was being done the pistols were redirected at the guard and the outside passengers. These also were silently signalled to descend from the top of the coach. Then the pistol was pointed at the indignant face of Major Bellamy whose head had been thrust out of the open window.

The Major quickly sank back into his seat muttering a curse. As he did so he felt a pistol being pressed into his hand. He heard a softly murmured, 'It's loaded. Not cocked. You're better placed for a shot at him than me!'

Bellamy was quick on the uptake. 'Thanks, Doctor,' he said softly. 'If I can get the bugger, I will!'

Having satisfied himself that all but the inside passengers were on the ground and had no weapons, Paul made them move some yards from the coach and then holstered one of his pistols. His next move was to peer into the coach window. When he had seen where Felicity was sitting and that she was very conveniently placed he withdrew a rather crushed rose from under his cloak and kissed it. Then he gave the semblance of a bow and manoeuvred his horse so that he could drop the flower through the window and into the girl's lap. A quick touch with his spurs to the horse's flanks had Paul away from the side of the coach almost instantly but he was not quick enough. Before he was more than a couple of dozen yards from the coach the sound of one pistol shot being fired was closely followed by another. Paul rocked in his saddle and almost fell from the horse but somehow straightened himself up to gallop off into the mist.

'Got him!' exclaimed Major Bellamy jubilantly. 'I got him! I know I got him!'

It was almost as if some dam had broken as a torrent of sound erupted from the watching outside passengers, the guard and the coachman. They noisily gathered around the coach door to congratulate the excited Major but inside the coach frantic efforts were being made by Mansell and Mrs Bellamy to revive Mrs Barker who had slumped back in a fainting fit. Barker himself, white-faced and ineffectual, sat in his corner nervously wringing his hands.

'Brandy! Has anyone any brandy?' Mansell was asking.

Bellamy, pistol still in hand, turned sharply from the window to say, 'Brandy? Aye! I've brandy. Never travel without it.' Putting the weapon down he produced a large silver flask with a cap serving as a small beaker. 'Give the old girl some of this,' he said. 'That'll do the trick!'

Whether it was the Major's words or his brandy being forced between her lips which brought results Mansell was not sure but Mrs Barker came to with fluttering eyelids and a shrieked, 'Has he gone? Has he gone?'

'Yes, Ma'am, he's gone!' The Major was chuckling as he retrieved his flask. 'Gone with something to remember us by! He won't be back, I'll warrant that!'

'My rings! My rings!' Mrs Barker frantically felt at her fingers. 'They're there! He hasn't taken them!'

'He took nothing,' said Mansell. His voice was soothing. 'He took nothing. Nothing from anyone.' He himself was thankful that the package he was carrying had not fallen into the man's hands and was still safe in his pocket.

'Damnably peculiar, I say!' exclaimed Bellamy. 'Damn peculiar and bloody frightening for the ladies!' Turning to his wife who was now back in her seat he added, 'Not that you were scared, were you, my love?'

'No, my dear. I knew you'd protect me, Herbert.' Mrs Bellamy placed her hand over that of her husband and pressed it affectionately. 'No, I wasn't even a little frightened.'

Bellamy then turned to Felicity and asked, 'What about you, m'dear? It was you he seemed interested in.'

'Yes, I was frightened a little.' The girl was fingering the

damaged rose with a puzzled expression on her face. 'Why did
he drop this in my lap?'

'Why? You're a pretty girl, and he was being gallant, I would
say. What say you, Doctor?'

Mansell only nodded a half-hearted agreement. 'Perhaps, perhaps not. But whatever his reason we haven't been robbed and
it remains very puzzling. No real harm has been done but there
is no doubt in my mind that we must report the matter to the
justices as soon as possible and set up a hue and cry for the
rascal.'

The coach driver, who had just opened the door of the coach
to make certain all was well with his inside passengers, spluttered an agreement with this proposal. 'Aye, guv'nor, we'll report
it. I want that bastard cotched! Cotched and bloody strung up!'

'Reporting it is a matter you can leave to me!' called out an
aggressive-looking young man from among the outside passengers. 'I'm going to borrow a horse or a pony and trap from the
innkeeper back there and make for Hitchin immediately. My
business in London can wait for tomorrow; reporting it can't if
the villain is to be caught! I'll get my father on to it straightway!'

'Thank you, Mr Oakley,' said Mansell, recognising the speaker
as the eldest son of one of the Hitchin magistrates. 'We're much
obliged to you, I'm sure.'

'Aye! That we are!' said the coach driver. 'If the young gentleman'll do that we can get on our way without further delay.
Everybody had best get aboard.'

Within a few minutes the coach was London bound once
more. Mansell, however, made no attempt to resume the sleep
from which he had been awakened by the pulling up of the
vehicle. Play acting, he was thinking, the occurrence had the
flavour of play acting. The old-fashioned costume of the highwayman rang a false note. The throwing of the rose into the
Quint girl's lap also smacked of the theatre or some cheap novel.
He shook his head and looked intently at Felicity. She was, he
was sure, an innocent player in a farce which might still end in
tragedy. He was beginning to develop a rather uncomfortable
feeling about the matter.

*   *   *

The bullet from the first shot had whistled unpleasantly close to Paul's left ear. The second bullet had thumped him hard high in the left shoulder and nearly unseated him. To his surprise he felt little pain, only a numbness in his neck and arm. When he had felt over the area as best he could with his right hand he looked at his fingers and was relieved to see there was not much blood on them. When he reached the ruined chapel he dismounted awkwardly and divested himself of the cloak. Suddenly he felt the agony of his wound. Pain swept across his body in a series of waves and fear welled up within him as he sank to a sitting position on a pile of broken stonework. Eventually the waves gave way to a fierce, dull ache. Somewhat relieved, but now very sorry for himself, Paul packed the borrowed pistols, the hat and cloak into a saddlebag and prepared to remount his horse. He was far from sure of his ability to get home and wondered what he could do if he did get there without being apprehended. How was he going to get a surgeon's help without the justices being informed? The one doctor he might have been able to trust was not going to be available. Unfortunately Mansell, as he had just seen, was aboard the coach which was bound for London.

16.   Solomon Abram

The coach arrived at the Greyhound Inn in Smithfield at only ten minutes later than its scheduled time of two o'clock. Waiting there were Quint and Mrs Lestrange, and Mansell was thankful he was able to hand over the still much excited Felicity to her father and that he would not have the bother of escorting her to the tea merchant's premises in Mincing Lane. Leaving her gabbling out her tale of the highwayman and the robbery that never was he quickly made his way to Hatton Garden.

He had no difficulty in finding the residence of Solomon Abram. A brass plate by a heavy, iron-studded door indicated that enquiries for the diamond merchant should be made on the third floor of the tall building. Mansell ascended the steep, narrow stairs and found, in the corridor off the third floor landing, a door bearing the nameplate of the man he was seeking. His first rap on the knocker brought no response. A second tattoo resulted in the muffled sound of movement from behind the door and the sliding back of a small eye-level panel. Two deep-set eyes peered at him and there was a murmured, 'Who is it?'

'Mansell. My name is Mansell. Doctor Mansell.'

'Your business with me?'

'I come on behalf of Mrs Bonnamy.'

'Of where?'

'Of Hitchin in Hertfordshire.'

'Stand back from the door please, so that I may see you better.'

Mansell complied with the request, conscious of the close scrutiny to which he was being subjected.

'One moment, if you please, Doctor Mansell.'

After the panel was closed there came the noises of heavy bolts being drawn and a key being turned. Then the door was opened to reveal to Mansell a small, heavily bearded man of about his own age who was wearing on his pate a black skullcap. He was smiling a warm welcome as he ushered the doctor into a pleasant book-lined room in which, despite the comparative warmth of the weather, a tiny fire was burning in a highly polished grate.

'Please take a seat at the desk while I rebolt the door. One cannot be too careful in my line of business. Robbers abound these days and London has far more than its fair share of villains.'

'True, Sir, very true.' Mansell sat himself in a comfortably padded chair. 'I take it, Sir, that you are Mr Solomon Abram?'

'Yes. At your service, Doctor.' The Jew moved silently and quickly to occupy a chair on the opposite side of the desk to Mansell. 'And how is Mrs Bonnamy? Is she not well?'

'Well enough in herself but she has a badly sprained ankle and I have advised her not to walk on it for a while. She has sent you her love and has asked me to transact her business with you.'

'Dear Madeline! I am indeed sorry to hear of her mishap. You may give her my love on your return. She is often in my thoughts, she and the two boys.'

'Peter and Paul?'

'My nephews by blood if not by marriage. My brother's sons. I haven't seen them for a year or two, they must be young men now.'

'Yes, two fine young men. I too am very fond of them. I have been ever since I saw them into the world. They are inclined to mischief though from time to time.'

'High spirits? Is that it? I like young men of spirit. Their father had it. Please tell Madeline that it is high time that she and the twins came to see me again. Those nephews of mine will soon be of age and I have plans for them. I have no children of my own nor am I likely to have and Paul and Peter will take their place.' Solomon Abram paused for a moment and then said, 'I am assuming that Madeline has sent you with something she wishes me to buy from her?'

'She has.' Mansell produced the small handkerchief and carefully undid the knot in the corner.

'Please place them here, Doctor.' A square of black velvet was being spread on the desk. Beside it a brass balance was being set up.

Solomon Abram's first inspection of the stones brought the comment, 'Nice. Very nice!' Each stone was examined carefully through a magnifying glass and carefully weighed; then what Mansell assumed to be Abram's estimate of its value was entered on a notepad. At the conclusion of this silent assessment the merchant looked up and asked, 'And what does Madeline expect me to pay for them? I don't doubt that she has given you some idea of their worth?'

'Eight hundred pounds!'

Solomon Abram smiled and reversed the notepad so that Mansell could see the total which had been cast.

'Eight hundred and twenty?'

There was a nod of agreement. 'It could possibly be slightly more but you can see how good a pupil Madeline was during those few happy years she had with my brother Jacob. If she would like the money immediately that is no problem. She can either have it in gold or by a draft. Did she give you instructions on this point?'

'A draft would be the most satisfactory to her and to me. I have no desire to have that amount of gold in my keeping overnight and with me on my journey home. Believe it or not we even had a highwayman stop our coach from Hitchin only this very morning.'

'You said stop your coach. You did not say rob it. If he had you might easily have been left with no diamonds!'

Mansell quickly, and with a smile, related the incident and his intrigued listener said, 'A rose? He left the girl a rose and then quietly made off?'

'Not entirely quietly. One of my travelling companions put a bullet in his back. He still rode away but he could be dead by now or captured!'

Solomon Abram shook his head sadly from side to side. 'Folly,' he said, 'and all for a moment's folly!' Then he began to write on his notepad.

Ten minutes later Mansell bade him a warmly handshaken farewell and was ushered out with two drafts in his pocket. One for Madeline Bonnamy and a second for Mansell to cash and from which he was to give to each of her sons ten pounds.

'Give it to them with my blessing. Cambridge is an expensive place, so I'm told, and I've no doubt the money will be welcome. They will, I know, write and thank me. Madeline, I'm sure, will have brought them up to observe the proper courtesies of life.'

That night, in his room at the Greyhound Inn, Mansell tossed and turned in his bed, with his mind constantly returning uneasily to the happenings that morning on the road to London. What was behind what he now was sure was some silly charade? Who was it masquerading as a highwayman? Had Felicity Quint some suitor other than the gypsy lad? He was certain of one thing. The rider had not been Nelson Draper. He was an older man. If it was some kind of jape it might have been Hitchin's best known japer, Henry Hawkins. The incident had the stamp of young Hawkins on it. But did Hawkins know Felicity Quint? Then the thought occurred to him: Peter and Paul! They were closely associated with the lawyer's son. One of them might have been led into the folly by him. The twins would know of Felicity's proposed trip to London. And the voice? Only three words had been uttered by the highwayman. Stand and deliver! That in itself was curious; it might be that the speaker felt if he said more his voice would be recognised . . . Paul, the stuttering Paul! Suddenly Mansell was sure he knew who it was who had held up the coach. Paul Bonnamy!

'Fool! Bloody young fool,' he said to himself. 'Poor Madeline! Paul might well be dead or dying and in a way I'm damn well responsible. If I hadn't been carrying that bloody pistol he wouldn't have been shot!'

At eight the following morning Mansell boarded the Hitchin coach and gloomily took his seat for the return journey.

17. The End of an Escapade

After a night of drugged sleep Paul woke up to find himself in his own bed, with his mother, his brother and Mathilde gathered around him. As he emerged from his woolly world of slumber with an aching head and an unpleasant taste in his mouth he heard Peter saying, 'Good! He's coming to!' and Mathilde's acid comment, 'About time he did. Perhaps we shall get some sense out of him at last. We got precious little last night!'

There was a groan from Paul as he shifted his position in the bed.

'Shoulder hurting?' asked Peter.

'It b-b-bloody well is! It's d-d-damned painful!'

'It's fortunate it's no worse,' said Mrs Bonnamy. 'You've been foolish, Paul. Very foolish! So has Peter. He's told us, Paul, about the whole silly business. Unhappily it hasn't finished yet!'

'Not f-f-finished? In what way, M-M-Mother? In what way?'

'There's a hue and cry out for you!' said Peter.

'F-F-For me? But do they know it was m-m-me?'

'No, brother mine, they don't, thank God! Nobody recognised you at the hold-up and what they're looking for is some unknown rogue they're certain was wounded in the get-away. There's a reward out of twenty pounds for information leading to his arrest. The Oakleys have offered it.'

'The gypsies! The two gypsies?'

'The pair that helped you to get home? Gypsy Draper and his son Wellington?'

'Yes! They c-c-could g-g-give me away!'

'They won't! Mother has paid them more than the reward money for getting you home. They won't talk. They're not all that fond of the law. They'll stay silent.'

'Did they tell you how they f-f-found me?'

'They did! They told us they came across you slumped by a gate in a field where you'd fallen off your horse.'

'I must have passed out!'

'You had but you came round enough, so they told us, to ask them to hide you somewhere until it was dark. You promised them that they would be well paid if they assisted you. They really wanted to get you to a surgeon but you wouldn't let them.'

Paul gingerly felt at his shoulder. It was padded and covered with a bandage. He asked, 'Has a s-s-surgeon been here, Mother?'

'No, Paul. Mathilde and I looked at the wound and decided it was not so serious it couldn't wait until we were able to get Doctor Mansell. Between us we cleaned you up and bandaged you. Then we gave you two of the pills the Doctor had left with me so that I could get to sleep with my painful ankle.'

'How did I manage to get home? I can remember being h-h-hidden in a h-h-haybarn but not m-m-much about the ride into Hitchin – only that it was dark and it was r-r-raining a lot.'

'You passed out again on the road home,' said Peter. The wound must have opened with the jolting and you lost a lot more blood. You'd fallen out of the saddle if the Drapers hadn't roped you on and propped you up from time to time. But nobody seems to have seen you riding through the town. It was late, it was dark and it was too wet for even the watch to be about.'

Paul sank back in his pillow as though exhausted. Mathilde intervened with, 'That's quite enough for the time being, Peter. Quite enough. Your brother must rest now and gather his strength for when Doctor Mansell arrives and attends to him. He will need it.'

'Just one more thing, Mathilde, p-p-please.'

'What, Paul?' asked Peter.

'What have you told Henry and Mark, Peter? Do they know I got back safely last n-n-night?'

'Not yet. They were very worried yesterday when they heard what had happened but I shall see both of them later this morning and tell them you are here. They're not likely to say anything to anyone. I'm sure of that. They won't want to get involved. Now sleep if you can and we'll just wait for the Doctor.'

Peter Bonnamy met Doctor Mansell off the London coach on its arrival at the Swan Inn and over two tankards of ale in a quiet corner of the taproom he revealed what he knew of the practical joke which had gone so badly wrong.

'So it was Paul?' said Mansell. 'I thought it was him who had held us up; several things pointed his way. But why did he do it and why did you let him? You are a lot of young fools!'

'He wanted to impress Felicity Quint. He thinks he's in love with her. He gets that way about girls every now and again. And as for the rest of us, we just thought it would be an amusing jape. It wasn't as though anybody was going to be robbed.'

'No! But the coach passengers weren't to know that. I for one didn't and I'd got your mother's diamonds in my possession! But enough of this talking about what has happened. If Paul needs surgical attention I had better go and collect my bag. You go home and tell your mother that I shall be with her shortly.'

Half an hour later Mansell, with his patient lying face down on the bed, was closely examining the wound. The entry hole of the bullet was not large and fairly clean but the flesh around it was badly bruised. Mansell, after he had straightened up, said, 'You are a fortunate young man, Paul. There seem to be no broken bones and no vital organ has been touched. A few inches to the right and the bullet might have smashed into your spine and you would now be dead or badly crippled for life. As it is it just lies buried in your shoulder muscle and I should be able to get it out without too much difficulty.'

Paul gulped and asked, 'Will it hurt much?'

'Yes,' said Mansell, who was removing his frock coat. 'It will be painful but I shall give you some laudanum which should help a little and I shall also give you something to bite on whilst I am operating. We don't want you screaming out and alarming the young ladies of the academy, do we?' Mansell turned to Mrs Bonnamy to ask, 'I suppose they know nothing of this silly matter?'

'Nothing, William, nothing.' Mrs Bonnamy was quite emphatic. 'The girls were all in bed when Paul returned last night and they are not allowed in this wing of the house without invitation. There is no need to worry about them seeing or hearing anything.'

'Good!' Mansell carefully poured a measure of laudanum into a wineglass and gave this to Paul to drink. He then set out several surgical instruments and his tray of diluted tar-water. Each of the instruments was carefully dipped and dried.

'Now, Paul, bite on to this wad of bandage please and turn over on to your face again.'

A somewhat drowsy Paul did as he was told. Then Mansell looked at Peter and Mathilde. 'You two,' he said, 'must hold him down firmly. The less he moves, the quicker I shall be!'

It was over in less than a minute but even so Paul had passed out.

'Better so!' said Mrs Bonnamy, looking down at her unconscious son as Mathilde and Peter relaxed their grip on him. Then to Mansell she said, 'Thank you, William, that was really quick.'

'It went well. Not too much groping for it and not a lot of bleeding.' Mansell held out his forceps showing her the ball he had extracted. 'Would you like it, Madeline?'

'As a souvenir of a very worrying occasion?'

'You could produce it each time either of the boys showed signs of some other folly in the offing.'

Madeline Bonnamy shook her head and Mansell busied himself padding and bandaging the wound. As the bandaging was completed Paul came round. He spat out the gag.

'Where am I?' he asked.

'Safe in bed,' said Peter, 'and it is all over. You'll live!'

Mansell carefully repacked his bag and resumed his coat.

'What now, William?' asked Mrs Bonnamy.

'Rest and light meals for a few days and I'll give you some more sleeping pills for him. His arm will have to be put in a sling as soon as he's on his feet but I shan't do anything about that until the day after tomorrow.' Mansell then turned to Peter. 'And you, young man, had better continue with the alibi masquerade. Paul mustn't be seen in the town with his arm in a sling or some people will begin to ask questions and tongues will wag. If a whisper of anything gets to the Oakleys they'll be on to it at once. They're not fools and I can well believe they'll take any steps they can to get the miscreant brought to justice. So while Paul remains in hiding here, you, Peter, must play his part from time to time in some of the shops and inns.'

It was a while later, when Mrs Bonnamy was settling with Mansell the business he had transacted on her behalf with Solomon Abram that she enquired, 'How soon do you think Paul will be able to travel without his arm being in a sling?'

'After about a week at most. What have you in mind, Madeline?'

'Packing the pair of them off to their uncle in London. He'll have them, I'm sure, and they'll be away from the bad influence of young Henry Hawkins.'

'And they won't be here casting eyes on your young ladies, will they?'

Mrs Bonnamy sniffed. It was an expressive sniff. 'Felicity!' she exclaimed. 'Of all my girls it had to be Felicity Quint. Damn the little hussy! I hope her father finds a suitable husband for her and she doesn't come back here. I really do!'

But ten days later, when Paul was leaving for London with his brother, Felicity Quint was no longer a dominant image in his mind. A certain Miss Sarah Barker, who had been engaged by his mother as a music teacher at the Academy, had taken her place in his thoughts. Although he had done no more than view her from his bedroom window he was convinced that this dark-haired young woman was the most beautiful girl he had ever seen and he was eager to make her closer acquaintance. Smiling inwardly as the coach rumbled its laborious way up the steep hill out of Hitchin he recalled how, early that morning, he had clambered, in stockinged feet and at considerable risk, from his bedroom window and across an outhouse roof to the open window of the music room in the far wing.

He had entered the music room and laid there, on the piano, a single rose and a small card on which he had carefully printed –

> *To Sarah,*
> *My love is like a red red rose*
> *That's newly sprung in June;*
> *My love is like a melody*
> *That's sweetly played in tune.*
> *Robert Burns (and so do I!)*
>
> *From your Ardent Admirer*

This, he hoped, would intrigue her but he also hoped that she would not show the note to his mother.

18. The Widow

(I)

Almost the last man to be hanged for sheep stealing in Britain was George Martin, a smallholder of Temple End, an outlying part of the hamlet of Charlton. He dropped to his sudden end on a gallows which had been erected just outside the gate to Hertford Gaol at eight in the morning of Wednesday 21st March 1832, and at his dropping an odd, almost sullen murmur went up from the crowd of three hundred who had gathered to watch this public spectacle. Jenny, his wife, well advanced in her first pregnancy, waited at the edge of the crowd with a horse and a low flat cart. On the cart was a crudely made coffin.

Those who passed her by on their way from the scene stared at her more in curiosity than in sympathy but one craggy-faced man in much soiled clothes did stop to ask, 'Would yer like me to give yer an 'and when they takes 'im down?'

Jenny Martin murmured her thanks and the man seated himself on the cart beside her and with some difficulty lit an evil-smelling clay pipe. Having for a moment puffed at this he said, 'Got ter wait, y'know. They won't let yer 'ave 'im fer a bit. They 'as ter be sure 'e's dead, they does.'

'So the gaoler told me last night. It is good of you to wait with me.'

The man let smoke dribble from his mouth, removed the pipe and spat on the ground before saying, 'I ain't in no 'urry, Mistress. Time's me own this morning.'

'What do you do?'

'Me? What do I do?' The stem of the pipe was pointed in the direction of a distant church spire. 'I'm sexton over there.' There was silence for a moment and then the pipe stem was directed at the hanging body. ''E were a 'Itchin man, weren't 'e?'

'Yes, we come from just outside the town.'

'Weren't 'e a good 'usband? Yer don't seem ter be weepin' much fer 'im.'

'He was a very good husband but I've shed what tears I have to shed.'

The woman's jaw seemed to set in a hard line. 'Now I intend paying back the man who brought him to this!'

"Ow come, Mistress? ''Ung the wrong man, 'ave they? Didn't yer 'usband do what they said 'e did? Sheep stealing, weren't it?'

'It was and he was caught red-handed at it. But he was given away.'

'Somebody peached on 'im?'

'Yes. He'd come to an arrangement with the shepherd but there were men waiting for him in the field. He didn't stand a chance.'

'The shepherd 'ad told, 'ad 'e?'

The woman nodded and then said bitterly, 'I'll get him for it if it's the last thing I do. I promised my husband that last night when they let me say goodbye to him.'

When she had said this she seemed to have withdrawn into herself with her memories of that last hour with her husband. They had talked mainly of what she should do when she got back to the farm. He had reckoned that she and his one-armed brother, a veteran of the Battle of Waterloo, should be able to run it between them and he was sure if they continued to pay the rent regularly the landlord, Delme-Radcliffe, would not turn them out. Next he had told her what to plant in the spring, what to buy in the way of stock and what to sell. Then he had sprung something of a bombsell whispering, 'Don't worry about money. Feel up the chimney on the left-hand side and you'll find a loose brick. Behind it there's a tin with a hundred and twenty sovereign in it. That should be enough for you and Hooky to keep going for a while!'

She had asked him where it had come from and he had grinned and replied, 'Sheep money! I've been getting it together to buy the farm. I wanted the boy to have something when we've gone.'

He had been sure it was a boy she was carrying right from the time she had let him know she was pregnant.

Then her thoughts and memories were interrupted by the sight of two men who had come from the gaol and climbed up on to the gallows.

"Aving a look,' announced the sexton. 'If they're sure 'e's gorn they'll 'ave 'im down an' let yer 'ave 'im. Yes! 'E's gorn all right. They're calling yer over.'

It was the sexton and the two hangmen who put the still limp body into the coffin. Before the lid was put into place Jenny Martin peered down into the distorted face of her dead husband and said, 'I'll find some way to make him pay, George. I promised you last night and I promise you again now. He'll pay for what he did!'

'Who, woman, who?' asked one of the hangmen.

'Josiah Thickpenny! The bastard who betrayed him!'

'Well, Master Thickpenny, if that's yer name,' said the sexton taking over the hammer the woman had been holding, 'I don't reckon I'd like ter be in your shoes!' Then one by one, he hammered home the nails Jenny Martin was giving him.

When the last nail had been secured and the hangmen had returned to the gaol the woman tried to press some coins into her helper's hand but he refused them firmly saying, 'No, Mistress, yer'd best keep yer money and if yer don't mind I'll just see yer safe out of the town. Yer've a long way ter go and wiv the state yer in yer'd best 'ave some one wiv yer part of the way 'ome.'

It had been more than half of the way to Hitchin before they parted company.

The next morning the body of the hanged man was laid to rest in the burial ground of the Back Street Meeting House in Hitchin and the minister there, the Reverend William Wayne, a good and kindly man, said a few words at the graveside.

Later that day, Doctor William Mansell helped deliver Jenny Martin of the dead man's son.

* * *

(II)

Anne Mansell was busy making mince pies when her husband, well wrapped up against a chill December wind, pushed open the outer kitchen door and deposited, almost at her feet, a heavily weighted rush basket. She waited until he had closed the door and removed his cloak before asking, 'What have you got here, William?'

'Christmas dinner, my dear! A good Christmas dinner!'

'From the Martins?'

'Yes. The most handsome capon you're ever likely to see! Better than a fee for my services.'

'Dressed?'

'Plucked and dressed and ready for the oven! A good ten pounder I should think.'

Anne wiped her hands free from flour and took the featherless bird from the basket. With her hands she carefully assessed its weight. 'Near enough twelve,' she said. 'Did you have to carry it all the way from Charlton?'

Mansell, who was standing with coat tails raised and his back to the kitchen fire, shook his head. 'No, Hooky Martin brought me back in the trap. Jenny Martin insisted that he did.'

'How is the boy? What did you find the matter with him?'

'Nothing more than a chesty cold but you know what she's like with that boy. Sends for me at the least sign of anything wrong.'

'He should be getting over childish ailments now. He's nine isn't he?'

'Not quite. He will be in March.'

Anne had disappeared into the larder to put the capon on the largest of her platters. She emerged to say, 'How time flies. Nearly nine years is it since they hanged his father? It just doesn't seem possible.'

'The older one gets, Anne, the quicker the years seem to roll by but they've been good years for the Martins. Jenny Martin has got that farm into a fair shape with Hooky's help and several good seasons.'

'From what you've told me they seem to have worked hard, both of them. You say that there isn't much Hooky can't do although he's only got one arm and a steel hook and as for Jenny she never misses a market with her fowls, her eggs, her butter and other things when they're in season.'

Seating himself by the fire Mansell said, 'Now let me tell you the latest news. Jenny is buying the farm!'

'Delme-Radcliffe is letting her have it?'

'He is. It will be hers from Christmas Quarter Day, so she told me today. It's something George always wanted, to actually own the farm.'

'So she's a satisfied woman now?'

'Satisfied? Far from it, Anne. She'll never be really satisfied until she's settled the score with Thickpenny but how she can do that I do not pretend to know. Since Quint made him bailiff at Manley Court he seems to have got further than ever out of her reach. It might have been easier if he was still only a shepherd.'

'But if she feels that badly about him she'll find a way. There'll be something one day she'll be able to do. Now, I suppose, William, you'd like your dinner?'

'Aye. That I would. I'm ready for that if it's ready for me! What is it?'

Anne smiled as she began clearing the table in readiness to set it for the meal. 'Shepherd's Pie!' she said.

*   *   *

In the lamplit barn Jenny Martin, Hooky and a grinning Gypsy Draper were gathered around a recently cleaned and well oiled mantrap which had been set with open jaws on the ground between them. Hooky was holding aloft a heavy log of wood and looking towards his sister-in-law and awaiting her order to drop it on the triggering platform of the menacing device.

'Now!' she snapped. There was a loud clatter as the toothed jaws seized the log and held it fast in an iron grip.

'That's set fine enough,' pronounced the gypsy with satisfaction in his voice. 'You won't do better than that. Hooky.'

'Sure?'

'Sure enough. I wouldn't fancy my chances if I stepped on it. I'm bloody glad the law's agin such things nowadays. It weren't when I was a lad.'

'Does anyone know that you found it?' asked the woman.

'No one, Mistress. No one, that is 'cept us three. It was in a pile of scrap iron in a barn. Preston way. It aren't likely to be missed and nobody saw me take it. I've been looking for one ever since that bastard beat up Nelson, and knowing how Hooky felt about what he did to his brother I told him what I'd got in mind and asked him to help.'

'Where do you and Hooky intend to set it?'

'On the path 'tween his back door and his privy. It's dark under the trees these mornings and we shall cover it with dead leaves, shan't we Hooky?'

'Aye! He won't see it till it's too late and it's got him by the leg!'

'And you'll be setting it tomorrow night?'

'Yes, tomorrow night. We know his two boys will be away for

a few days. We heard that from Ralph Ashton at the Highlander. They're going to London to pick up a load of stuff for old Quint. There'll be nobody at the cottage except their father until Christmas Eve.'

Jenny Martin said, 'Good! It's him I'm after. Not his boys and I want to be sure he suffers.' She paused and then said to Hooky, 'Try it again. I want to be really certain it will work!'

Hooky grinned. Then, assisted by Draper, he prised open the jaws of the trap with an iron bar. The much mutilated log, now freed, rolled across the barn floor. The trap was then immediately reset.

19. The Trap is Sprung

A loud knocking at his back door disturbed Mansell at his belated breakfast and on hastening to answer the summons he found the agitated knocker was a groom he had sometimes seen passing through the marketplace driving a carriage and pair.

'Well?' he asked.

'Doctor! Doctor! You've got to come quick!'

'Where and why, man?'

'You've got to come to Manley Court. Mr Quint wants you. Bailiff's been hurt. Hurt bad. I've the dog-cart in the road outside. It'll be quicker than you walking!'

Questioned by Mansell as they set off at a fast trot through the streets of Hitchin, the groom had a little more to add to his original announcement. 'I just heard one of the maids say bailiff hadn't been up to the house for his breakfast at the usual time and when Mrs Lestrange had sent to find him there he was with his leg in a trap!'

When they arrived at Manley Court Quint was waiting by the steps to the front door of the house.

'We've brought him here, Mansell,' he said leading the way up and into the hall, 'because there's more room for you to deal with him than there is in his cottage.'

'How did it happen?' asked Mansell.

'We don't really know. He's far too dazed and in too much pain to tell us much but it seems someone had set a man-trap in the path to his privy and chained it to a tree. He must have been trapped for an hour or more before we found him and released him.'

Thickpenny had been laid on a blanket-covered hall table and Mrs Lestrange, who was standing beside him scissors in hand, had just finished cutting away the boot, stocking and breeches from his injured leg. Having taken a quick glance at the torn and gaping wound Mansell removed his hat and frock coat and handed these to the housekeeper. Then he rolled up his shirt

111

sleeves and began to make a closer examination of the leg, shaking his head as he did so.

Quint asked, 'Will it have to be amputated?'

Mansell straightened up. 'No, I don't think so,' he said. 'I may be able to save the leg though I doubt whether he'll ever walk properly again. The bones, so far as I can tell, are not broken but the calf muscle is badly torn and will need a lot of stitching. He'll also require some careful nursing. He's no wife, has he?'

'No, his wife is dead. There's only him and his two sons. They get their meals here and one of our women keeps his cottage clean.'

'We can cope with the nursing,' said Mrs Lestrange. 'That will be no problem. Now, I take it, Doctor, you'll need hot water?'

'I shall. And soap and towels. Also an old sheet which can be cut into bandages.'

It took considerable time for Mansell to trim and suture together the appalling wound and to dress and bandage the leg. Thickpenny came round sufficiently just before he was finishing off the bandaging to answer Quint's questioning, 'Who do you think has done this to you, Thickpenny?' with a bemused, 'I don't know, Guv'nor. I don't know.'

'Think man, think! Who owes you a grudge?'

A curious look came into Thickpenny's eyes. 'Those gypsies!' he snarled. 'Those bloody gypsies! They could have done it!'

Mansell tied the final knot in the bandage but ventured no opinion. He had no liking for his patient and saw no need to do more than provide his surgical services and collect a fee from Quint.

On his return home, however, with one of Quint's guineas in his pocket, he voiced his own suspicions to Anne.

'The Martins?' she said. 'You think they may be behind what happened?'

'They might well be. They've good reason for hating him and they won't have forgotten what he did. They could just have bided their time and I'm saying nothing except good luck to them. Thickpenny deserves all he's got! Now to more cheerful things. Is Susan home yet? The Academy is supposed to be breaking up for Christmas this morning, isn't it?'

'She's home, William. She came in half an hour ago and has

gone up to her room – I rather think to wrap up the Christmas presents she'll be giving. She brought some gossip!'

'She did? And I can see you're wanting to pass it on!'

Anne smiled. 'It will amuse you,' she said.

'Well? Out with it, woman! Who is it about?'

'To start with, the Bonnamy twins. They're back from Cambridge and Paul's been caught by his mother kissing the new music teacher under the mistletoe!'

'Miss Sarah Barker?'

'Yes, the prim and proper Miss Sarah, but listen, Peter – '

'What's Master Peter been up to?'

'Mathilde found him in bed yesterday morning with one of the kitchen maids! Susan and Amanda saw him being chased down the corridor with his breeches in his hand and his shirt tails flying!'

'Young devil! Fine goings on in an academy for the daughters of gentlemen!'

'That's not all, William!'

'Not all?'

'No. Felicity Quint came back to the school last week. She told Susan that there was no one she liked among the young men in London who'd been presented to her by her father and she wouldn't consider the idea of marrying any of them. She's now sharing a room with Susan and Amanda.'

'So?' Mansell sensed there was more to be told.

'So, William? It's very much so! Late last evening there was a whistling from under their bedroom window and Felicity got out of bed, wrapped a cloak over her nightdress and hurried out of the room. Susan says she and Amanda rushed to the window and looked down into the yard but there wasn't much of a moon and they didn't see much, only two dark figures making for the stables.'

'Go on!'

'Felicity didn't return until after the hall clock had struck midnight! She didn't say anything to anyone but left her cloak across the bottom of the bed. Susan said when she saw it this morning it had straw on it!'

'Are you thinking that it was young Nelson Draper she met?'

'Yes, William, I am!'

'But he should be at Royston.'

'Perhaps he's returned to his family for Christmas. Suppose his employer has loaned him a horse for a few days? It's possible, isn't it?'

'It's possible, Anne. Sir Arthur is a kindly man who might do something like that if he's taken to the boy but how could Felicity have known that it was Nelson waiting for her in the yard?'

'That puzzled me until Susan mentioned three gypsies had called at the kitchen door a few days ago selling clothespegs and baskets. She's sure Felicity spoke to one of them.'

Mansell was smiling broadly as he sat down. 'Well,' he said, 'If they are rolling about together in the straw again, and anything comes of it, Quint will either have to let them marry or call me in once more!'

'He'll never agree to them getting married, surely?'

'Never, my dear? Never is a long, long time!'

20. The End of a Year

It was New Year's Eve, and just after ten of the clock a tired and dispirited Mansell returned home to remove his cap and fling off his cloak before dropping wearily into his chair by the side of a still brightly blazing log fire. After a few moments he eased off his snow-sodden boots and stretched out his stockinged feet towards the warmth.

When he saw Anne coming from the kitchen bearing a tray on which was a steaming jug and two beakers he gave an appreciative sniff and said, 'Bless you, my dear, you're bringing me what I fancy most. It is mulled wine, isn't it? By God, I need something to warm me and cheer me up. It's bitter out there – '

'And things haven't gone well, have they, William? I could tell that by the look on your face as you came through the door.' Anne set down the tray on the table and then filled the two beakers. One she gave to Mansell, the other she took with her to the chair on the opposite side of the fireplace.

He sipped at his beaker gratefully before replying. When he did his voice was tinged with sadness. 'Not well at all, my dear. Not well at all.'

'You lost the baby?'

'I lost both!'

There was silence for a while and Mansell seemed to be more intent on watching the shadows cast by the fire dancing on the walls and ceiling than on elaborating on his sorry news.

'Both?' Anne prompted.

'Yes. Both. We did what we could but the girl was far too young and the baby far too large and needing turning.' Mansell paused, 'We could do no more.'

'We? Someone was helping you?'

'Yes. Big Lil. The girl's mother was useless and the father dead drunk on the floor. There was scarcely a thing we needed in the house. Lil fetched what we wanted from her own place and even lit a fire with her own coal!'

115

'But the Riddens aren't Chapman's Yard people! They're Back Street proper.'

'True but Lil seems to know the family well and I have a feeling they may even be related. She was very sorry for the girl and God help the man who fathered the child if Lil ever gets her big hands on him!'

'Does she know who it was?'

'She's sure it was the uncle, the mother's brother. The one who has just been transported for life for thieving.'

'But you are not so sure?'

'Who can be sure of anything the way most of them live in Back Street and those stinking yards? Six or seven to a tiny room, boys and girls together and parents sleeping with them. There's scarcely a house where incest isn't common between brothers and sisters and fathers and daughters. With that amount of interbreeding it's no wonder so many there are imbeciles. The girl who died tonight was a twelve-year-old simpleton. She had no idea of what was happening to her. She was just terrified out of what little wits she had when the birth pangs started.'

'How terrible, William.'

'Yes, I've had bad cases before but this one tonight really sickened me. I did what I could but I failed.'

'Then you've nothing to reproach yourself with. Perhaps it was for the best after all. What sort of life would they have had in Back Street?'

'Not much of one, I know, but I hate failure. As to Back Street I shall have another word with Delme-Radcliffe. He knows my views and the views of Hawkins and the other doctors in the town. I have a feeling that he agrees with us.'

'You're wanting to see most of the ale-houses closed?'

'More than that. It's not just the beer and the gin those who live there drink to forget the poverty and other miseries of their lives but the overcrowding, the dirt and the diseases which have brought about a squalid, quarrelsome underworld of crime and depravity. We've got some of the worst slums in England! The whole damned lot should be pulled down. Every house, every miserable little shop and every drinking den should go!'

Mansell's voice had risen almost to a shout. Anne touched his arm. 'But what of those who live there?' she asked. 'What is to become of them?'

.

'They should be rehoused on the outskirts of the town. Better cottages, fresh air to breathe, clean water to drink and better sanitation. It could be done!'*

'But that would take a deal of money. Who would pay?'

'There's plenty of money in Hitchin. Plenty. It's a prosperous little town and getting even more prosperous for many, especially the Quakers. They're not short of guineas!'

'But will they part with them?'

'If Delme-Radcliffe takes the lead and shames them into it they might well do so.' Mansell held out his beaker for a refill and smiled as he added, 'But enough of the miseries, Anne. Let us be thankful for our own good fortune in this nearly passed year and be ready to welcome in the new one.'

'I am thankful, William, very thankful. We have lacked nothing, nor have any of ours lacked anything. Pray God, we shall want for nothing in the year that is coming.'

'Aye. It's been a good year. We've been able to save a little and there's good money deposited at Sharples. We've acquired another daughter and it looks as though we may even get another daughter-in-law!'

'You are thinking of our Dick marrying?'

'I am. At long last he's settling down. Now he's taken that live-in job with Charlie Wingrave at Charlton and is courting his daughter, I've high hopes of him!'

'You can hear wedding bells ringing next year?'

'I can! And that reminds me, Anne. I saw Dick earlier today on his baker's round and he told me he'll be with the bellringers at St Mary's tonight. A team of them will be trying to ring in the New Year with a full peal and Charlie Wingrave, who is going to conduct them, thinks Dick has learned enough now to be trusted with a bell.'

'Our Dick a bellringer! It doesn't seem possible! He was never much of a churchgoer but this ringing seems to have done him nothing but good.'

'Yes. Well, he was quick and eager to learn the ropes, wasn't he? It's no wonder Charlie took a liking to him. Still, it was a real

---

*The Hitchin slums were demolished in the 1920s and the inhabitants rehoused on the edges of the town.

stroke of luck for Dick, Charlie offering him the roundman's job after his brother died.'

'It was that! And now it's Charlie's daughter Dick's after!'

'So it would appear. From what I know of the girl she's pleasant enough. But plain rather than pretty.'

'Pretty is as pretty does, William. All I hope and pray for is that she will make him a good wife and that they will both be happy.'

'I hope so too. If they do wed they'll want for nothing. Emma is the apple of her father's eye!'

'He's rich, so they say.'

'Strangely so for just a country baker. He seems to have a proper knack for making money!'

'That's a knack we seem to lack, William, but we're not poor either. We're snug and warm in our cottage, we've enough to eat, we've a fine family, some very good friends – '

'And we've just had a wonderful Christmas! The best ever I can remember!' Mansell took a cigar from the box on the table. The fifty had been a seasonal present from Delme-Radcliffe. Having lit the cigar with a spill lighted at the fire he sat back relaxed and at ease to enjoy the fragrance of the smoke. Anne too was silent as she closed her eyes and thought back to Christmas Day when her family, the whole family, had gathered round the laden festive table. Daughter Mary with husband Timmins and young Daniel, son Thomas with his obviously pregnant Charlotte, and little Polly-Sue, the bellringing Richard and last, but far from least, Susan, their ward.

What a feast it had been! The giant capon had been cooked to a tender, succulent turn for skilful, surgical carving by William. The plum pudding had been the richest and the fruitiest she had ever made and there had been oranges, sweetmeats, nuts and wine in plenty. Mrs Bonnamy had to be thanked for the wine. She had sent a hamper containing a variety of delectables and a whole dozen bottles of fine French wines. And there had been presents from other grateful patients – even a present from Nathaniel Quint, two pounds of tea in a small chest. And what jollity there had been after the meal, with party games which always seemed to lead to forfeits whereby the ladies had to be kissed by the gentlemen or the gentlemen kissed by the ladies or the gentlemen and the children blindfolded and made to bob for apples in a water-filled tub!

Anne had seen Susan's eyes sparkling with tears of laughter and delight as she entered wholeheartedly into the fun and the frolics. Never before had the girl been to such a party or kissed so often. Never before had she been so happy. She had loved the red velvet dress her 'Uncle William' and 'Aunt Anne' had bought for her and she had been delighted with the presents she had received from the other members of her acquired family.

Breaking out of her pleasant reverie Anne prodded her contentedly smoking husband and said, 'What about those bells tonight, William? Will they wake Susan and keep her awake. I do hope they won't. I want her to have a good night's sleep. She's back to school tomorrow.'

Mansell took the cigar from his mouth and carefully eased away the ash into the small silver tray Susan had presented to him early on Christmas morning. He said, 'It's not likely, my dear. The wind is strong and from the east. It will carry most of the sound over to the other side of the town. I doubt if any of those in the Churchyard houses, or in Cock Street or Bancroft will get much rest until well after three tomorrow morning. It's a three-hour peal that's planned!'

'My goodness! Dick will be tired! Are we sitting up to see the old year out and the new one in?'

Mansell shook his head. 'That is not my intention. I've had too much of today already and as soon as I've finished this excellent cigar and we've emptied the jug we shall – '

Anne, recalling the phrase they had used so often when their children were small, said, 'We shall go up Wooden Hill and down Sheet Lane – '

A smiling Mansell finished it off with, 'And enter the Land of Nod!'

21. Ring Out the Old

An hour before midnight nine bellringers and the Vicar, the Reverend Henry Wiles MA, had assembled in the ringing gallery of St Mary's Church. Two brass oil lamps and two hand lanterns hanging from brackets on the walls cast a warm yellow light over the lower part of the gallery but little of this light penetrated the velvety blackness filling the body of the great church beyond the wooden balustrade. Somehow this brooding darkness seemed, not holy, but malevolently threatening and hiding ancient evils. Dick Mansell, who was peering over the balustrade, felt a coldness running down his spine. Shaking off this grue he turned and went to where his fellow ringers were gathering in a half circle before the clergyman, who was preparing to call down a blessing upon them for the mammoth task they had set themselves to do at the coming of the New Year. This task was that of faultlessly completing a peal of five thousand and forty Plain Bob Triples. It was to Dick a daunting prospect. But it was one which had been done in the tower before and a tablet on the wall recorded the event. It had taken place in February 1782 and it had taken three hours and twenty minutes to complete. The names of the eight ringers were listed. Providing no one made a mistake and embrangled the bells there would be another peal board on the wall in January and his name would be on it. It would be something of which he could be proud.

At the conclusion of the short prayer Dick joined in the ragged chorus of amens and stood waiting patiently for the now handshaking vicar to reach him at the end of the line. First for that limp grip was Charlie Wingrave, puller of the mighty tenor bell and the team's captain and conductor. Next was Jimmy Jeeves, brother of the town's leading undertaker. Mark Everett, the hatter's son was third, fourth George Barker the blacksmith, and fifth Philip Allen who worked for Newtons the builders. There was a slight delay and a smiling exchange of words when Wiles reached Tom Rumball the stonemason and another when it came to the turn of William Kefford, the fishmonger, who for some reason best known to himself insisted on first wiping his hand thoroughly on the backside of his breeches before taking that of the Vicar.

Last but one in the line was Walter Primrose. The old man's face broke into a tooth-gappy grin when the Vicar enquired, 'Well, Walter, how many times have you rung the old year out and rung in the new?'

'Fifty-six, Vicar. Fifty-six. This'll make fifty-seven. I were twenty when I started and now I'm seventy-seven an' I ain't missed one in all that time.'

'A fine record, Walter. Very fine indeed, but isn't a peal a little more than you should be trying to do at your age?'

The gappy grin broadened. 'Aye. It would be if I was 'tempting it, but I ain't. No, all Charlie is letting me do is strike the old year out with the nine tailors and the twelve strokes fer the months.* Then I'll just do the first ten minutes of the peal before I 'ands back the tenor to Charlie.'

'Then you'll go back to home and your bed, I hope.'

Walter shook his head. 'Shan't do nothing of the kind. I ain't going till the peal's done. Got to relieve on the ropes from time to time – and keep my eye on young Dick 'ere. It's his first big peal and we don't want no mistakes. Not that me and Charlie reckon 'e'll make one cos we've learnt 'im proper, ain't we, Dick?'

Dick Mansell, thus appealed to, gave an embarrassed nod of affirmative as the Vicar turned to him saying, 'So it's to be your first peal, is it, Mansell?'

The proffered hand was shaken gently. It felt to Dick like a piece of Kefford's cod and he released it quickly. 'Yes, Vicar. My first.'

'You are now working for Mr Wingrave, I hear?'

'Yes, Sir. I do a daily round for him. In the villages mostly. It's a big round.'

'I expect your father is pleased to see you in steady employ-

---

*The Passing Bell. Thrice three struck on the tenor bell notifies the passing of a male adult or the passing of the year. Thrice two, on the middle bell, the death of a female adult. Thrice one on the lightest bell, the death of a child.

ment now. How is the good Doctor? As busy as usual, I suppose, with all the babies being born in Back Street?'

Dick only replied with, 'He's busy all right.'

The Vicar smiled his thin smile before turning to address the hovering Charlie Wingrave, 'Then I shall leave you and your men to your labours. I hope you will succeed. Yes, I hope you will be successful. Goodnight, Wingrave – goodnight to you all. Bless you again.'

There was a muttered response of 'Goodnight, Vicar' from the bellringers and audible sighs of relief arose as the door from the gallery to the winding staircase closed behind the clergyman.

'Now he's gone,' said Wingrave, 'we can make a proper start but before we raise the bells I want a word with you, Mark.'

Mark Everett grinned and said, 'You do, Charlie? What about? What have I done?'

'You were in the Red Cow tonight before coming here, weren't you?'

'I was. So were you. I saw you and Walter come in to get the jugs of beer and the tankards for our refreshments tonight. So what, Charlie? What of it?'

'You were in bad company!'

'Me? I was only with Henry Hawkins and the Bonnamy twins.'

'That's what I mean. Bad company. Young buggers always up to tricks. They knew you were ringing tonight, didn't they?'

'They knew. Why shouldn't they have known?'

'They were trying to get you drunk weren't they? So tight you couldn't ring properly. They would reckon it a good prank if they got you to wreck the peal!'

Mark chuckled. 'They tried,' he said, 'tried hard. But I wasn't going to let them. Don't worry, Charlie, I only had one. Honest! I only had the one.'

Somewhat re-assured Charlie ordered the ringers to take off their coats and stand by their bells. Walter sat himself down on the bench close to the refreshment trays and watched the proceedings with brightly beady eyes. Dick grasped hold of the treble bell's rope and, at a nod from Charlie, pulled it gently downward, gathering in the slack with his left hand. Overhead, high in the tower, the smallest of the eight bells began to speak in soft, tremulous tones. Then, one by one, her sisters joined in the chorus and the eight brightly coloured sallies rose higher and higher as the clamour grew.

With his bell up and deftly set at back stroke Dick glanced at old Walter for approval and was rewarded with a nod and a grin. When all the bells were up and silent, Charlie called out, 'Right lads, we'll just have a few rounds and a touch of Grandsire Triples to get the feel of things, then we'll take a break afore Walter rings out the old. Ready?'

Once more, at a nod from Wingrave, Dick pulled on his rope and led the bells into rounds. The now much more harmonious sounds were flung from the tower by the snow-filled, gusty east wind across the snow-covered roofs of the town. They heard them in Tilehouse Street and the sleeping Quakers there turned grumpily in their beds. The shopkeepers in the Market Square and its offshoots of Cock Street, Bucklersbury, and Sun Street tried without success to stop their ears under the bedclothes. All to no avail. Most of those who lived in Golden Square and that end of Bancroft wished they lived further from the church and its bells while those, like Mrs Bonnamy, who did live further away were thankful they lived no closer.

Anne and the doctor, still not in bed when the rounds commenced, could only hear the sound of the bells intermittently.

'The wind is carrying the sound of them away from us,' explained Mansell. 'And I expect the louvres of the belfry windows on our side will be choked with snow. We'll not be disturbed much.' He added a, 'Glory be!' But Anne expressed some disappointment. 'I would have liked to have heard them properly. After all it is our Dick who is one of the ringers. Not that I understand what bellringers try to do. They don't play tunes, do they?'

'No, my dear, they don't. They just keep changing the sequence of the bells in various kinds of mathematical exercises. It's beyond me. They call it music, but I don't, I'm afraid. What I am thankful for is that Dick has taken to it and that it has got him out of that part-time work at the Angel. I was getting worried about him.'

Laying aside the tiny remnant of his cigar Mansell rose from his chair. Anne, taking the hint, lit a candle, turned out the lamp and preceded him, candlestick in hand, to the stairway.

* * *

Walter Primrose, confident of his ringing prowess, stood with the rope of the tenor bell firmly in his grasp as he waited for the nearby, watch-in-hand Charlie to give the order for him to swing the one-and-a-quarter tons of metal over the balance for the first of the nine tailors. As 1840 slipped into the past Charlie's cry of 'Time!' was pursued almost immediately by the mighty, solemn booming of the bell.

'Boom! Boom! Boom!' Three clearly defined strokes followed by three more and then a further three. There was a pause followed by the strokes for the months of the year which had gone. Walter was unhurriedly moving with a smooth, machine-like rhythm, only bending his back slightly with each pull. He silently mouthed the names of the months as he struck them off. 'January – February – March – April – May – June – July – August – September – October – November – '

As December hovered on his lips a surprised look came upon his face and he slowly pitched forward to fall first to his knees and then face downward to the floor. The rope was violently wrenched from his hands and then, wildly and wickedly lashing out in all directions, it was whipped up to the ceiling of the gallery as the bell was overthrown and its stay broken.

Charlie Wingrave's loud cry of 'Stop! Stop! Stop!' was scarcely heard by the seven waiting ringers as the clangour of the huge, loose bell filled the gallery and church with an awesome sound but they hastily relinquished their charges and cowed back to the walls to get away from the madness of the flying rope. Gradually the bell ceased its frantic bellowing and at last its rope hung still, the red, white and blue sally high out of reach.

Then, and only then, did Charlie and the other ringers gather round the recumbent Walter. Two of them, George Barker and Philip Allen, carefully turned him on to his back.

'Is he dead?' asked Charlie.

'Don't reckon so,' replied the blacksmith. 'He's breathing but it don't look too good to me. Here, one of you, give me a rolled up coat or something to put under his head.'

As Philip Allen placed the coat under the old man's head his eyelids flickered momentarily and he made a slight gasping noise. One side of his much crinkled face appeared to have slipped and become fixed to give the appearance of a lop-sided grin.

'He's had some sort of stroke,' was Charlie's opinion, 'we'd best get hold of a doctor.' Looking round for Dick Mansell he told him to fetch his father. 'Old Walter trusts him,' he said, 'he's been looking after him for years. Off you go, Dick.'

By the time Dick had returned with his father, who, when summoned, had just been getting into his bed, Walter had been moved to the side of the ringing gallery and was covered by blankets brought over from the Vicarage. The remaining seven bells had been rung down for safety and now hung mute in the belfry.

The Vicar, his frilly nightshirt stuffed into his breeches and enveloped in a thick dressing gown, was standing by Walter looking rather at a loss. He greeted the doctor effusively, 'Thank God you've come so quickly, Mansell. You'll know what's best to be done for the poor old man.'

Mansell bent over Walter listening intently to the laboured breathing. He felt his pulse carefully then momentarily eased back an eyelid before announcing, 'An apoplexy. A bad one, I am afraid and there is little I can do for him here or anywhere else, but we had better get him home and into a bed.' But as he finished speaking Walter breathed his last and the gasping ceased.

'Just as well,' said the Doctor, but then to confirm what he was sure had happened he felt for a heartbeat. There was none and after slowly shaking his head he gently lifted the top blanket and pulled this over Walter's lined but now completely relaxed and peaceful face.

An uneasy shuffling of feet among the bellringers was brought to a halt by Charlie Wingrave saying, 'Quiet, while the Vicar says a prayer for him and for us. You'll do that, Vicar?'

Wiles said a few words and then led them all into the Lord's Prayer. At its conclusion he was asked if he wanted the body removed that night.

'No, Wingrave. Let him rest here in peace until the morning. He couldn't be in a better place. I'm sure he died happy here but someone must go and tell the daughter he lived with in the

Swan yard. I think you live closest, Barker? Perhaps you'll do it?'

The blacksmith nodded. 'Aye, Vicar. I'll do it but ain't we forgetting something? Something important, seeing what Walter did for years when it were wanted.'

'No, it hasn't been forgotten,' said Charlie, 'and if the Vicar don't mind we'll do it now.'

'You want to ring him out?' asked Wiles.

'Yes, Vicar. Ring him out. We'll send him on his way with the nine and then his seven and seventy. They'll have to be struck on number seven as number eight is out of it but Walter will understand.'

The bell was not far into the seventy-seven solemn strokes when Mansell emerged from the church and began trudging through the now deep snow on his way home. In his pocket was a crown piece given to him for his services by Charlie Wingrave. It was a bright and shiny one.

*   *   *

Contentedly asleep in her small, neat bedroom Susan Deamer heard nothing of the bells nor of the calling out and return of her beloved guardian. She had settled down well to her new way of life and her memories of the past and its hardships were fading fast. She loved being at Mrs Bonnamy's Academy and had acquired two firm friends, Amanda Fostring and Felicity Quint. She had also developed an adoration for the new music teacher, Miss Sarah Barker. Each night when she said her prayers she asked God to bless her Uncle William, her Aunt Anne, Amanda, Felicity, and Miss Barker. She never forgot her mother and she included, on occasions, a plea that her Aunt Ada might be forgiven.

Amanda too had gone to bed happy that night. Under her pillow was a neatly printed card inviting her to a 'Young Person's Birthday Ball' to be held at the Priory on Friday the eighth of January commencing at five o'clock in the evening, carriages at ten. It had been addressed to her as Miss Amanda Radcliffe-Fostring and when she had been given the card by the gruff but kindly lawyer, John Hawkins, she had been told that in future she was, according to Mr Delme-Radcliffe's instructions, to be known by that hyphenated name.

'He has been delighted with Mrs Bonnamy's reports of your progress,' Hawkins had said, 'and that is why you have been given this invitation to his niece's birthday party.'

'But it says ball!' Amanda's reply had brought a smile to the lawyer's lips as he said, 'It will take the form of a ball. There will be supper and dancing as well as games. I know you have been taught dancing at Mrs Bonnamy's.'

'Yes, Mr Hawkins, I have. I know how to do the quadrille, the cotillion and how to waltz,' she said with pride.

This had brought an amused snort from the portly bow-legged Hawkins. 'Waltz, can you Amanda? That's more than I can manage but then I shan't be at this ball. I haven't been invited!'

'Who will be there, please?'

'Mr Delme-Radcliffe's own two youngsters, his nieces and nephews from the Holwell rectory and the younger sons and daughters of local gentlefolk and professional people like myself. Two of my boys and two of my girls will be going and I have blank invitations for two of your friends from the Academy. I expect you have made some.'

A delighted Amanda had given him the names of Susan Deamer and Felicity Quint and Hawkins had nodded his approval and smiled again when asked, 'But what shall I wear, Mr Hawkins? What shall I wear?'

Amanda, he noted with pleasure, was fast losing her cockney accent and her voice was no longer strident but low-pitched and pleasant. Being something of a mimic had helped her considerably in her steps towards gentility.

'What will you wear, Amanda? That has been thought of by Mr Delme-Radcliffe.' Hawkins had produced a cardboard box from a cupboard in his office and said, 'Here you are, here's your ball-gown, your slippers and your stockings. Real silk stockings. Mrs Bonnamy chose them and she also bought a small gift for you to present to Miss Amelia. You must take a gift. That is most important!'

Meanwhile, Felicity Quint, in her bed at Manley Court lay tearful and angry. She had made up her mind. She would never forgive Nelson. Never! Never! She never wanted to see him again. He had been hateful. It had been wonderful when he had come to Mrs Bonnamy's that night before Christmas and they had gone to the stables and made love in the hayloft. Twice he had pleasured her. Then things had gone wrong. Badly wrong. She had suggested to him that they should elope and take a coach to a place called Gretna Green. There they could be married without anyone's consent but their own. She had some money, more than a hundred pounds in fact, and she had her jewellery which could be sold. She was sure that they would have enough to live on until her father came round to accepting Nelson as her husband. He could take him into the tea business and they could all live happily ever after.

There had been an emphatic refusal by Nelson to this madcap scheme. 'Supposing he doesn't?' he had said. 'Then what? Your money won't last for ever.' Gypsy life, if they were reduced to that, he had continued, was not for her. It was a poor way of living. It could be wet and cold and horrible sheltering for the night under a hedge or an old piece of canvas. He wanted something better than that for her. And there would be no chance that Sir Arthur would take him back at Royston. No chance at all.

A quarrel had ensued, when bitter things had been said. Nelson had left her and she had told him as he had pulled on his breeches before leaving, 'Never come back!'

'I shan't!' he had shouted.

Remembering this Felicity turned her face into her already damp pillow and wept again.

PART TWO

1847

1. A Man of Secrets

There was no ringing out of 1846 nor a ringing in of 1847 by the bells of St Mary's Church. An epidemic of influenza sweeping through the town had laid low four of the bellringers, including the captain Charlie Wingrave, and at midnight on the last day of December Charlie lay hovering at death's door.

Mansell, like the other Hitchin doctors, had been kept over-busy by the epidemic, which had started just before Christmas, and he was wakened from a sleep of near exhaustion when, at one in the morning, Dick, his son who had married Charlie's daughter, rapped loudly upon his front door.

It was Anne in her nightgown who answered the summons. Having greeted her son, but not very warmly, she asked, 'What is it, Dick?'

'It's Charlie! We think he's going! He looks really bad and we want father to come! Come at once! I've got the pony and trap.'

Mansell, partway down the stairs and still struggling into his coat, called out, 'I doubt if there's anything much more I can do for him, Dick. I expect Emma and her mother are doing what I told them to do the other day, aren't they?'

Dick, as soon as he was face-to-face with his father, said, 'Yes, they are. They're keeping him warm with a fire in the bedroom and they're giving him plenty of hot drinks but – '

'But what, boy?'

'He can't drink them now. He's breathing badly and he doesn't seem to know anyone. Sometimes he babbles as though he is out of his mind!'

'Delirious, is he? That is bad. Well, I shall come at once and have a look at him but I can't promise you anything. If it is pneumonia, nature will have to take its course. It could go one way with him or it could go the other.'

Having wrapped his cloak closely around himself Mansell picked up his bag and his cap. In the trap, as they trotted through the empty moonlit streets and country lanes on their way to the

131

bakery at Charlton, nothing more was said and Mansell's mind traversed the years back to that New Year's morning when he had stood by Charlie Wingrave's side in the ringing gallery at St Mary's Church and they had seen old Walter Primrose die. Was it six or seven years that had passed since then? Whichever it was they had for him been good and pleasant years. Early on Dick had married Emma Wingrave, and the newly-weds had settled down in a cottage, close to the bakery, presented to them by Charlie. More recently his ward, Susan Deamer, had married Mark Everett, the haberdasher's son, and those two had taken over the living quarters above the shop in the Market Square. Theirs had been one half of a very pretty double wedding. At the same time, Paul Bonnamy, now a partner with his Uncle Solly in the diamond business, had married Sarah Barker, with twin brother Peter, a solicitor with John Hawkins's firm, being best man to both grooms. Their one-time bosom friend, Henry Hawkins, had not been there. He had been banished to London sometime before by his exasperated father. John Hawkins had suffered this 'limb of Satan', as he called him, long enough, and after some irate townsfolk had seized young Henry and threatened to duck the mischievous youth in the Priory horse-pond not once, but a dozen times, he dispatched his son to where he could study for the Bar at a safe distance from Hitchin.*

'It's sink or swim for you, Henry!' his father had growled, 'and mind you, if you sink, your fate will be on your own head!'

Mansell smiled to himself at the memory of the occasion. He had been standing close to the door of the coach at the time of this parting admonishment and had thoroughly approved of the action John Hawkins had taken.

'Thank God!' he said to himself. 'I've never been greatly troubled by my children's behaviour, even young Dick's, and now I can settle down and enjoy my grandchildren!' His much loved Mary already had three children, Thomas had four and Dick two. Susan Everett, who he fondly regarded as his second daughter, had one and another well on the way. He was still musing on these happy family thoughts when Dick brought the trap to a slithering halt in the bakery yard.

Minutes afterwards Mansell stood with a grave face by the

---

*Henry Hawkins, after a distinguished career as a barrister, was made a judge in 1876.

bedside of a mumbling Charlie restlessly tossing and turning and having great difficulty in getting his breath.

He asked, 'How long has he been like this, Bella?'

'Since about seven o'clock last evening,' she answered and there was much anxiety in her voice.

'You should have sent for me sooner. Now if we are to save him we must act quickly!' Mansell began to issue orders which Bella and daughter Emma, who had joined her, hastened to obey. Three-quarters of an hour later, when he and the two women stood back from the bed on which Charlie now lay beneath a tent-like structure, quietly breathing in strong aromatic fumes from a steaming bowl by his pillow, the battle for his life seemed on the way to being won.

Bella Wingrave looked at Mansell thankfully as she said, 'God bless you, William. It's a miracle!'

Mansell smiled wearily. 'Yes, Bella, truly a miracle. We caught things just in time. Now, God willing, he should pull through, but he'll need careful nursing in the coming weeks.'

'He'll get that, you can be certain of it. Now we shall carry on as you have asked, replacing the bowl every hour and keeping a steaming kettle on the hob.'

'Good! And remember, a full spoonful of the menthol with each bowl when you change the water – I've left you enough to last until I return this evening – but above all, Bella, you must keep this room warm.'

Before Dick took his father back into Hitchin the two shared a pot of tea in the kitchen. After Dick had pushed a mug of the brandy-laced brew across the table to his father he asked, 'How long do you think it will be before Charlie will be able to come back to the bakery?'

'How long, Dick? Several weeks, I'm afraid.'

'Then we ought to be thinking of getting some help?'

'You should. You and young Charlie may be able to manage for a few days doing the baking and the rounds but you won't be able to go on for long.'

'Charlie won't like it. He hates strangers in the bakehouse.'

Mansell laughed. 'Is he afraid of someone finding out what he puts in the bread? Is he using some secret recipe? That bakery already holds secrets from the days when the Bessemers used the building as a foundry. Has Charlie some of his own?'

'He's got secrets all right. Several! Although I'm his son-in-law I don't get told everything. Not by a long way. Neither does young Charlie, nor Emma! There have been several occasions when I've come back from my rounds to peculiar smells in the bakery. Smells that don't come from baking bread. I'm certain of that!'

'Have you asked Charlie about the matter?'

'Only once! He told me pretty sharply to mind my own business! Another thing – ' Dick hesitated for a moment and his father asked, 'What?'

'There's a room or a big cupboard close to the side of the oven which is always kept locked and Charlie hides the key!'

'So?'

'I asked young Charlie if he knew what was in there. He said he wasn't sure but he thought from something he'd overheard said by his mother that there were still things inside belonging to the Bessemers.'

'Things left behind when they closed down the foundry and went to London? That's nearly twenty years ago!'

'I suppose so.'

Mansell rubbed his chin thoughtfully. 'If I remember rightly,' he said, 'Bella was a maid in their employ when she married Charlie.'

'Yes. So I've heard tell from Emma. She says her mother stayed on as a maid until she was born. Her father was then a foreman in the foundry and in the typecutting workshop.'

'That was when I first met him. He was supposed to be very good at his work. So good I was surprised he didn't go to London with the Bessemers, particularly as at that time he was as thick as thieves with young Henry Bessmer. I was even more surprised when he and his brother set up the bakery together. Bread-baking wasn't Charlie's trade.'

'That may have been true then, Father, but it was his brother's and now we have the best rounds in Hitchin and Charlie seems to be making a fortune.'

'And investing it wisely in bricks and mortar if rumour is right, Dick!'

'Yes. Not only does he now own the bakery buildings and the two cottages adjoining, but Emma and I believe he owns as many as twenty shops and houses in Hitchin, including one of the mansions in Bancroft.'

'And all from selling bread?'

'It must be! But as I told you earlier, Father, Charlie can turn quite nasty if you start asking him questions about his business and I have certainly never dared ask him where he has been to when he comes back from London every month or so.'

'He may have rents to collect up there, Dick, or perhaps he goes to see the Bessemers.'

'Somehow I don't think it's rent-collecting or anything to do with the Bessemers. He's only there for a short time. He gets young Charlie to take him into Hitchin for the eight o'clock coach and then he has to be picked up off the last coach from London on the same day. He never stays overnight.'

Mansell chuckled. 'Well, I'm sure it's not a woman involved. Charlie is not that sort! But I'll tell you this, Dick, he won't be going to London this month nor next. I suppose he could send Bella. She may be privy to his secrets even if you and Emma and young Charlie are being kept in the dark.'

There was a snort from Dick. 'If he wants to keep his secrets, let him. I don't suppose they amount to much anyway. He just likes being secretive. Now, Father, let me drive you home before I have to start work in the bakery. I expect young Charlie is already at it!'

It was well past five in the morning before the exhausted doctor was able to fall asleep again in his own bed.

2. The Lasting Silence of Slithy Tobbs

Inspector Rudd and the stout Sergeant Pegg making their way to the Islington Police Station paused on the pavement on the opposite side of the road to the Windmill Inn to watch the Hitchin coach being reined in at the hostelry's front door.

'Strange,' commented Rudd, 'we don't often see the Kershaw Flyer pull up there. I wonder who is getting off?'

As the coach came to its brake-creaking stop one of the outside passengers, a small man in shabby clothes, stood up, and after saying something to the guard began to clamber down to the ground. The guard delved deeply into the luggage boot and with considerable difficulty retrieved a small but heavy leather handbag. This, when the passenger was safely on the ground, was lowered into his upward stretched hands.

'It's Tobbs!' exclaimed Rudd, 'Slithy Tobbs, his own nasty little self! I think, Sergeant, that you and I had better see what the rascal has got in that bag he's just lifted down!'

Hastening across the road closely followed by Pegg, Rudd called out, 'Hold it, Slithy! We want a word with you!'

Tobbs, about to put the bag on the ground as the coach began to roll away, turned sharply to face the oncoming Inspector and Sergeant, a look of apprehension in his cunning, blackcurrant eyes belying the quavering smile on his lips. 'Why?' he said, 'if it isn't Mr Rudd and Mr Pegg! I 'opes yer both well and yer not bein' troubled by these nasty March winds. Proper cold journey I've 'ad.'

'Enough of that, Slithy. What have you been up to out in the country? What have you got in that bag?'

'Nothing much, Mr Rudd.'

'It looks rather heavy for nothing much, Slithy. Tell me what you've really got and if I believe you I won't even bother to look. Not even if you say it's the Crown Jewels!'

'It ain't them, Mr Rudd. You know it ain't. It's just a few

things I 'ad ter pick up for a friend wot couldn't pick 'em up fer 'imself.'

'Helping a friend, are you? Not one of your friends in the Somers Town lot, I suppose, Slithy? I hear you've been seen in bad company since you were let out last month.'

Tobb's reaction was immediate. 'Me, Mr Rudd? That's a lie yer bin told! It ain't true. I don't 'ave nuffing ter do with that mob. Them's racecourse! Real narsty them lot! Yer know me, Mr Rudd. I ain't never bin vilent wiv my bits of trouble. I ain't looking fer no long stretch in the 'ulks or in that 'Stralia place!'

'I'd like to believe you, Slithy, but I don't. You were seen in the Half Moon last week with half a dozen of the Rizzi gang including Jack Rizzi himself. You know you were!'

'I were only 'avin' a drink in there! Honest I was! But if Jack arsts yer ter 'ave one wiv 'im, yer 'as ter 'ave one. Yer daren't say no, not ter 'im. Not if yer got any sense.'

'Was it him who sent you out to the country for what you've got in your bag?'

A really scared look appeared on Slithy's face. After hesitating with his reply he suddenly made up his mind and dropped the bag so that it fell on Rudd's right foot. He then took to his heels, frantically pushing his way through the small crowd which was beginning to form. Pegg immediately pounded after him, leaving Rudd hopping around on one leg and obviously in considerable pain.

But the puffing Pegg returned almost immediately to report, 'Lost the little bugger! He got to the corner too quick for me and I couldn't see which way he went!'

Rudd gingerly lowered his foot to the ground. 'We'll get him later,' he said. 'Little bastard! We know where he hangs out. Let's get to the station and have a look at my bloody foot and find out what's in this bloody bag!'

Limping badly the Inspector led the way up the hill, closely followed by the bag-laden, still heavily breathing, Pegg.

Once in his office Rudd removed his boot and stocking to reveal some badly bruised and swollen toes. 'Sod him!' he said looking down at his foot. 'Just wait until I get my hands on him. I'll give him something he won't forget in a hurry! You see if I don't! Now! What was it he didn't want us to see?'

The bag was not locked and when opened by the Sergeant

was found to contain six blue material bags, each secured by a knotted string. Pegg cut the string of the first bag taken out and poured the contents on to Rudd's desk.

'Blimey!' he exclaimed, as a cascade of crown pieces spread themselves before the Inspector's astonished gaze. 'Blimey! It's a bloody fortune!'

'It will be if the other five bags contain the same. You'd best check and see, Pegg.'

Taking out the remaining bags Pegg opened them one by one to report, 'It looks like the same in each, Inspector. But do you reckon they're good ones?'

Picking up one of the coins Rudd examined it closely. Having put this down he looked at another coin taken from the pile and then another. 'I can't see anything wrong with them,' he said. 'They look good to me but I think perhaps we had better get an opinion from the bank across the road. Let us see what Mr Thompson has to say.'

Ten minutes later, with Rudd's damaged foot in a soft slipper, he and the Sergeant entered the bank and were shown immediately to the manager's office. After a few words of explanation, Mr Thompson, a grey-headed gentleman in sober Quaker-grey suiting, began inspecting the dozen specimen coins which Pegg had placed before him using an immense magnifying glass.

Having looked at each of the coins he said, 'They appear genuine enough. If they had been presented at the counter we should have taken them in. They look right, they feel right, but do they weigh as they should? That we can check.'

Ten of the suspect coins were put on a fine balance and set against ten of the bank's coins taken from a bag which had obviously come straight from the Mint.

There was a difference; the bank's coins gently but positively tipped the scales. Mr Thompson shook his head and looked at Rudd. 'The weight is not quite right and I do not now think that they are silver. But what they are made from I do not know. As counterfeits they are the best that I have ever seen. They would pass undetected anywhere.'

'They would?'

'Most certainly. But there is one curious thing and that is the date.'

'Yes. I had noticed it. They are all William IV coins of 1837 but there is nothing wrong with the date, surely?'

'No. It was the last year of his reign and coins were struck in it, but if the rest of your coins are the same date then it seems a little peculiar that such a large batch should have remained together for such a long time, particularly as these appear to have been in circulation. They are discoloured, scratched and slightly worn. Something doesn't seem to make sense, Inspector. It is not only the weight which is wrong that disturbs me but other things combined with that. How many of these coins have you acquired?'

'We haven't counted them yet.'

'Then let me have them counted for you by one of my clerks. He can do so in the presence of your Sergeant, and while we are waiting for this to be done, you I hope, will join me in a glass of Madeira.'

Pegg fetched the leather bag and the remaining coins and took them into the counting house with Mr Thompson's senior clerk and Rudd and the bank manager, with glasses of excellent wine in hand, sat and waited for the count to be completed. In a short time Pegg entered the manager's office and handed his superior a slip of paper. Rudd glanced at it and passed it across to Mr Thompson, saying nothing.

The bank manager's eyebrows gave a twitch. Then he said, 'That will make six hundred with what we have here on the desk?'

'Yes!' replied Rudd. 'To the value, if they were genuine, of one hundred and fifty pounds!'

'A serious matter, Inspector.'

'Very serious. The coiners and those passing the coins must be caught as soon as possible. We have one lead through the man Tobbs and I've no doubt that we shall soon lay him by the heels but we must get to the source of the supply. I expect the Mint will be able to identify the metal being used. Knowing that may help.'

'I have a customer, Inspector, who may be able to give us a quicker answer than the Mint. He's a metallurgist who is still fairly young but fast making a name for himself in several fields. If you would like me to do so I will send him a few of the coins for testing.'

'I should be much obliged if you did, Sir. Very much in the debt of you and your bank.'

'Think nothing of it. We too are involved when it is a matter of counterfeit coins. It is to our advantage if the miscreants are dealt with speedily. You say you know this man Tobbs?'

'Yes. We know him, don't we, Pegg.'

'Yes, Sir. We do. He's been through our hands twice before. And when we get him this time we'll soon get him talking or my name's not Josiah Pegg!'

But when they found Slithy Tobbs the following morning he was lying face downwards in a ditch on the outskirts of Islington and was in no condition to do any talking. He was very dead. His throat had been cut almost from ear to ear.

3. The Hunt Begins in Earnest

A full week has passed and Slithy Tobb's body already lay beneath six feet of earth in the Islington cemetery. Rudd had pulled in several of Jack Rizzi's gang for questioning but Jack himself had conveniently disappeared and not one of those asked admitted to knowing his whereabouts.

'And even if we do find him,' said Rudd to Pegg, 'I doubt if we shall get much out of him. He's more cunning than a fox and he'll produce a cast-iron alibi we shan't be able to break. Unless someone comes forward and admits to being present when the murder was committed we are not likely to get much further forward with that investigation.'

'So you think we ought to drop it?'

'No, Pegg, just shelve it and concentrate for the time being on what Tobbs was carrying.'

'The coins?'

'Yes, the coins – and of course the counterfeiters.'

At that moment there was a tap on the office door and one of the duty constables entered to say, 'There's a gentleman at the counter, Sir, who says he's a Mr Henry Bessemer and he would like to see you.'

'Bessemer?'

'Yes, Sir, Bessemer.'

'Did he say what he wanted to see me about?'

'Yes, Sir. Them coins.'

Pegg said, 'It must be the metallurgist Mr Thompson was asking to examine the crown pieces you left with him.'

'Yes. Show him in, Coddles. And you, Pegg, set a chair for him.'

A tall, well dressed gentleman in his early thirties but with a slight stoop was ushered into the office. Having greeted Rudd and Pegg and shaken each by the hand he seated himself on the chair indicated by the Sergeant and placed his hat and a small glass jar on the desk. The jar appeared to contain some pieces of coin and what looked like metal filings.

'Yours, Sir,' said Rudd, 'is a most opportune arrival. We were just discussing the case of the counterfeit coins. I take it they are not silver?'

Bessemer nodded his head and smiled. 'Not a trace of silver in them, Inspector,' he said. 'They are made of a clever mixture of copper, nickel, lead, tin and antimony. Particularly clever because the weight nearly matches the weight of the metal used for coins of the realm.'

'And, I suppose, not costing much to produce?'

'A mere fraction of the coin's purported value!'

'Where could you buy such a metal?' asked Pegg.

'I know of nowhere, Sergeant, where you could buy an alloy of this nature. The metal used for these coins has been especially produced by someone with a considerable knowledge of smelting and alloys but what is of significant interest to me is the quality of the dies used to stamp out the crown pieces.'

'The dies for the two faces of the coins?'

'Yes. They have been sunk to perfection. My father has been most impressed.'

'Your father, Sir?'

'Yes. Yes he is a great expert in the matter of coin production. For some years before the French Revolution he was with the Paris Mint.'

'Hm!' Rudd sat back and, after a thoughtful moment, said, 'So we now have to look for men who are skilled in both die sinking and creating alloys?'

'That is so, Inspector, and I do not envy you your task. I cannot, for the life of me, imagine where you will start. Perhaps the man who was carrying the coins will lead you to them. I take it that you have him in safe custody? He will talk, surely?'

Rudd grinned. 'He's in safe custody, Sir. It couldn't be safer! But he's not going to say a word! Mr Tobbs is dead and under the sod!'

'Dead?'

'Murdered! But we have been questioning the driver and guard of the coach which brought him to London with his bag and we know where he got on the coach.'

'Where was that, pray?'

'A place called Hitchin, Mr Bessemer. You may have heard of it?' There was a sudden silence and Rudd after a moment, added, 'You seem startled, Sir?'

'I was! I was! I was born near Hitchin. I know the town well.'

'Then you probably know the Swan Inn, the starting place for the London coaches?'

'I do.'

'Well, Tobbs was seen talking to a woman there a few minutes before he took his seat on the coach.'

'You've traced the woman?'

'Not yet. We only heard about her yesterday. According to the guard, who says he saw her and Tobbs exchanging words, she was wearing a hooded cloak and much of her face was concealed.'

'A woman of mystery. She may not be easy for you to find.'

'I have high hopes, Sir, high hopes! Tomorrow I shall be going to Hitchin and seeking the help of the police there. If we can find the lady we may be able to make some progress. If we can't then we must look for another lead.'

'Well, I wish you good fortune in your hunt, Inspector. May you be successful in it.' Henry Bessemer rose from his seat and picked up his hat. Rudd held out a restraining hand. 'Before you go, Sir, you must let me know the fee you require for your services rendered.'

'Fee, Inspector? Fee? You have no need to worry about that. I have been amply rewarded by the bank. Mr Thompson has seen to the matter. The bank has been most concerned. Counterfeit coins of such fine quality are a grave threat to the banks. They are a grave threat to all of us!'

But it was a very perturbed Henry Bessemer who left the police station that morning. He did not like the thoughts that were passing through his mind.

4.   Inspector Albyn Joins the Hunt

The next day Inspector Rudd was met off the London coach by Inspector Leonard Albyn who commanded the Second Division of the Hertfordshire Police and who was stationed at Hitchin with two constables.

Having exchanged pleasantries the two officers strolled gently along Cock Street and past the cattle market in Bancroft, continuing until they reached the Bridewell and the small Police Station which served the town and its surrounding district.

Once safely within its walls, Rudd opened up and told Albyn about the murdered Tobbs and the spurious coins.

A startled Albyn said, 'So you think we have a nest of counterfeiters in our midst?'

'I do! And I have a killer loose in my district!'

'Nasty!'

'Very nasty! These won't be the kinds of crime you are accustomed to round here.'

'No, thank God, they're not. There's poaching in plenty, a little thieving and occasional cases of stack burning. As much as we can manage with the few men I've got and the big area we are expected to cover.'

'Well, I'm afraid I shall have to push the matter of the dud coins over to you with the hope that you'll let me know of what progress you are making. I shall be dealing with the murder as a London matter. I'm sure I know who was responsible for silencing Slithy Tobbs but I do need proof to get a rope round Rizzi's neck.'

'Do you really think that if we can establish a connection between Rizzi and the coiners it will help with your case?'

'Yes, Albyn, I do. If your counterfeiters can be found and made to squeal they will probably supply the missing links in my chain.'

'I hope they will. I shall certainly be following up the lead you've given me as soon as I possibly can.'

'The cloaked and hooded lady?'

'Yes. The mystery woman!'

That evening Albyn waited at the Swan Inn for the return of the daily coach from London with a view to questioning the guard about the woman, who, according to what he had told Rudd, he had seen in conversation with Tobbs. Albyn also had in mind finding out from the guard who else from Hitchin had been on the coach with the little man and his heavy bag. They also could be questioned.

Over tankards of ale in a private room at the inn the guard, Alfred Figgis, was not able to add much to what Albyn had already learned through Rudd in so far as the cloaked woman was concerned.

'No, Inspector, I didn't really get much of a look at 'er. The pair of 'em were right up the yard. Not far from the smithy – an' that's a fair distance from where we loads the coach as yer must know.'

'And you don't think she gave him a bag?'

'I ain't saying that. I'm only saying I didn't see 'er pass no bag to 'im. What I am sure is that when I first saw 'im in the yard 'e 'adn't got a bag an' when 'e got on the coach 'e 'ad!'

'Hm! That's something I suppose, but we'll forget him for the moment and you can tell me who else from Hitchin was on the coach that morning.'

'From 'ere?'

'From Hitchin, yes. There may be someone else who saw the two of them together. Someone who may even know who she is. It's possible!'

Figgis removed his low-crowned hat and vigorously scratched through his thick crop of greying hair as though trying to rouse his memory cells into active life.

'That were more 'an a week back, Guv'nor. I've 'ad a lotter passengers since then but I does mind that Mr 'Awkins were a hinside that morning.'

'The lawyer?'

'Yes, Guv. The lawyer, not the doctor, but there were a doctor aboard. You know 'im. The one wot ain't a proper doctor but just as good.'

'Mansell?'

'That's 'im. Houtside 'e were. Sat next ter the little man wiv the bag.'

'Did he, by God!' Albyn made two entries in his notebook and then asked, 'Anyone else?'

There was a broad grin from Figgis. 'There were an' all! 'Er ladyship! She were hinside wiv Mr 'Awkins.'

'Who do you mean? Lady Who?'

'Betsy Barker! Fancies 'herself more 'an a bit does our widder Barker. Even more since 'er 'usband went and 'er gal married that Mr Bonnamy an' 'e were took up by 'is uncle in Lunnon wot's in the sparkler bus'ness. She were going ter Lunnon that morning ter see 'er gal and Mr Paul. Proper rude ter me she was when I 'elped 'er up an' shoved 'er in wiv 'er bum!'

A smiling Albyn made another note. 'No one else?'

'Not proper 'Itchin, Guv. Not wot comes ter mind. There wos some from the villages but not many. We weren't hoverful that morning. I does know that.'

Having thanked the guard and bought him another tankard of ale, Albyn made for his home, his supper, and his bed, knowing he had a busy day ahead of him on the morrow and one which would include a close encounter with a dragon.

His first interview that morning was with John Hawkins at the lawyer's Portmill Lane office. Unfortunately Hawkins only had a very slight recollection of Tobbs.

'Yes,' he said, 'I did see him get off the coach at Islington and I saw him being apprehended by the police. I certainly didn't see him at Hitchin. Nor did I see any woman dressed as you describe. Not much help I'm afraid, Inspector. No, the only lady I remember that morning was Mrs Barker and she was being her usual forceful self!'

Mrs Barker, when she was questioned at her Tilehouse Street home, sniffed and said, 'Woman in a hooded cloak? Yes, I saw one, Inspector, what of it?'

An elated Albyn then asked, 'Do you know who it was?'

Mrs Barker gave another of her eloquent sniffs. 'Who was it? Of course I do not know who it was! She was a common-looking woman! Certainly not one of my acquaintances!'

Doctor William Mansell, who Albyn fortunately spotted entering Mrs Bonnamy's Academy, was more helpful. He remembered Tobbs quite well.

'He sat next to me on the coach. We had outside seats just behind the driver. Not that he was much company. Hardly got a civil word from him the whole way. I wasn't sorry when he got off at Islington and I watched the police approach him.'

'He escaped Doctor, but only to get himself murdered. The police found his body the next morning. His throat had been cut.'

'Not nice! Not nice at all!'

'Did you see him talking to anyone at Hitchin before the coach left?'

'Yes. I'm sure I did. A woman.'

'Do you know who it was?'

Mansell shook his head. 'No, they were too far away and her back was towards me. She was, if I remember rightly, wearing a heavy-looking blue cloak with a big hood. It was a cold morning and she was well wrapped up.'

'Damn. I'd hoped for more from you.'

'What has the woman got to do with Tobbs being murdered?'

'We think she gave him the bag he was carrying.'

'I'm sure he had no bag when I saw them speaking together, but he did a few minutes later when he came to the coach. What was in the bag? Do you know?'

Albyn produced one of the crown pieces which had been given to him by Inspector Rudd before his return to London. Mansell took it and looked at it closely.

'Six hundred of 'em!' said Albyn. 'All wrong 'uns and it seems possible that they were made in Hitchin!'

Mansell's, 'Does it, indeed,' sounded casual enough but something was whirring in his mind like a clock gone mad. The whirring continued after Albyn had left him. Crown pieces! Charlie Wingrave and his secrets! The Charlton bakery which had once been a foundry! The locked room! The Bessemers and the rumours about them when they had lived at Charlton! Things were beginning to add up to a very unpleasant total. Dick and Emma might well be involved. He must see Bella at once. It would be useless talking to Charlie, who, since his illness, had deteriorated into a doddering shadow of his former self. He was old now. He was old beyond his years and inclined at times to be quite silly. No, it would have to be Bella. He was almost certain that she was the woman who had been at the Swan Inn that morning, enveloped in the hooded cloak, and she would know if there was evidence of counterfeiting concealed at Charlton. If there was, it would have to be got rid of immediately. Inspector Albyn was no fool. He might, even before the day was out, find somebody who had recognised Bella. Seeing her as soon as possible was imperative.

Mansell, as soon as he had finished examining, and prescribing for, the three of Mrs Bonnamy's young ladies who had coughs and colds, set off on foot for Charlton, wishing, and not for the first time in his life, that he could afford to keep a pony and trap.

5.   The Last of the Secrets

Bella Wingrave was busy in the kitchen preparing a meal when the door opened and Mansell, very much out of breath, burst in on her.

'William!' she exclaimed. 'You are in a state! You've been hurrying, haven't you? You of all people! You ought to know better at your age!'

'Never mind that, Bella! Where's Charlie? Is he in the bake-house?'

'No. In the privy. Do you want him for something? Something urgent? Do, for heavens sake, sit yourself down. He'll be back in a minute or two.'

Mansell seated himself on a chair by the table at which Bella was working. He said, 'It's perhaps just as well that I have got you on your own. It's you I want an answer from.'

'Me? Answer?'

'Yes. You, Bella! An answer! Were you in the yard of the Swan Inn a week back last Tuesday? In the morning? About the time the coach was leaving for London?'

Her eyes suddenly became wary. Her nodded 'Yes' was only given after a momentary hesitation.

'You were?'

'Yes. I took the pony and trap into Hitchin and left them in the yard near the blacksmith's place. The pony had a loose shoe and I wanted it attended to. Why? Why are you asking, William?'

'Did you give a leather bag to a man? A bag containing six hundred crown pieces?'

It was almost as though the question had been a hard blow. Bella reeled sideways and then collapsed on to a stool. Her face was ashen.

Recovering herself slightly she said loudly and emphatically, 'No, William! Of course I didn't. Where would I get all that money? No! No! No! It's ridiculous!'

'You're lying, Bella. You were seen!'

'I couldn't have been! I wasn't even there when he took it from the trap!'

Suddenly Bella realised the implication of what she had just said. Her hand went to her mouth.

'Then,' said Mansell, 'you must have told him where to find it when he spoke to you.'

Bella nodded then she murmured wretchedly, 'Yes. It was hidden under a blanket.' She burst into sudden tears, weeping into her apron, her face hidden.

It was at that moment Charlie entered the kitchen. He was still doing up the buttons on his coat, a coat that was now too large for his shrunken and emaciated frame. His walk as he came through the doorway was nothing more than an old man's shuffle. He looked first at Bella and then at Mansell.

'What's going on?' he asked in a querulous tone of voice. 'What is it, Bella?'

Bella raised her tearstained face and said, 'He knows, Charlie, he knows!'

'Knows? Knows what, woman? What have you been telling him, you fool?'

Mansell intervened quickly. 'That's enough, Charlie! Quite enough! Sit down and I'll tell you what I know and also what I strongly suspect. If I'm right then we have all got to move and move quickly or there will be big trouble for everyone!'

A shaking Charlie lowered himself into a chair close to Bella on her stool. They looked a guilty and pathetic pair and it seemed as though Bella had aged a full ten years in only a few minutes. When they were settled Mansell said, 'Before I start in this matter. How about Emma and Dick?'

'They know nothing,' said Bella. 'Nothing! Nor does young Charlie. There's been no one else involved since Charlie's brother died seven years ago.'

'Thank God for that! Now, what I do know is this. That a bag of coins was taken from your trap by a man named Tobbs. He sat by my side on the coach to London that morning. When he got off at Islington he was picked up by the police – '

There was a gasp from Bella. 'Police! The police know about the coins?'

'Not everything. Tobbs escaped before he could be questioned but he didn't get far before he was murdered. He was found the next morning with his throat cut! Someone made sure he wouldn't talk! The London police have the coins of course, and they do know they are counterfeit. They also know that Tobbs picked them up from somebody in Hitchin. Further, they suspect a woman is involved, as he was seen speaking to one in the Swan yard. The London police have now put the Hitchin end of the matter in the hands of Inspector Albyn of the local police and he is already looking for that woman. I know it was Bella because I tricked her just now into an admission. Albyn doesn't know that yet but I do not think it will be long before he gets on her track!'

Charlie asked, 'How do you know all this, William?'

'I was questioned by him only two hours ago and it wasn't until he questioned me that I became suspicious and began putting two and two together. This is what I think is the truth of the matter and you can correct me if I am wrong. You have been making counterfeit coins for a long time, haven't you?'

Charlie nodded. 'Yes. Ever since the Bessemers left here seventeen years ago and me and my brother set up the bakery.'

'Then I'll continue. You had learned about mixing and melting metals when you worked for the Bessemers. You knew what was secretly added to the type metal alloy to make it longer-lasting in use.'

'Yes, I did. Still do. And I was there one day when young Mr Henry was in charge and made a mistake in the mixture and we got something out of the furnace which looked exactly like silver.'

'Which later gave you the idea of counterfeiting coins?'

'Yes. You can't see the difference between the alloy and what the Mint uses for proper coins. That's not all silver, you know that?'

'Yes, so I've been told. But who made the dies for stamping out your coins?'

There was a sly grin from Charlie. 'I did!' he said with some pride. 'Old Mr Bessemer taught me die sinking. He was a good teacher and after a time he said I was better at it than him – and that's saying something seeing he was at the French Mint in Paris before the Revolution. I cut the first set in 1831 and the second in 1837 when the first set wore out!'

'Good God! However many coins have you made from them?'

Another grin appeared on Charlie's face. 'How many? Thousands! I've lost count!'

'But how on earth have you managed to get them into circulation? And how is it they look as though they have been in use?'

'Making them look used was Bella's idea. Before we issued any we put them in a small butter churn with sand and water and a little acid and gave it a few turns. They came out just as we wanted them to look. Ready for sending out!'

'Sending out to who or to where?'

'Nothing local. That could have been risky. No, I used to take them to London to someone who had connections with the bookmakers on the race courses. He bought them from us at about half the face value so he did well and so did we. We didn't want to be greedy and neither did he. It's been a nice steady business until now but Bella and me decided last year that we'd made enough out of it to be able to retire. We dismantled the furnace and got rid of the press and the dies and began selling off the final batch of coins we had made. When I was taken ill at Christmas I wasn't able to go to London and I haven't been able to go since.'

'Why didn't you send Bella?'

'He wouldn't let me go,' put in Bella. 'He said it was a man's business. He reckoned they were a rough lot he'd been dealing with and he wrote to – '

Charlie said sharply, 'No names, Bella, no names! Yes I wrote and asked for someone to come and collect six hundred from a woman in a blue cloak who would be in the Swan Yard when the London coach was getting ready for the morning trip. The rest you seem to know.'

'Was that the last of the coins?'

'No,' said Bella. 'Not quite. We've still got four hundred left.'

'Have you, by God!. More than enough to get you hanged or transported for life! Where are they? In the bakery?'

'No! There's nothing in the bakery. Nothing that shouldn't be there. Nothing at all. The coins are here! In the kitchen!'

'Here? Where?'

'In the milk churn in that corner. We were getting them ready for the final delivery – ' Bella was interrupted by the sounds of hurried clip-clopping into the yard, and almost as soon as

Mansell's eyes had turned from staring at the churn to looking at the door there was a loud and urgent knocking.

At Mansell's nod to the gaping Bella she rose and went to lift the latch, but before she could do so the door was burst open and Inspector Albyn pushed his way into the kitchen leaving, on the threshold, his two constables and a tall gentleman with a grim look on his face.

'It's the police!' Bella's voice rose to a shriek. 'It's the police and Mr Henry!'

Charlie and Mansell both stood up. Charlie's pale, haggard face went even whiter as Albyn announced in a loud voice, 'Charles Wingrave, I have a magistrate's signed warrant to search these and any adjoining premises for – '

The Inspector stopped abruptly as Charlie slumped back into his chair and then slid slowly down into a sprawling heap on the floor like a marionette with suddenly severed strings.

Mansell quickly crossed to the stricken man and bent over him. Almost immediately he straightened up and addressed Albyn. 'I think he's had a heart attack,' he said in a low voice.

'Is he dead?' asked Albyn.

'No, but I'll be surprised if he lives for very long. He was a very sick man before the shock you have just given him and I cannot see him surviving it.'

'Then he'd best be got to his bed. We shall try not to disturb him but we've our duty to do and search we must. Can you manage to get him up the stairs?'

'He will have to be carried.'

'Then my two men will assist you. Afterwards they will search this house and whilst they are doing so Mr Bessemer and I will search the bakehouse.'

Less than an hour later Charlie Wingrave died. Mansell broke the news to Albyn as he, his men and Henry Bessemer reassembled in the kitchen.

'Dead, is he?' said Albyn. 'Well, I'm sorry, Mrs Wingrave, very sorry, particularly as we have found nothing anywhere here whatsoever to connect him with the crime we are investigating. That, despite the information laid before us by a certain gentleman,' the Inspector glowered at Bessemer, 'and the matter, so far as you and your late husband are concerned, can be considered as closed. Without evidence we have no case.'

Followed by his two men he stalked angrily from the kitchen, leaving Henry Bessemer to face Bella. After a moment she said without anger, 'I'm surprised at you, Mr Henry.'

He replied, 'I had to say something, Bella. I voiced my suspicions to the London police last evening and I was asked to catch the morning coach to Hitchin and inform Inspector Albyn. I did it reluctantly but it had to be done. It was very wrong of you and Charlie to do what the two of you must have been doing and it has lead to a terrible thing. Murder! It just had to be stopped.'

'It was being stopped!'

'But being stopped too late! . . . You can assure me, Bella, there will be no more of it and that you have really got rid of everything?'

'All but a few coins in the churn over there and I promise you, Mr Henry, that those will not be circulated.'

'Good, Bella, good! I shall say no more. With Charlie's death you have been punished enough.'

'Will you tell your father about what has happened?'

'I shall. He is old now and it will make him very sad. He was very fond of you both and he often speaks of the days when we lived here and you were with us. They were happy times.'

'They were, Mr Henry, they were. And will you come to Charlie's funeral if I let you know when it is to be? You were good friends once.'

'Yes, Bella, very good friends and I will come. Now I must say goodbye and return the horse to the police at Hitchin. Then I will catch the late coach to London.'

Bella and Mansell stood together outside the kitchen door and watched Henry Bessemer ride out of the yard. Before he turned the corner and on to the Hitchin road he tipped his hat to Bella and she raised her hand in acknowledgement. As soon as he was out of sight she said, 'Now, William, what do we tell Emma and Dick and young Charlie?'

'Where are they?'

'Dick and young Charlie are still on their rounds and Emma is in Hitchin with the children. They should all be back soon at about the same time.'

'I suggest we tell them nothing except that Charlie is dead and died rather suddenly. There is nothing more they need to know but if it should come to their ears that the police have been here just say it was a big mistake. The past is best forgotten.'

Bella nodded her agreement and then tears welled into her eyes as Mansell gently led her into the house.

A week later Charlie's body was taken for burial in the graveyard at St Mary's Church in Hitchin. A plot had been found for him close to the tower and the bells he had loved and rung so often and so well. The cortege when it left Charlton was an impressive one. Following the ornate hearse with its black-plumed and black-beribboned horses were four closed carriages. In the first rode Bella, Emma and Dick Mansell and young Charlie. In the second were Doctor and Mrs William Mansell and Mr Henry Bessemer. In the third and fourth an assortment of Charlie's cousins, aunts and uncles.

Two men standing outside the Swan Inn as the cortege crossed the market place respectfully bared their heads.

One asked, 'Who is it, Albyn? Do you know?'

'Yes, Mr Oakley,' said the Inspector. 'I do. It's Charles Wingrave.'

'The Charlton baker?'

'Yes. The baker.'

'Hm! A rather grand funeral for him, isn't it? Was he such a wealthy man?'

'Wealthy enough, I'm told! But what is wealth, Mr Oakley, when you are going to your grave. You can't take it with you. You can take nothing!'

But Albyn was not quite right so far as Charlie was concerned. The night before the funeral, Mansell, assisted by Bella, had removed the coffin lid and packed the remaining four hundred counterfeit coins around the body. Charlie's last secret was to go with him to where it was never likely to be uncovered.

6. With Murder in Mind

The tall young man who stood beneath the ancient Bancroft archway in the very early morning of what promised to be a really hot July day had not the past in mind but the future. A future when the old farm barns and buildings which, with his father's permission, he was already converting would develop from the present small beginnings into a distillery producing large quantities of the finest galenicals available in Britain. He, William Ransom, would see to that. Only the best would be good enough to meet the standard he proposed setting as a manufacturing chemist. His Quaker father was funding him to the full in his purchases of stills, percolators, condensers, refrigerators, vats, tubs and retorts, and all the other things needed for the great project. Also his father was allowing him to use corners of the home farm fields for the cultivation of aromatic and medicinal plants such as belladonna, aconite, squirting cucumber, chamomile, henbane and lavender, the raw materials he required for processing. In August and September each year, and he had in mind starting this year, he intended to pay local women to go out to the harvested cornfields and bring in dandelion roots. He was aware that the drug he could distil from these was now much appreciated by the medical profession as a laxative and a tonic, and it had been found to be especially useful in the treatment of liver complaints.

Suddenly his attention was brought back to the present by his seeing the momentary emergence of a woman from the doorway of the cottage at the distant end of the yard. It was the cottage which he had made available to the man he had taken into his employ as his principal assistant.

So the rumour he had recently heard was true. Arthur Winthrop was a womaniser and to Ransom, with his stern Quaker upbringing, fornication was a sin difficult to forgive. Perhaps the appointment had been a mistake. Philanderers were not to be trusted and the darkly handsome Winthrop would either have to promise to mend his ways or go. It would be a pity if he went. The man had the right qualifications for the post, having been one of the foremen at Southalls in Birmingham where he himself had learned the art and mystery of a manufacturing chemist, and undoubtedly Winthrop was an expert in producing a wide range of galenicals.

Sadly Ransom unlocked the door to the office he had set up in the archway building and having removed his tall hat sat down at his desk to think further about this disturbing matter. He decided he would raise it with Winthrop when the man reported to him for their usual eight o'clock meeting. There was no doubt in his mind that the woman had spent the night in the cottage but he would at least give Winthrop the opportunity to make a clean breast of the affair, although he would not be pressed to reveal the name of the woman. A severe reprimand would then be given, followed by the threat of instant dismissal if there was a repetition of the misdemeanour. With this course of action settled in his mind Ransom opened up his stock book.

At the cottage the woman's hasty return startled Winthrop who, bare to the waist in the kitchen, was shaving himself at the sink.

'Hell!' he exclaimed as he nicked his cheek and blood began to trickle down towards his chin. 'Hell! Now look at what you've made me do, woman! Get me that towel quick!'

She picked up and handed him the towel he had indicated saying, 'He saw me! I know he saw me!'

Winthrop holding the towel firmly to his face asked angrily, 'Who saw you? Who?'

'Young Mr Ransom!'

'Are you sure? It's early for him! He doesn't usually get in until seven!'

'It was him! He was standing under the archway staring this way!'

'Damn! You should have looked through the window before you went out of the door.'

'I did, but he was in the shadow and I didn't notice him.'

'Hm! Just what I didn't want to happen. It won't do me any good nor you, Lavinia, if anything gets to the ears of that holy brother of yours and he finds out that we spent the night together.'

Lavinia's pretty but weak-chinned face crumpled and she burst into tears. Winthrop, ignoring her distress, carried on shaving but he was obviously seething inwardly with anger.

Eventually, Lavinia, still dabbing at her eyes with her small handkerchief, said, 'But Obadiah won't mind quite so much, Arthur, if I tell him we are going to get married soon. He wants to see me married before he dies. He told me so only yesterday, just after Doctor Foster left him.'

'He did, did he? Well, that's up to you now. You know what you've got to do first, and if he's as bad as you say he is you've got to do it quick, while he is still alive. It's no good if she doesn't go first.'

'But it's murder, Arthur!'

Winthrop put down his razor and wiped the remaining lather from his face before replying, 'Murder? That's an ugly word Lavinia. It's only murder if it looks like it. What we are going to do won't. Nobody will know it wasn't a natural death except us.'

'You're sure, Arthur?'

'Quite sure! I know what I'm up to, my dear.' Winthrop's voice was cajoling and there was no trace of temper in it. The smile on his face brought a warm glow to Lavinia's cheeks and she thought how handsome he was and how strong-looking. So different to poor Obadiah wasting away in his bed at Manley Court.

Winthrop's cajoling continued with, 'And do remember, my darling, when that unfortunate brother of yours passes on you'll be a really rich woman, with your own carriage and pair and all the jewellery and clothes you could ever want. We shall be together and if you like we can even go and live in Italy or somewhere else where it is warm all through the year. It will be worth it, won't it, just doing what we've talked about. You don't like her anyway, do you?'

'No! I hate her! She's been horrid to poor Obadiah ever since she married him. When will you give me the – '

Lavinia hesitated over the word and Winthrop said quickly, 'Tomorrow, my dear, tomorrow when I see you at the cricket match. I've got to get it first from a locked cupboard in Ransom's office. I've got a key, I had one made specially.'

Having kissed Lavinia with what seemed a sudden burst of

passion Winthrop took her to the door saying, 'Now you must get off and back to Manley Court. Where are you supposed to have been last night? The usual place?'

Lavinia smiled. 'Yes. With the Bedford aunt, the one who brought up Obadiah and me. I said I'd be back on the first coach this morning.'

'Clever girl!' Winthrop kissed her again and Lavinia released herself with reluctance from his arms. Watching her as she scurried up the yard, under the arch and out into Bancroft. Arthur Winthrop's pale eyes were cold, calculating and completely without pity. One, at most two, years married to Lavinia would be as much as he thought he could endure. And there must be no brats. Then she could go the same way he intended Felicity Pring to go and the Quint fortune would be his to do with as he pleased. He completed his dressing with care and prepared himself for what he thought might be an awkward meeting with William Ransom.

But the young Quaker's admonishment was astonishingly mild. In fact when Winthrop told him that he was shortly going to marry the woman who Ransom had seen leaving the cottage earlier he offered his congratulations and said, 'I am most pleased to receive thy news, Winthrop. My father says that marriage has a steadying influence on a young man and that I too should be considering it, so I will wish thee every happiness with the young woman. It does occur to me though that I must find thee somewhere else better to live than in the yard. That is no place in which to bring up a family. I will speak of the matter to my father. He has, I think, a house becoming vacant in the lower part of Bancroft which might suit you well.'

Winthrop thanked him profusely and then reminded him of the cricket match which was to be played on the morrow.

'No, I had not forgotten that I had promised thee the day to thyself and if I find it possible to get away from here I may come to Butts Close myself in the afternoon. I too have a liking for the game. It is a pleasant, honest sport.'

So, on the most amicable of terms, the two young men went on to discuss the workplan for the day, which included the setting up of two new evaporation pans and the making of arrangements for the storage of the first loads of lavender expected late that afternoon from the fields on the Gaping Hills to the west of the town.

7. The Curate's Wife

In 1845 Felicity Quint, much to the surprise of many, and not entirely with her father's approval, had married the Reverend Obadiah Pring, one of the St Mary's Church curates. With his slightly bulbous eyes and protruding Adam's apple, Obadiah was not a good-looking young man but he had a kindly manner and a pleasant voice and he was well liked in the parish.

Nathaniel Quint, after the curate had approached him to request permission to seek Felicity's hand in marriage, had asked his daughter, 'Couldn't you find someone better than him? He's no looks, no money and no prospects. You'll be a fool if you throw yourself away on him!'

Her reply had been a shrugging of her shoulders and, 'Well, I like him and if I can't have who I really want then Obadiah will have to do. Looks aren't everything, and, as for money, I've no doubt you'll help us and even let us live here at Manley Court.'

'Aye, girl,' he then replied, 'I'll even do that. At least he's not the gypsy scum I've a fancy you're still hankering after, so take him and forget that boy for good.'

But the marriage had been a disastrous one from its very beginning. Three months after it had taken place Felicity sent for Mansell, and the doctor, who went to Manley Court expecting to be consulted about a pregnancy, received something of a surprise.

'Me, pregnant?' Felicity had said when they were together in her bedroom. 'Pregnant? Not likely! He can't!'

'Can't what?'

She was frank in her reply and Mansell looked at her in astonishment as she told him what had happened, or rather had not happened, during the Paris honeymoon.

'You did that, and he still couldn't?'

'No, he still couldn't! There wasn't a sign of life in it!'

'What's the matter with the man? He's not – '

'No. I know what you're thinking. I do know there are some

peculiar men. One of the girls at Mrs Bonnamy's had a brother like it, so she said. No. I'm sure he's not one of those. He just can't! That's it. He just can't, and I want you to give me something I can put in his food or his drink which will change things.'

Mansell shook his head. 'Sorry, Felicity,' he said, 'there isn't anything. A lot of people think there are pills and potions which will work miracles in that way but they are wrong, and I'm not going to waste your time or your money in giving you any of them. I assure you there is nothing. Nothing!'

'But I want a child!'

'Then I suggest that you get an annulment of the marriage on the grounds of non-consummation and marry someone else.'

'Hm! That will take time and cause a lot of talk. I'll have to think about it.'

But there had been far more pressing matters to occupy Felicity's mind. Within a week of her consultation with Mansell her father was killed in Mincing Lane by a runaway carriage and pair and a month after that Obadiah was diagnosed as having tuberculosis. The taking over of her father's share in the tea and shipping business had not proved difficult to the astute Felicity and she soon showed the doubting ones in the trade that she was quite capable of carrying on in Nathaniel Quint's place. However, Obadiah's illness and the nursing he required when he was confined to his bed was not a problem quite so easily solved when so much of Felicity's time was taken up in London. She was much relieved when his sister, Lavinia, offered her services and said she was prepared to live at Manley Court and help look after the ailing man. Not that Felicity took much of a liking to the simpering Lavinia, but she was prepared to tolerate – what she called – her silly ways and to pay her a very generous quarterly allowance.

Nearly two years later, in the Spring of 1847, when Arthur Winthrop appeared on the scene and began courting Lavinia, Felicity was by no means pleased. She found the chemist both obnoxious in his manner and far too familiar with the woman servants in the house.

'He's nothing but a lecher,' she confided to Mrs Lestrange, and the housekeeper said that she agreed with her. 'He'd put his hand up anyone's skirts!' she said, 'even mine!'

Later on, the same morning as William Ransom caught sight

of Lavinia leaving Winthrop's cottage, Felicity called in Mansell to attend to her bailiff, Thickpenny. The man's leg wound had never completely healed and eventually became ulcerated. After Mansell had seen to it and Thickpenny had hobbled away on his crutch Felicity said, 'Now I want your advice on another matter.'

'Obadiah? You know he's not my patient. He's Doctor Foster's and I wouldn't like to get at cross purposes with him. In any case I don't think I could do more for him than Foster is already doing.'

'I've always thought you *could*, but it is not Obadiah I want to talk to you about. It is his sister.'

'Is Lavinia not well?'

'Well enough, I suppose, in body if not in mind. No, she is behaving like some sort of madcap. She came in about two hours back all flushed of face and unnaturally excited. It was almost as though she had been drinking. She gabbled out that she was getting married next month and she was going to ask the Vicar to start calling the banns next Sunday!'

'So? She's been courting for some time, hasn't she? That damn chemist fellow at Ransom's, so I believe?'

'Yes, Winthrop – though God knows what he sees in her. She's nothing but a dried-up spinster of thirty-five or more, years older than him, and' she added spitefully 'with precious little under her petticoats for any man!'

'Well? How do I come into this, my dear?'

'If she is going I shall have to replace her, and I thought you might know somebody with nursing experience. Now Obadiah is so ill Mrs Lestrange can't attend to all his needs on her own, and you know how much time I now spend in London most weeks. Damn Lavinia! Damn Winthrop! It's all very inconvenient!'

'Damn him by all means! Insolent young puppy! Only last week when I called at Ransom's he told me to clear off. He wasn't prepared to let me have small quantities of drugs for what he had the cheek to call my quack medicines and I could go to a chemist in the town!'

'You wouldn't take kindly to that!'

'I didn't! He's a most unpleasant fellow. I'm surprised that you are including him in the Manley Court team for the big match tomorrow!'

Felicity smiled ruefully. 'Needs must but I'm short of players this year. He told me a few weeks ago that he had played regularly for a Birmingham team when he was working there and I offered him a place.'

Something her cricket-enthusiastic father had started, and which Felicity was determined upon continuing, was a match between the Manley Court and Mincing Lane workers and the Hitchin Town team captained by Mr Delme-Radcliffe. This had been played since the inception of the challenge on Butts Close, the open space not far from the centre of Hitchin and bounded on one side by the road to Bedford. Cricket had been played on this common ground, but in a desultory fashion, ever since archery had ceased being practised but it had been Delme-Radcliffe who welded a Hitchin team together to face all challengers. He had even dressed his team in his own racing colours in his effort to give the game a vigorous life. When Quint's first challenge had come, with its offer to meet all the expenses of the day, the Squire had taken it up with alacrity. The fixture had now become a regular one, to be played, weather permitting, on the second Saturday in July each year. It had also become one of the highlights of the town's social calendar.

'And this year,' said Felicity as Mansell prepared to leave her, 'we shall win. I'm determined on it! I shall be seeing you and Mrs Mansell in the guest tent, of course?'

'Yes, my dear, you certainly will. And if I do find a possible replacement for Lavinia I shall let you know tomorrow. I think I know of someone who would suit you admirably but I shall have to speak to her first.'

'Then I hope that you will be bringing me good news tomorrow.'

'I'm almost sure that I shall!'

8.   A Match is Played

On the sunlit morning of the great day Felicity, accompanied by Lavinia, arrived at Butts Close at exactly ten o'clock. Her carriage with its pair of greys was followed by three wagons containing the Manley Court team and some of their supporters. This small cavalcade was greeted on its arrival by loud cheers and some catcalls from the large crowd of townsfolk already assembled on the ground.

The two ladies were helped to alight from their carriage by a smiling Delme-Radcliffe, who said, when they were safely down, 'Well, Mrs Pring, you've organised things beautifully for us again, I see, and the good Lord is going to be kind to us with the weather. We couldn't wish for a better day and my only regret is that your father is no longer alive and able to be present to witness the match. From what I hear of your team the game is likely to be a close one!'

Felicity was looking around her with critical eyes. Then she smiled with approval at what she could see. Everything seemed to be as she had ordered. The turf had been shorn to a nicety and the huge marquee, where a mid afternoon meal would be served to the teams and invited guests, was of a snowy whiteness and brightly decked out with flags. There was, by arrangement with the Lucas Brewery, a beer tent for the refreshment of the grown-ups and several booths where soft drinks and sweetmeats could be bought for the children.

'Now, Mrs Pring,' said the Squire, 'before you join your guests perhaps you will allow me to introduce my team, and I hope, after you have met them, that you will have the Manley Court team introduced to me. I understand that you have some new young gentlemen from your London office?'

Felicity's wicked ripple of laughter caused many heads to turn in her direction. She said, 'Yes, Mr Radcliffe, I have. My two cousins. They play regularly for the Marylebone Cricket Club!'

'Do they, by Gad! Then we shall certainly have to look to our laurels today, shan't we? That is, if we're going to beat you!'

Lined up to meet Felicity were the members of the Hitchin team, all wearing blue and gold sashes. They were respectfully bareheaded, with their beribboned top hats held in their left hands. First to be greeted was Mark Everett, the haberdasher; next in line was the smiling solicitor, Peter Bonnamy; he was followed by George Barker, the blacksmith, and by Tom Allam, Alfred Allingham, Jack Lewis and Joseph Lewis, all sons of the Squire's tenant farmers; and Lofty Barham, the gunsmith and John Timmins and Percy Butt, two of the Priory gardeners, brought the line to an end.

When all their hands had been shaken Felicity asked her cousin and team captain, David Quint, to take the Squire down the line of the Manley Court players. These were sporting red and green favours. There beside David's brother were two of the Mincing Lane clerks, six of the Manley Court workers and the smiling Arthur Winthrop.

'Haven't I seen you somewhere before, Winthrop?' asked the Squire as he shook the chemist's hand.

'Yes, Sir.'

'I thought so. At the distillery in Bancroft, was it not? You are Mr Ransom's assistant, aren't you? You were there when I was being shown around the new laboratory?'

'Yes, Sir.'

'How is it that you are playing for the Manley Court team today?'

Winthrop explained that he was engaged to be married to Felicity's sister-in-law. The Squire nodded and said 'Congratulations. Well, if you prove yourself today, man, I shall be asking you to join the Hitchin team. We can always take on a good man and I think you are more rightfully mine than Mrs Pring's even if you are marrying into her family!'

When the courtesies had been completed Felicity sat down among the invited guests in the reserved section by the refreshment marquee and the two captains were joined by the umpires for the spinning of a coin. The toss was won by Delme-Radcliffe and, as he chose to put in his side to bat first, it was David Quint who had to lead out his team to bowl and field.

In due course, and to a gentle clapping from the spectators,

Delme-Radcliffe and Mark Everett walked, bat in hand, to their respective wickets. After the umpires' guidance had been given in respect of middle and leg they prepared to face the onslaught of the bowlers. The fielders, with bent backs and hands on knees, waited anxiously while David Quint took up the ball, applied it to his right eye and then made his first delivery. This was fast and true and straight. The Squire treated it with caution – merely blocking the way to his wicket. The second ball was looser and bounced a little. Delme-Radcliffe struck out boldly. There was an admiring gasp from the spectators as the ball passed over some of their heads, over the skirting Bedford Road and into the cornfield beyond. The scorer notched up six runs on his tally board and two fielders hurried to retrieve the ball from the standing corn. Those who had witnessed this mighty stroke clapped vigorously.

Mansell, who had settled down with his wife just behind Felicity, touched his hostess on her shoulder. She turned a smiling face to him and said, 'That's a very good start for your side, Doctor!'

'My side?'

'Well, your son-in-law is playing for it and I can't expect you to favour my team today, can I? You have something worthwhile to tell me, I hope?'

'Yes, I'm sure it will please you but it will keep until we break for the meal.'

Felicity nodded and turning to the front saw that play was about to start again. Slowly but very surely the score mounted, with both batsmen looking well set. When seventy appeared on the tally board the bowlers were changed and wickets began to tumble fast. First to go was Delme-Radcliffe, with a respectable forty to his credit; next went Mark Everett with thirty-two. He was followed quickly by an indignant Peter Bonnamy with a duck. Ten minutes before two o'clock the Hitchin team was out for a total score of one hundred and twenty-four runs. Its downfall had mainly been brought about by the inspired bowling of Arthur Winthrop. He had taken six of the wickets and it was he who took the miraculous catch which brought the innings to a close.

As the now jubilant Manley Court team followed the last two batsmen from the field, Winthrop was greeted with a round of applause for his performance, and he was still smiling broadly when he took a place at one of the tables in the marquee next to a bright-eyed and adoring Lavinia.

'Damn the man!' exclaimed Mansell as, with his wife on one arm and Felicity on the other, he lead them to the specially reserved seats at the top table. Felicity responded with a chuckle. 'Now, Doctor,' she said, 'that is not sporting of you at all. You must admit that he played well even though you don't like him. But what is your news, now that Lavinia is out of hearing?'

'I've found a replacement for her.'

'Good! Who?'

'A young woman named Lucy Bongers. She's the daughter of an old friend of mine who rules one of the Back Street yards with a heart of gold and rod of iron!'

A slight frown crossed Felicity's face. 'Back Street?' she asked dubiously. 'Back Street? Surely not?'

'Yes, Felicity, Back Street, but Lucy has been living and working at Doctor Hawkins' Infirmary ever since it started seven years ago. She is now one of his most valued nurses. Although she is nearly as huge as her mother she is very gentle and kindness itself. You won't regret employing her. I don't doubt Hawkins will be unhappy to lose her, but you know as well as I do that it is not likely to be for long and she can go back to him when the time comes. While you have got her you can pay her rather better than Hawkins can afford to, so she will benefit and so will you.'

'When can she start?'

'A week today, I would suggest. Lavinia will still be with you and can show her what has to be done.'

'Good! Now look at Lavinia. It's disgusting the way she is fawning over Winthrop. She's completely infatuated! The silly little fool!'

But Winthrop was showing sings of acute embarrassment at the attention he was getting from Lavinia. 'Don't, my dear,' he implored. 'People are staring at us and I don't want to attract too much attention at the moment because I want to pass you something.'

A little later, when Delme-Radcliffe rose to thank Felicity for sponsoring the event and eyes were directed at him, Winthrop slipped a tiny phial into Lavinia's hand containing a small amount of colourless crystals. She dropped this, without a word, into the reticule reposing on her lap.

After quite a splendid meal of cold meats and salad, followed by a strawberry and cream confection, cricket was resumed, with the Town team going out to field.

The opening batsmen for Manley Court were the two Marylebone Cricket Club players, but within ten minutes both had been dismissed by George Barker, Hitchin's demon bowler, with balls which had sizzled off the turf to send the stumps flying.

'Hell and damnation! Bloody Hell!' exclaimed an unladylike Felicity, as the second of her star players left the field with only three runs recorded on the tally board. The third and fourth men in, the Mincing Lane clerks, fared slightly better, and gradually, but far too slowly, the score rose to thirty-one. Then came more disasters. Two easy catches were taken and the clerks were back in the dressing tent. Fifth to face the bowling was a sturdy groom from Felicity's stables and sixth was Arthur Winthrop. This pair soon began amassing runs. Sixty was passed, then seventy, then eighty. At one-hundred-and-one the groom fell to a sneaky ball from Delme-Radcliffe, and Ezra Thickpenny, the shepherd, took his place.

The match was now truly in the balance, and Mansell could see Felicity had acquired a more hopeful look on her countenance. After a hesitant start, Thickpenny, obviously heeding some whispered instructions given to him by Winthrop, did no more than block the ball's getting to his wicket and left the scoring strokes to the chemist.

At a quarter to six, with the afternoon shadows of the bordering trees lengthening across Butts Close, a magnificent drive to the boundary by Arthur Winthrop took the Manley Court score to one-hundred-and-twenty-six and the Hitchin Town team conceded defeat.

Felicity was jubilant, Delme-Radcliffe congratulatory and Lavinia, with stars in her eyes, ecstatic with happiness. In her mind, as she saw her lover being chaired from the pitch by the fellow members of his team who had rushed out to greet him, she was crying out 'He's mine! All mine! It's me who sleeps naked in his arms! It's me he is going to marry! It's me he loves and it's our child already in my belly! Ours! Ours!'

She felt in her reticule for a handkerchief with which to wipe away the tears of joy which were trickling down her cheeks and in doing so her fingers touched the small glass phial. This made her turn sideways to look at Felicity, who was chatting still with Delme-Radcliffe. She suddenly felt an increased loathing for her sister-in-law and realised that it was becoming easier for her to do what Arthur wanted her to do. Once again she went over in her mind the plan he had devised. It seemed foolproof if she did exactly as he had instructed her – just drop the crystals in the warm brandy grog which Felicity took up to her room each night to help her to sleep and which, on occasions, she was asked to make up.

'I don't care now whether it's quick or not or even if she suffers,' she said to herself. 'Just as long as we can't be found out, that's all that matters!' Then once again she touched the phial to reassure herself it was there.

9. A Potion for the Parson

Lavinia told Winthrop of her condition on the Thursday follow-ing the week-end of the great match, but instead of responding tenderly as she had hoped he said, 'Then you'd better do what you've got to do as quickly as possible or you'll find the child will be born a bastard, won't it?'

'But Felicity is not here!'

'She's in London, I suppose?'

'Yes, she went on the early morning coach on Monday.'

'You had Saturday night and Sunday night, didn't you?'

'She mixed the grog herself, Arthur. She didn't let me do it.'

'Damn! When will she be back in Hitchin?'

'On Saturday morning. There's a nurse coming in who'll be replacing me when we get married. She wants to introduce her to my brother.'

'What sort of nurse?'

Lavinia told him and after a momentary silence Winthrop said, 'Well! Watch out for the bitch. She might be dangerous. You'll just have to be extra careful from now on, but if you can't get what I gave you into the grog then get it into something else. We can't afford to wait too long, can we, my dearest?'

Again Winthrop's mood had apparently changed to one of tenderness as he kissed her, and Lavinia left him feeling both happy and contented.

When Lucy Bongers was introduced by Felicity to her patient early in the afternoon of Saturday, Obadiah took an immediate liking to the huge young woman. Lying back in the immense four-poster bed, which had once been Nathaniel Quint's, the ailing man said between bouts of coughing, 'I don't think that I shall be bothering you for long', and there was a flash of a pleasant smile, 'I shall try not to make too much of a nuisance of myself in the meantime, Nurse, or shall I call you Lucy?'

'Lucy, if you please, Mr Pring. That's more friendly-like and we want to be good friends, don't we?'

'Then Lucy it shall be! I like the name Lucy.'

At this point Lavinia entered the bedroom with an armful of flowers and began filling vases and Felicity, with a look of dislike on her face, walked out. Lucy whose sharp eyes missed nothing, decided that if the two women were at odds with each other it was none of her concern. Her concern was for her patient – and she did not like the way he was almost continuously coughing.

'May I give him a dose of this linctus, Miss Pring?' she asked, indicating the large bottle on the bedside table.

'You may, Nurse. Not that it will do much good but it's better, I suppose, than nothing. A tablespoonful will suffice.'

But the evil-smelling syrup seemed to irritate rather than alleviate the cough, and Lucy decided that she would raise the matter of the mixture with the mistress of the house as soon as she could have a quiet word with her. She knew her patient was in the care of Doctor Foster and it was his prescription she was questioning but she was sure Doctor Mansell's mixtures were far more effective and it would be worthwhile trying a sample bottle from him.

However, it was not Lucy's word with her which induced Felicity to send one of the grooms to bring back Mansell but the irritating cough she herself seemed to have developed almost immediately after the cricket match.

When Mansell arrived, and she and he were in her bedroom together, she voiced her fears to him. He very carefully sounded her chest and her back and listened to her breathing before reassuring her, 'No, my dear, I don't think you've much need to worry. I'm certain that it is not the early stages of what Obadiah is suffering from, although that is known to be infectious. You don't seem to be losing weight, you are obviously not debilitated, and from what you tell me, you do not have any sweating at night. No, it is not tuberculosis – you are not likely to get it as you don't sleep in the same room with him and are only rarely now in close contact with him even. No, I suspect it is just a summer cold which has brought a nasty cough.'

'Can you give me something for it, please?'

'Of course!' Mansell delved into his carpetbag and brought out a medium-sized bottle containing a golden brown mixture. Holding out the bottle to Felicity he said, 'This should help. Take a large spoonful three times a day and you should find the cough disappearing within a few days.'

'And Obadiah?'

'The same. It can't cure his cough but it will ease it and it is at least pleasant enough to take. Now, Felicity, while I am here I should like to have another look at Thickpenny's leg. That ulcer of his is getting much worse and if the leg is to be saved it will have to be cleaned out and dressed daily. Now Lucy is here she can attend to it; if you will ask her to join me in the kitchen with Thickpenny I will show her exactly what to do each day.'

The bailiff, after the bandage had been removed from his leg, groaned at the sight of his ugly affliction.

'Damn those bloody gypsies!' he exclaimed bitterly. 'Damn them! Damn them! Damn them! Damn the buggers to hell!'

'Keep your curses!' said Mansell. 'You be thankful, Thickpenny you didn't lose your leg at the time. And how do you know it was the gypsies who set the trap you walked into?'

'It must have been! It were them all right. I just know it were! If I ever catch any of them bloody Drapers trespassing again I'll shoot 'em! I'll shoot 'em! I swear I will!'

'Quiet, Thickpenny,' said Felicity, who had just come into the kitchen. 'I'll have no such shootings on my land, so be quiet and don't utter foolish threats. If Doctor Mansell thinks rest for a week or so will help with the healing I suggest that you get off to your bed immediately after the leg has been dressed. I can run the estate myself for a few days without your assistance.'

When the leg had been dressed by Lucy and re-bandaged, the bailiff, still muttering, went off to his cottage and Felicity informed the big woman about the bottle of linctus which Mansell had provided and which was now standing on the bedside table in her room. 'And the Doctor says you may give a spoonful of it three times a day to Mr Pring.'

'And Doctor Foster's bottle, Mrs Pring?'

'Put it to one side for the moment, Lucy, and in the meantime, and until I tell you otherwise, just give Mr Pring Doctor Mansell's linctus.'

'Then I shall give some to the master immediately,' replied Lucy. 'The sooner he has something to help him the better it will be, poor man.'

There was a flurry of her skirt and Lucy hastened off upstairs.

Felicity regarded her disappearance with a smile, saying to Mansell, 'I think you've found me a treasure. Now if you will come into the library with me, Doctor, I will settle your account and order one of the grooms to bring the trap round to the front door ready to take you home.'

It was while Felicity and Mansell were saying goodbye at the open front door that the loud screaming of a distraught woman was suddenly heard from the upper floor. Moments later, Lavinia rushed headlong down the stairs and brushed past them in the doorway screeching 'What have I done? What have I done?'

Too much surprised to stop her, Mansell and Felicity watched as the demented woman almost threw herself down the front steps and shot off in the direction of the stables.

A quieter, but still urgent voice, summoned them from the stair landing. It was Lucy's. 'Doctor! I think you'd best come at once, Sir, and you, Madam! It's Mr Pring! I think he's dead!'

Mansell, pursued by Felicity, rushed up the stairs and followed Lucy into Obadiah's bedroom. The curate, well propped up on his pillows, was staring towards the door with sightless eyes and an incongruous grin on his face which bared his teeth – there was little doubt that his life had come to a rapid and shocking end.

Mansell's quick examination only confirmed the obvious and he hastily drew the sheet up over the distorted countenance before asking, 'What happened, Lucy? Can you tell me?'

'It was the cough mixture, Sir' I just gave him a spoonful and he suddenly gasped and stopped breathing.'

'He did what?'

'He just stopped breathing. It was as quick as that. Then Miss Lavinia came into the room and saw me standing over him with the bottle and the spoon in my hand and shouted out "You've killed him!" before she dashed the bottle out of my hand. There it is on the carpet. Next she started screaming and then she rushed out of the room and down the stairs! She must have passed you!'

'She did! But what on earth has she been up to?' Mansell picked up the bottle, sniffed at it and then stoppered it with his finger to take a small sample of the linctus. Applying the fingertip to his tongue he felt a strong tingling sensation and looked aghast at Felicity and Lucy.

'This bottle has been tampered with,' he said. 'By God, it has! And there is little doubt who did it. It's that sister of his!'

'Lavinia? But why?' asked Felicity.

'Can't you guess? She thought the linctus was just for you as it was on your bedside table – '

'But why kill me? I've done her no harm!'

'Have you made a will, Felicity?'

'No, I haven't.'

'So if you die before Obadiah the estate will go to him, and as he was dying the money would soon pass on to her. You just had to die first to make her a rich woman!'

Felicity was looking at him with a horrified expression on her face. 'But poison! How could she? Wouldn't it be traced?'

'Some poisons are very difficult to trace and I suspect this is one of them. What's more I think I know who could have supplied it and probably hatched the plot. The man who is planning to marry her!'

'Arthur Winthrop?'

'Yes. The chemist. He would have access to various poisons and would know how they would act. The sooner we get Inspector Albyn here and the matter in the hands of the police the better!'

'What about Lavinia?'

'We must find her at once. She'll be wanted for questioning.'

Lucy, Mansell and Felicity joined the servants in the search for the missing woman, while one of the grooms went off post-haste to fetch someone from the police station. It was Silas Thickpenny, the gamekeeper, who eventually found Lavinia. She was hanging by her neck from a beam in the hayloft. Mansell it was who cut her down and pronounced life extinct.

One of Albyn's constables discovered the empty phial in the dead woman's bedroom fairly late on the afternoon of her death, and as Mansell had already voiced his suspicions to the inspector, Albyn rode off with this to the Ransom distillery immediately.

William Ransom, when the phial was handed to him, sniffed critically at its open end before saying, 'I think it contained aconitine.'

'Is that poisonous?'

'It is indeed! It can only be used sparingly in medicines.'

'Medicines for what, may I ask?'

'Alleviating neuralgia, mainly.'

'Do you produce it here?'

'We produced some for the first time last autumn. It comes from a plant called Monkshood, and we grew a crop of it alongside the Bedford road just outside the town. What is thy interest in this aconitine, Inspector?'

'We think someone has been poisoned with it!'

'That is bad. I am saddened by thy tidings but surely thou dost not think it came from here?'

'I'm afraid I do and I've good reason for believing so, Sir.'

'But the only stock we have remaining is a small sample I keep under lock and key in a cupboard in this office.'

Ransom felt in his pocket for a bunch of keys and having selected one opened a cupboard door to reveal a number of clearly labelled jars. He took one from the top shelve bearing the word POISON in large letters and placed this on his desk. Then he referred to his stock book.

'I know what there should be,' he said. 'Now let me see how much the jar contains. Quickly, but with extreme care, Ransom weighed the contents of the jar on a fine balance. When he had ascertained the weight he turned, white-faced, to Albyn before saying solemnly, 'There is nearly an ounce missing!'

'That doesn't sound much, Sir.'

'It would be enough to kill a dozen people!'

'Good God! Who has a key to that cupboard beside yourself?'

'No one! Only I have a key to it.'

'Not Winthrop?'

Ransom stared at Albyn. 'Winthrop? You suspect him? No! He has no key, I can assure you, and I have never had the cupboard unlocked when I was not in this room. Never!'

'Then I am certain that he has had a key made to fit the lock. Has he ever borrowed your bunch of keys for some purpose of his own elsewhere?'

'Yes. He has had them once or twice for unlocking the drawers in the laboratory. The last time was a month ago.'

'That's when he must have taken an impression for a locksmith to work to.'

'I cannot believe it. We must send for the man at once, Inspector, for you to question him.'

But Winthrop was to be found nowhere in the distillery. News must have reached him that something had gone awry at Manley Court and the chemist had fled. Enquiries made immediately revealed he had been seen boarding the London coach which left the Swan two hours earlier and there was no hope of catching up with it.

That was the last ever heard of Arthur Winthrop by that designation, but three years later a chemist's assistant by the name of Albert Wheeler was hanged in the Somerset town of Taunton for the murder of his wife and wealthy mother-in-law by aconitine poisoning. Wheeler had been a cricket player of considerable local repute.

PART THREE

1857

1. The Return of Nelson Draper

The town of Hitchin saw many changes in the ten years following the deaths of Obadiah Pring and his sister. The Great Northern Railway line from London to Peterborough, passing through Hitchen, was opened in 1850, and soon afterwards the town had rail links also with Royston and Cambridge and with Bedford and Leicester. Within days of the railway's first opening John Kershaw's Hitchin Coach *Perseverance* ran to London for the very last time and soon all the public coaches had gone. Also hit were the carriers, except the few who maintained a service to local towns and villages without stations.

Industry began to flourish in the town. Although Hitchin's outgoings were still mainly corn, straw-plait and wool, the tanning of leather and the production of galenicals and fragrant oils by the Ransom distillery became increasingly important. In the summer months more and more of the fields around the town were being taken over by the lovely hazy blue of the lavender crops and the variegated colours of the medicinal plants, belladonna, squirting cucumber, chamomile and henbane.

In 1853 an engine house and a reservoir were built by the great windmill on the steep hill overlooking the town, and sewers and pipes were laid in the streets. On Christmas Day of that year water from the springs near the hamlet of Charlton was connected to many of the houses, and the sounds of flushing lavatories were for the first time heard in the better parts of the town.

Sadly, in 1855 Mansell's wife died. She was buried in St Mary's Churchyard one cold November afternoon, when a dank, yellowish fog hung menacingly over the rooftops threatening to descend any minute and blot out the town. The now aging doctor never recovered from this grievous loss, which even his skills had been unable to avert, and he began to neglect his practice and seek what solace he could from alcohol.

Some eighteen months after Anne's dying, one Friday in May 1857, he was seated in the taproom of the Swan Inn reminiscing with two other disconsolate drinkers. One was John Kershaw, the former coach proprietor and the other Isaac Newton, the builder, who had retired some while before after thirty-six years of superintending the town's fire brigade.

'Damme, John!' said Newton 'Nothing in this bloody place is the same. Nothing! Everything is changing but nothing is changing for the better! Do you know what my successor has done now?'

'What?' asked Mansell.

'Moved the bloody fire engines from our yard in Tilehouse Street to the old Maltings in the Wratten!'

Kershaw laughed and said, 'Is that such a bad thing, Isaac? You know how many times you had to cut down your wife's washing lines to get the engines out in a hurry. She must have singed your ears a time or two when the sheets and the shirts went into the mud!'

'It was a damn sight easier to get the engines out on to the road than it will be in the Wratten, and minutes matter when you've got a blaze to attend!'

Mansell raised a placatory hand before saying, 'Yes, I know they do, Isaac, and I know how you liked to be at the scene as soon as you could, but now, my old friends, how about refilling these pots?'

There were nods from Newton and Kershaw and Mansell called the barman over. It was while they were being served that someone entered the room and crossed to the bar. Mansell, whose back was towards the newcomer, did not bother to turn to see who it was. When, however, he heard a man's voice asking for a room to be reserved for the night he reversed sharply on his bench.

'Nelson!' he exclaimed.

The tall, youngish man, elegantly dressed in a dark blue frock coat with bright buttons, well cut breeches and highly polished brown riding boots, spun around on his heel. Then with a broad smile on his darkly handsome face he said 'Well! Well! Well! If it isn't Doctor Mansell! How are you?' In a few strides he was across the room to grip the Doctor's outstretched hand warmly.

'My word!' exclaimed Mansell. 'What a swell you've become, Nelson!'

Nelson Draper's smile broadened even further. 'Yes. Things have changed a lot for me, Doctor, since we last met.'

'But you are still with Sir Arthur at Royston?'

'I am. He's more or less retired now and I've largely taken over the running of the stud as his partner.'

'You've been fortunate.'

'Very! But I've worked hard and studied hard to get where I've got now. It hasn't been the easiest of roads.'

Mansell introduced Nelson to Kershaw and Newton. Both remembered his father well, and John Kershaw asked, 'And where's your father now? We haven't seen him about these parts for years.'

'Father? The last I heard of him was that he had gone back to somewhere Henley-on-Thames way, where he was born, I believe, but I haven't had news of him myself for ages. He never really approved of me forsaking gypsy ways and settling down to steady employment in one place. The last time we met we had words about it!'

'What are you doing here in Hitchin?' asked Mansell, after an extra tankard of strong ale had been ordered for Nelson.

'Doing here? It's business with the Squire. He's not very satisfied with a mare he bought from us last month which he thought would make a good hunter. We warned him that she had a really nasty temper but he would insist on having her.'

'And you'll be taking her back, I suppose?'

'Yes. By train, I expect.'

'Train! Train!' Kershaw snorted. 'By bloody train! Those damn things almost ruined me, they did!' He snorted again before downing the remnants of his tankard. 'Dirty bloody things, trains. Who wants 'em? They should never have been allowed!' He rose to leave. Newton also rose.

When they had gone Nelson asked quietly 'And Felicity, Doctor, what has happened to her? Is she married now?' His voice was anxious.

'She was.'

'Was?'

'Yes. She was married for a short time to a curate by the name of Pring.'

'He died?'

'Better put it that he was accidentally murdered!' Mansell then related the circumstances of Obadiah's death.

'So she's a widow now?'

'She is. And a very wealthy one too, Nelson. She took over the tea business when her father was killed and enlarged it considerably and now, despite the fact that she's a woman, she is a force to be reckoned with in the City. She spends more time in London nowadays than she does at Manley Court, but I still see her fairly frequently.'

'I'd like to see her again.'

'You would?' Mansell was regarding Nelson through narrowed eyes and hesitated before asking, 'You've not married?'

'Me married? No, there's never been time for that. Nor have I ever wanted to marry anyone except her.'

'You haven't?'

'No.'

'Then see her by all means. I know she is at Manley Court today. Her groom was here a short while ago. He had come into Hitchin with the pony and trap and was on his way to the station to pick her up off one of the London trains.'

'Hm! I'll think about it. After I've seen Delme-Radcliffe I may even try out the mare with a ride up to the Court and back.'

Shortly afterwards Nelson departed on his way to the Priory. Some time after he had gone and two tankards later Mansell also left the Swan. His gait, as he crossed the Market Square and passed along Sun Street, was not altogether steady. Samuel Lucas, who was watching his progress as he skirted the brewery building, shook his head rather sadly.

2. Journey's End in Lovers' Meeting

Felicity Pring was furious.

'You are a liar, Thickpenny!' she said in a raised voice. 'A liar and a thief!'

'It's a mistake, Ma'am, just a mistake! I'm sorry!'

Felicity who was seated at the big desk in the library glared across at the cringing bailiff and pointed again to the entry in the account book open in front of her. She said, 'Sixty pounds you've entered here and this letter from the butcher says you had ninety pounds for the sheep we sold him. You've been robbing me. God knows how much you've made out of me during the past ten years. Your father was a rogue and a brute but he was honest. When he was dying after having his leg off I promised him that I would give you a chance to prove yourself in his place but I was a fool to do so. You are not even a good gamekeeper! I should have known better!'

'But – '

'But me no buts! Get out! Get out and take that brother with you. I expect he's been in it with you. No wonder the farm hasn't been paying its way for so long. Out! Out! If either of you are on my land tomorrow by this time of the day I shall call in the police and have you prosecuted!'

Silas Thickpenny scowled at her and said in a cold, grimly menacing way, 'Prosecute, will you, you bitch? Sent packing, are we? You'll be sorry! Bloody sorry! I'll see you pay for it! By God, I will, if it's the last thing I do!'

Felicity's hand went to a bell cord. 'Out! Out!' she shouted. 'One more threat and I'll call the grooms to have you horse-whipped!'

The white-faced and angry-looking Thickpenny turned and flung open the door. Then without attempting to close it, he stomped off through the hall and out of the house. Mrs Lestrange glided into the room in her quiet way and shut the door before

185

going to Felicity and putting a comforting arm around her shoulders.

'Now, my dear, you'd best calm down. I heard most of what went on and you did what was right in ridding this place of him and his brother. I shall never forget what they did to Nelson and I've never trusted any of the Thickpennys from the day I first set eyes on them.'

'No, I made a mistake in ever keeping them on here. I see that now. But the business has upset me, Annabel. Perhaps you would get me some brandy. I feel I need it.'

With trembling fingers Felicity took a long, thin cheroot from the silver box on the desk and the housekeeper, after fetching a small glass of brandy, went to the fireplace and lit a taper and passed it to her mistress.

'Not that I approve, Felicity, I don't and I never shall. Smoking is not ladylike!'

Felicity smiled. She seemed to be recovering quickly from the vexatious encounter with the bailiff. She said, 'You are a goose, Annabel. A real old goose! It's perfectly proper for a lady to indulge nowadays, providing of course that she doesn't do it in a public place. Dozens of us do it. You must try it yourself one day!'

Mrs Lestrange quickly riposted with, 'What, and be sick? Just as you were when you were caught out at school. Mrs Bonnamy was furious! Not likely!'

There was a knock at the door of the room and the housekeeper answered the summons. After a momentary conversation with the elderly manservant who had knocked she turned to Felicity saying, 'It's Frost. He says you have a visitor. He won't give his name but he looks a real gentleman and insists that he's a very old friend of yours.'

'Intriguing!' Felicity allowed smoke to drift from the corner of her mouth. 'An old friend, is he? And a gentleman? Well, Annabel, if he is such an old friend we must receive him. It may even be somebody you also know. Have him shown in but stay with me.'

When the visitor briskly entered the library the startled Felicity widened her eyes and took the cheroot from her mouth. As she rose from her chair she exclaimed, 'It's Nelson! By God, it's Nelson!'

The smiling Nelson went forward and, taking her free hand, lifted it to his lips. As he relinquished it she said, 'So my gypsy boy is now a gentleman of manners.'

'Yes, and position and property! And you, so I hear, my dear, are now a tycoon in the great City of London!'

At that point, having exchanged warm smiles with Nelson, Mrs Lestrange discreetly left the room. When she had gone Felicity rested the cheroot in an ashtray and Nelson held open his arms. Without the least hesitation she stepped into his close embrace.

'It's been so long,' she said. 'So very long!'

Several minutes later Felicity at last asked 'Why have you waited?'

'I had to make my way, my dear, and have something better to offer you than a hedgerow to sleep under – '

'I would even have done that, Nelson, I loved you so much. When you left me that night I was angry. Angry and foolish and then, one day, after I had given up all hope of ever seeing you again, I married – '

'Yes, I know. Mansell has just told me.'

'The doctor has been a good friend over the years, Nelson.'

'Yes, he's been a good friend today. It was he who insisted that I saw you. But what now, my dearest?'

'What now?' Felicity's face was alight with mischief. 'I suggest that you propose, Sir, and that you do it properly! Down on your knees, at once!'

Nelson was still on his knees and laughing when Mrs Lestrange re-entered the room carrying a laden tea-tray. 'Like that, is it?' she said, putting the tray on the desk. 'I'm very glad to see it. You've been pining for him long enough, my girl! Congratulations to you both and I know the two of you will be happy together. I wish now that I had brought champagne and not tea!'

'The champagne can come later,' said Felicity. 'Nelson will be dining here tonight and – '

'Sleeping here?'

Nelson who, with Felicity's assistance had risen to his feet, was about to say he hoped so when Felicity said firmly, 'Yes! He certainly will! And if you dare to ask me where, Annabel, I shall shake you!'

But Mrs Lestrange was not to be outdone. As she was leaving the room she murmured, sufficiently loudly for the lovers to hear, 'Then you'll need two extra pillows on your bed, Madam!'

3. A Death in the Morning

The May morning was cloudless and bright, and as early as half past four the sunlight was flooding into the bedroom where the lovers lay together. With no servants yet astir the house was tomb-silent as two intruders quietly made their way through the kitchen and up the back stairs to the first floor landing. One was carrying a gun.

Slowly the gunman opened the chosen bedroom door, then, having closed it behind them the pair moved to the bedside.

'My oath!' exclaimed Silas Thickpenny softly as he bent over the sleeping Nelson. 'The bitch has got herself a man!'

'Don't you see who it is?' asked his brother.

Silas peered more closely at the face half concealed by a raised arm. Recognition dawned. 'It's that bloody gypsy!' he muttered. 'That bloody Darkie Draper!' Then, signalling Ezra to stifle, with his hand over her mouth, any possibility of screaming by Felicity at her awakening, he prodded Nelson with the gun.

Nelson's startled eyes looked up and saw Silas pointing a gun at his sheet-covered midriff. Felicity awoke struggling to free herself from the hand clasped brutally over her mouth.

'Keep quiet, both of you!' commanded Silas. 'Keep quiet or I'll blow his bloody balls off, and you wouldn't like that, would you, Mrs Bloody Pring?'

Felicity, when the hand had been removed from her mouth asked, 'And what do you want, Thickpenny? Money? There's none here!'

'Lying bitch! There's a safe in here, so I've been told. Hid behind a picture of roses. That's the one, over there. And I know what's in the safe. There's money and jewellery. You get up and unlock it or I'll pull this trigger and let him have it where it'll hurt most.'

'Then someone pass me my wrap.'

'Mother-naked, are you? I might have guessed as much. So is he by the look of things. Precious pair of bare-arsed Adam and

Eves, aren't you. Give her the wrap, Ezra, and take your eyes off her tits while she puts it on.' Then Silas added with a leer, 'And if we've a mind to it when we've got what we came for, we'll both have her across the bed before we leave!'

Silas then prodded Nelson again with the gun. 'You can get up as well, gypsy!' 'Go and stand by that window where I can see you!'

Felicity, having pulled her wrap tightly around her went over to the picture and swung it to one side on its hinges. Behind it a small safe had been let into the brickwork. She had in her hand a bunch of keys taken from the drawer of a bedside table and using one of these she opened the safe door. Nelson who had taken up the position indicated by the gun barrel was watching her movements closely.

'Stand back!' said Ezra, 'and let me see what's in there.' From his pocket he produced a hessian bag. Pushing Felicity aside he took out a velvet-covered box and tipped its glittering contents into his bag. 'Where's the money?' he asked. 'Where is it, women?'

'In the drawer at the bottom!'

Silas pulled on the drawer handle and swore. 'The sodding thing's locked!' he declared. 'Unlock it!'

Felicity did as she was bidden and stepped back as Ezra pushed forward again. When he had pulled out the drawer he turned and showed its contents to Silas, saying gleefully, 'Look! it's full of sovereigns! It's a bloody fortune!'

Silas eagerly craned forward and for a moment his gun no longer pointed at Nelson. It was the opportunity Nelson had been waiting for. With almost incredible swiftness he swept up a heavy bronze vase from the window ledge and in one continuous movement brought it down so that it struck Silas on his right shoulder. There was an involuntary tightening of Silas's trigger finger and as the weapon went off Ezra's face seemed to disappear in a welter of blood. It had received the close-quarters concentration of pellets and with a curious gurgling scream the stricken man fell to the floor, dropping the drawer as he fell.

The sounds of the explosion and the scream so paralysed the three onlookers that they stood staring for a moment and no one moved. Then Silas, still clutching the gun, backed towards the bedroom door, opened it and took to his heels, making for the back stairs. When he was halfway down he saw his way barred by Frost, the elderly footman. The night-shirted servant stood at the foot of the stairs waving his arms, but Silas fell upon him, wildly swinging his gun by the barrel. There was a sickening thud as the butt struck Frost across the head and the man fell to the ground. Silas bounded over his body and disappeared through the kitchen and out of the house.

In the meantime Nelson had gone forward; after he had knelt for a moment by the fallen Ezra he got up and said, 'He's dead, Felicity. You'd best give me a sheet to cover him up.'

By now Manley Court was fully aroused and Mrs Lestrange, with a housecoat over her night things, hurried through the open bedroom door just as Nelson was tucking his shirt into his breeches.

'What has happened?' she asked and then looked down to see the sheet-covered body in front of the open safe. 'Who is it?'

'It's Ezra Thickpenny!' said Felicity.

'Dead?'

'Very!' said Nelson, and then Felicity told the housekeeper what had happened in the bedroom and how Silas had run off.

'It must 'ave been 'im, Ma'am, what 'it Frost.' It was a man's voice from among the several servants who were clustering round the bedroom door in varying states of attire. 'We've just found 'im, with 'is 'ead cut open bad, at the foot of the stairs. 'Urt proper bad, 'e is!'

'Is he being attended to?'

'Yes, Ma'am. Somebody's getting 'im to bed but I reckon 'e do need a doctor!'

'Then one of you take the dog-cart into Hitchin and fetch Doctor Mansell' ordered Felicity, 'and you, Beamish,' she said to the head groom, 'you ride into the town and tell the police what has happened. I should like Inspector Albyn to come out here at once. The rest of you get dressed and back to your duties.'

By eight o'clock order had been fully restored in the house, Inspector Albyn had arrived with two constables; statements had been taken from Felicity and Nelson; the body of Ezra Thickpenny had been removed to one of the stables; and a hue and cry had been set up and the hunt was on for Silas Thickpenny. Doctor Mansell, who had arrived before the police and spent some time examining the injured Frost, now joined Nelson and Felicity in the housekeeper's room for a coffee and buttered roll breakfast.

'Will he be all right?' asked an anxious Felicity.

Mansell shook his head doubtfully. 'I can't be sure. His skull may be fractured and he's no longer a young man. He will need careful watching and will have to be kept still and quiet for a few days.'

'Then if you can stay here, Doctor, and remain overnight, I should be grateful,' said Felicity. 'He must have the very best attention. I feel he deserves it if he tried to stop Thickpenny getting away.'

'That, I promise, he shall have,' said Mansell, 'and what about you? A sedative, perhaps?'

Felicity made a face. 'Thank you, but no,' she said. 'I've my own prop to lean on at the moment.' She gave a fond glance at Nelson and held out her left hand so that Mansell could see the ring on her engagement finger.

'Does that mean he is going to make an honest woman out of you at last?'

Nelson laughed. 'It does, but I had to borrow the ring from Annabel.'

'Not borrowed,' said the housekeeper. 'I gave it you to give to her. I couldn't have you bedding her under this roof without some proof of honest intentions!'

'And when is the wedding to be?' asked Mansell.

'As soon as possible!' said Felicity. 'And you are to be there!'

'Me?'

'Yes, you, Doctor. I shall need you to give me away!'

4. The Fire

After their meal that evening Felicity, Nelson and Mansell were joined in the library by Inspector Albyn. As he entered the room their enquiring eyes brought his answering, 'No! We haven't got him. Where he is, God knows!'

'Could he have made his way to London?' asked Mansell. 'There are plenty of trains these days.'

'It is possible, I suppose, but I've had a watch on the station most of the day and he hasn't been seen.'

'Then he could still be in this area?'

'It's more than likely that he is. After all, he was once the gamekeeper here and he knows the woods hereabouts like the back of his hand. He might well lie low for a day or two and then make his escape. It's far too large an area for me to have searched by the few men I've got available. He may also have friends in the locality who will hide and feed him.'

'Supposing I offer a reward for his capture,' said Felicity. 'Would that help?'

'Better put as "information leading to his arrest" ' replied Albyn. 'If he has still got the gun we don't want anyone trying to tackle him. It wouldn't do. Wouldn't do at all! How much are you prepared to offer?'

'Five hundred pounds!'

It was while Albyn was considering this that a young maidservant entered the room and went across to Mansell, saying in a quiet voice, 'Mrs Lestrange thinks you'd better come at once, Doctor.'

'Where is she?'

'With Mr Frost. He's gone all peculiar-like. Mrs Lestrange, me an' 'is wife were sitting with 'im when sudden-like 'e sat up, an' then fell back with 'is eyes wide open, but I don't reckon 'e's seeing things.'

'Do you mean he's dead, girl?' Mansell rose from his chair. So too did Albyn.

The girl nodded. 'Yes,' she said, 'I reckon 'e is!'

'Then it's a murderer we're after,' said Albyn. 'And he'll hang if we catch him.'

The two followed the girl from the room, but they were back within a few minutes.

'Is he dead?' asked Felicity.

'Yes,' said Mansell. 'I'm afraid he is.'

'Increase the reward to seven hundred pounds,' said Felicity.

'I will, Madam,' said Albyn, 'and I'll have the notices printed in large type and circulated for display in Hitchin and the surrounding villages. For that sum we ought to get some result.'

Mansell stayed on that night at Manley Court to be on hand in case he was needed to attend the sedated but much distressed Mrs Frost. He had been provided with a room next to that of the housekeeper, one which, like hers, overlooked the stable yard. At about midnight, however, he was roused by a loud knocking at his door. Rising quickly – he had only undressed to the extent of removing his frock coat and boots – he went to see who was calling him.

Mrs Lestrange was there, candlestick in hand. Mansell said, 'Mrs Frost? Am I wanted?'

'No, Doctor, it's not her. But can you smell smoke?'

Having sniffed at the air Mansell went to the window of his room and raised the sash. Putting out his head and shoulders he could see orange tongues of flame leaping not only from the outhouses beneath him but also from what he thought must be one of the haylofts. The horses in their boxes had already scented the fire and were beginning to trumpet and scream in their panic and to kick out noisily at the wooden separating panels and doors.

'By God!' Mansell called out, 'the yard and the house are on fire! Let's get everyone out!'

Within a matter of minutes Felicity and Nelson and the rest of the partly clothed household were assembling by the front steps. As soon as it was known everyone was out and safe Nelson called for the grooms to help him rescue the horses. Felicity set about organising the rest of the servants to help her bring out the more valuable treasures in the house. 'I don't like the way the wind is gusting,' she said to Mansell. 'If we don't get help quickly I doubt if we shall save the house.'

Followed by the two grooms, Nelson rounded the corner into the stable yard, to be brought to an abrupt halt by a menacing figure silhouetted by the now leaping flames. There was a shout of 'Stop! Stop, Gypsy, stop! Stay where you are or I'll shoot you, you bugger!'

It was Silas Thickpenny, brandishing his gun.

The halted Nelson called out, 'Let us get the horses out! You're not going to let them burn, are you?'

'Burn? Let 'em burn! They can all burn! So can you, Gypsy, so can you! Stay where you are. Stay where I can see you and who you've got with you! All of you, hold your arms up!'

'But the horses!'

'Bugger the horses! And bugger you, Gypsy! I'll pay you back for what you did last night! Made me kill Ezra, you did! Now I shall kill you! And her! I'll kill you both! By God I will!'

As he was speaking the flames, fanned by the night breeze, seemed to be leaping up all around. Felicity's fears now seemed to be well founded. The house was in grave danger and Nelson was getting desperate. There was sufficient light for him to see the demoniac look on the face of Thickpenny and he knew it would be useless trying to appeal to him again. 'The man's mad' he thought, and he made a move to lower his hands with a view to taking a chance with a sudden rush.

Thickpenny, however, was watching him too closely and raised his gun to a firing position. 'Keep 'em up, Gypsy!' he almost screamed. 'I can't miss you and you'll die just like Ezra did! So will anyone else who tries anything!'

Suddenly a noise came from behind him; Thickpenny half turned to see what Nelson was staring at, but it was too late for him to do anything as Nelson's fierce, black mare, which had freed herself from her box and reared above him, dropped down to crush him with a flurry of wildly kicking forelegs. It was all over in a matter of noise-filled seconds.

Moving cautiously, Nelson went forward to within a few feet of where the trembling, wild-eyed mare stood over the still, recumbent body. As he neared her he began calling out in a soothing voice, 'Quiet, girl. Quiet. It's all right, girl! Quiet, you beauty. Quiet. Quiet. You're all right now.' The calming words were interspersed by a curious hissing, between-the-teeth whistle, and the mare made an almost immediate response, stepping over the body of the man she had just killed to nuzzle Nelson's outstretched hand.

'Blimey!' exclaimed one of the grooms. 'Who'd have thought it! 'E's bloody magicked 'er 'e 'as! Bloody 'ell!'

Nelson turned from caressing the mare's now arched neck to say quietly, 'See what you can do for the others. Get 'em out if you can. Hurry!'

The grooms ran to obey his order but it was already too late and they were quickly back out of the billowing smoke, coughing and retching. 'It's no good, Gov'nor,' said one of them. 'No bloody good at all! Them flames 'as got too big an 'old an' we can't get at the 'osses. But we did manage ter get into the 'arness room.' He was carrying a saddle, the other groom, a bridle. 'Thought they might be 'andy if yer was thinking of riding the black in the the town to get 'elp.'

While they were saddling up the now strangely docile mare Felicity arrived on the scene, accompanied by Mansell. Both were smoke-blackened from their forays into the house salvaging what they could.

'What's happened?' she asked staring at the crumpled figure on the ground. 'Isn't that Thickpenny? Is he dead, Nelson?'

'It's Thickpenny all right, and I should think he's as dead as mutton. The bugger tried to stop us freeing the horses but my mare freed herself and fortunately savaged him. Perhaps, Doctor, you'll make sure he won't be troubling us again.'

Mansell was already stooping over the body. When he straightened up he said, 'He'll trouble no one again! Not even Jack Ketch! The hangman's been cheated!'

By this time Nelson was up in the saddle, and without another word he galloped off. It was, however, a full forty minutes before he returned with help in the form of the town's fire brigade with two engines and thirty men under their captain, William Jackson.

Having set the pumpers to work, and ordered where the hoses should be directed, Jackson reported to Felicity, saying, 'Sorry, Mrs Pring, we should have been here fifteen minutes sooner if we hadn't knocked off a wheel rounding the corner out of the Maltings.' Mansell, who heard this, thought 'Old Isacc Newton was right. They shouldn't have moved there. It's not the right place for the fire engines. But the damage is done now. They're not going to be of much use here, by the look of things.'

His thoughts were confirmed by Jackson going on to say, 'I reckon it's gone too far for us to save more than your west wing, and we may not even do that. You've done well, Ma'am to get out all the things you have.' He was looking at the piles of treasures scattered along the gravel drive. 'Arson wasn't it?'

'Yes, arson, Mr Jackson, arson!'

As the fire brigade captain moved away shaking his head Felicity, Nelson and Mansell were joined by Inspector Albyn. They all went together to view Thickpenny's body. Albyn, rather to Felicity's horror, turned it on its back with his foot and stood looking down on the distorted face saying, 'It's a pity! I was hoping to watch you hang! Hang as high as Haman!' Mansell, for the sake of decency, fetched a salvaged rug and flung it over the corpse.

Morning, when it dawned, revealed a sorry scene. Almost all of Manley Court had been gutted, and smoke and steam were still rising from the ruins. Felicity, red-eyed and dishevelled, stood surveying the wreckage with Nelson's arm around her waist.

'Well,' he said, 'at least it solves one problem. We shan't be living here when we're married, my dear.'

'I had already made up my mind on that matter,' she replied. 'Even before the fire I had done that.'

'You had?'

'Yes. Royston is where your work is and that is where we shall both be going. We shall build a house or buy one near the stud farm.'

'And what about London and your business there?'

'No difficulty, my dearest. Nowadays it is only just over an hour's journey by train, and if I go twice each week that will be quite enough. In any case, I've a fancy for taking up with another business?'

'Such as?'

'Breeding!'

'Bloodstock?'

'Yes. If Sir Arthur wants to retire I shall offer to buy him out and become your business partner as well as your sleeping partner, and besides–'

'Besides what?'

Felicity laughed, 'If we do some other kind of breeding the

children will require my attention!' Felicity then looked across at
Mansell who was standing closely by their side.

Mansell chuckled, 'Children, my dear! Remember I charge five
shillings for each delivery but they come cheaper by the half
dozen!'

'Then, God willing, six it shall be!' said Felicity. 'And' she
added, 'I should like three of each!'

5. The Carpenter's Wife

When Mansell received a 'come at once' message from Joseph Fostring, the Ickleford village carpenter and general handyman, he hastened to the Swan Inn yard to borrow the blacksmith's pony and trap and set off at a smart trot to answer the summons thinking the Fostring baby was making an unfortunately early arrival. To his reckoning the birth was not due until the end of December, not now at the month's beginning, and such early first births were never to his liking – they usually meant trouble. It was, he hoped just a false alarm. He knew the bearded Joseph was an over-anxious father-to-be but as he had been a very close friend of his for many years he wanted to allay his fears even if they were misplaced.

Bowling bumpily along the badly rutted road out of Hitchin, Mansell thought back to twelve months earlier when, in the carpenter's shaving-strewn workshop, Joseph had broached the subject of marrying again. This he wanted to do with the object of fathering a son who could learn the craft and eventually take over the thriving business which he had built up.

'Maggie,' Joseph had said, referring to his late wife, 'couldn't have children, as well you know, William, but she's been gone these six months now and she won't grudge me the chance of getting a son. In fact, when she was dying, she begged me to marry again and to do it as soon as it was decent and respectful-like.'

Mansell had asked him his age.

'Fifty-five! And still hale and hearty!' had been the reply, and to the Doctor's enquiry if he had anyone in mind he had chuckled and said, 'Yes! Mary Walker. The innkeeper's daughter.'

Mansell recalled his surprise at this answer and his saying, 'But surely she's rather young for you?'

'Aye! She's only twenty, but she says she's willing.' Then Joseph had hesitated before asking, 'Perhaps you'll have a look at her, William. If you think she's all right for childbearing we'll get Vicar to put up the banns next Sunday.'

The girl, who was plain but pleasant enough, had readily submitted to examination by Mansell who, at its conclusion, had gone at once to Joseph and told him there was no reason why Mary should not be able to carry and deliver a child without difficulty. There had been a January wedding and in May, much to Joseph's delight, Mansell was able to confirm that Mary was pregnant.

Much to the astonishment of many of the more critical villagers, the marriage turned out to be a great success in every way. The placid, good-natured Mary kept the cottage spotlessly clean and was an excellent cook and she was an enthusiastic bed companion for her still virile husband. Joseph became a very happy man.

'Yes,' thought Mansell, as he brought the trap to a standstill outside the Fostring's cottage which was situated on the opposite side of the village green to the church, 'that Mary of yours, Joseph, is a treasure and you could have done a lot worse than take her for a wife.'

He was greeted at the cottage door not by Joseph but by Joseph's niece Amanda. But it was a very different Amanda from the little Cockney sparrow who long ago had come to him in the Market Square seeking a laxative for her grandmother. This Amanda Radcliffe-Fostring was a sophisticated young woman, quietly but expensively dressed, who had taken her place in the world and was now very sure of herself. Not only was she the deputy head of Mrs Bonnamy's Academy for the Daughters of Gentlemen but she also had two much praised novels to her credit. The first, *The Squire of Belmont* had as its principal character, a kindly but hard-riding, hard-drinking gentleman, with the language of a Billingsgate porter, who had obviously been modelled on Delme-Radcliffe. The second, *Latimer's Law*, much to the amusement of John Hawkins, was a mildly satirical representation of him and his legal practice in Hitchin's Portmill Lane. The bulky lawyer, on meeting the author for the first time after the books' publication, had gently reprimanded her, and then, following a great bellowing of laughter, had kissed her on both cheeks.

Mansell's enquiry: 'Amanda, my dear, what are you doing

here this morning?' was countered by a welcoming smile and, 'I've a day off from school, Doctor, and I was just visiting. When Uncle Joseph told me about Mary, and that you were soon likely to be here, I decided to stay on in case help was needed.'

'I hope it won't be, but how is Mary now?' asked Mansell, as Amanda led the way up the narrow stairway to the bedrooms above.

'Quietly sleeping when I looked in on her a few minutes ago. It seems a shame to wake her but Uncle Joseph was so worried when she had these stomach pains early today and said she felt sick he thought it best to send for you.'

Mary was wakened and a thorough examination gently made by Mansell. Afterwards he was quietly reassuring to the doe-eyed Mary.

'Nothing for you to worry your pretty little head about, Mary,' he said, but downstairs – and out of Mary's hearing – he admitted to Amanda that all was not well.

'The child is lying badly,' he said. 'It won't be before its proper time, I am sure of that, but it may be a very difficult delivery.'

'So?'

'Mary must take things very quietly from now on and rest as much as possible.'

Amanda accompanied Mansell to the adjoining workshop where they found Joseph and Isaiah Bird, his elderly assistant, both busy at their benches. Joseph who was assembling a beautifully carved cradle obviously intended for the coming child, looked up anxiously at their entrance. So too did Isaiah. Having seen who was at the open door, Joseph put down his mallet and went forward to clasp Mansell's outstretched hand.

'I knew you were here, William,' he said. 'I heard your trap pull up at the gate but I thought it better for 'Manda to take you up to Mary. How is she now?'

Mansell, well aware that the rheumy-eyed Isaiah was also closely listening, told Joseph what he had already told Amanda, and it was she who raised the matter of getting some immediate assistance in the cottage for Mary.

'If she's not to do much housework and cooking for the next few weeks, Uncle, then you'll have to get someone in at once.'

'That can be arranged, 'Manda.' Joseph nodded in the direction of Isaiah. 'His wife is standing by to help in the house when the baby is born, but I don't suppose she'll mind coming in early, will she, Isaiah?'

'That she won't, Master.' The old man's walnut-shell-wrinkled face had broke into an almost toothless smile. 'That she won't. She'll be pleased to come. Yer knows how Minnie an' me feel about that babbie. We don't want nothin' ter 'appen to it. Be sure we doesn't. It be too precious. None of us what believes don't want fer anything ter go wrong. We've been a-waiting a long time for the blessed day when He comes agin.'

A flash of anger crossed Joseph's bearded face.

'Enough of that nonsense, Isaiah,' he said. 'You go and get Minnie at once and stop your foolish talk.'

'It ain't foolish, Master, but you don' see what yer ought ter be seeing even though the signs are proper plain. You mark my words. I've got the gift of prophesy, I 'ave. He'll come on Christmas Day just like He did afore. Praise be the Lord, the Lord's name be praised!'

Still muttering, Isaiah shuffled out of the door and Mansell, somewhat bewildered, turned to Joseph for an explanation. The glowering Joseph gave a shrug and with a look at Amanda appealed to her to give it.

She said 'It's silly but it's simple. We have Uncle Joseph here who is getting on in years and is a carpenter, just like the Joseph in the Bible, and we have young Mary, who's his wife, and who's great with a child that is due to be born on or about the twenty-fifth of this month. In Isaiah's eyes, and in the eyes of the dozen or so chapel-going villagers he's been talking to, this points–'

Mansell smiled, 'To the Second Coming, I suppose?'

'It does!'

'But what if the child is a girl? It could be.'

'Then they'll all be sadly disappointed! So will Uncle Joe! Won't you, Uncle?'

'No, I shan't!' put in Joseph quickly. 'I shan't at all. I shan't be at all upset. She'll be right welcome and Mary might well give me a boy next time. Daughters can be a real blessing and no one knows better about that than you do, William. You'd be right lost without your Mary, wouldn't you?'

Mansell readily agreed. 'And that reminds me,' he said, 'I've promised my Mary I'd be back early today for her birthday party and I'd best be on my way. Remember, Joseph, keep that wife of yours away from any heavy work and make sure she rests with her feet up. She's to have no worry and to do as little as possible.'

Amanda, with her arm round her uncle's aproned waist, watched from the workshop doorway as Mansell unhitched the pony and mounted the trap. As he and his conveyance disappeared round the corner by the church Joseph said, 'Do you know what we shall do if the baby is a girl, 'Manda?'

'No. What?'

'We shall call her Amanda after you and–'

'And what, Uncle?'

'We shall ask you to be her godmother!'

6. The Swansong of Simeon Radcliffe

Just before four o'clock on the afternoon of the day of her Ickleford visit, Amanda entered the Everetts' gentlemen's shop in the Hitchin marketplace and was shown upstairs to the living quarters by a grinning apprentice. There she found her school-days friend, Susan, waiting to serve tea.

They exchanged kisses and Amanda, having removed her muff, cloak and bonnet, went to stand with her back to the fireplace, raising her skirt and petticoats to allow the heat from the blazing coals to warm much of her shapely legs.

'That is not very elegant!' declared Susan with a smile. 'You're showing your drawers! Mrs Bonnamy would certainly not approve!'

'She's not here!' replied Amanda with a mischievous grin. 'And I'm not so sure she wouldn't do the same if her legs were as cold as mine are. It's freezing outside and the fog is rolling in rapidly. It's going to be really thick tonight.'

Susan, who was pouring water into the teapot from a steaming kettle, said, 'That will mean Mark's train being delayed.'

'Is he in London?'

'Yes, looking at Spring fashions and ordering stock.'

'And the children? Not here?'

'No. They are at their grandparents' for a few days. They love going there and Mark's mother and father love having them.'

'And spoiling them, I suppose?'

'Spoiling them terribly. But isn't that what grandparents always do? You'll find that out for yourself one day – if you ever relent and marry that Peter of yours and have some children of your own!'

'My Peter? Peter Bonnamy?'

'Yes. Peter Bonnamy. You've kept him waiting long enough, Amanda. You know you are fond of him and what's more I've seen a broody look in your eyes several times since your Uncle Joseph got young Mary pregnant. How is she by the way?'

'One moment, my dear, and I'll tell all!' Amanda lowered her skirts and joined Susan at the table. Then, when settled, she gave her friend a full account of the morning's happenings.

'So there's likely to be a problem, Amanda?'

'Not one but two problems. The actual birth of the child and the peculiar behaviour of old Isaiah and his friends.'

'It's ridiculous! They can't be serious, surely?'

'They are. And if they get any more portents such as large stars in the sky at Christmas it could lead to a riot in the village. I've now discovered that it's not only the Ickleford villagers who are involved but people from Hitchin are also believing a miracle is going to take place.'

Susan, with an indignant sniff and a 'More fools them!' then began to talk about their times together at school, and after that gave Amanda a rundown on the latest local scandals. Their time together passed quickly and pleasantly until, at seven, Amanda reluctantly rose to leave, saying she was due back at the Academy to help supervise the younger pupils going to their beds.

'But you can't go home alone in this,' protested Susan, who had drawn back the curtains from the window to reveal the Market Square blanketed by dense fog. 'You really can't. You must wait for Mark to return and see you through the streets.'

'I shall be all right,' was Amanda's answer. 'It's not far and the street lamps will give me some help, so I shan't get lost. No. Go I must and go I will!' She continued with the buttoning up of her cloak and the adjusting and tying of her bonnet strings. 'Don't worry, my dear, it's just that I won't have Mark turning out in this again when he does get home. He'll have had quite enough of fog by then!'

Still protesting vehemently, Susan let Amanda out through the shop door and into the bewildering murk of the night. 'Do take care, Amanda!' she called, as her friend was swallowed up by the swirling fog. 'Do take care!'

Before she had gone more than a few yards Amanda began regretting her decision not to wait for an escort. Being Amanda she was too obstinate to turn back, and she pressed on, almost blindly, until she was about to pass what she was sure was the Red Cow tavern. Suddenly a door was flung open and a shouting man pushed out on to the pavement where he stood unsteadily for a moment still shouting obscenities. The door was quickly closed, cutting off the pale yellow light from the room's lamps and leaving the darkness seemingly darker than before. Then, to Amanda's horror, the man she had only momentarily glimpsed, reeled and bumped into her, felling her to the ground. As she collapsed the drunken man fell on top of her. His breath in her face smelled of beer and vomit and she was immediately nauseated.

Buff Birker, the town's bully boy and layabout was fighting drunk and in an uncontrollable temper. Clawing himself free from Amanda he managed to get to his feet and then drag her to her knees by the collar of her cloak.

'You bitch! You bloody little bitch!' His voice was lowered to a threatening growl. 'You tripped me up, you did. You bloody tripped me up!'

His words were followed by two, heavy, back-handed slaps. The first of these knocked aside her bonnet and caught her a stinging blow on her ear. The second was across her face. This brought the salty taste of blood to her lips. Her attempt to scream was frustrated by rough, strong fingers being clamped around her neck and two thumbs pressed hard into her throat.

'I'll larn yer to trip me, woman! I'll larn yer!' The snarling threat was scarcely heard by Amanda as she began to drift away into unconsciousness. 'I'll larn yer, yer bitch. Yer'll not do it agin! By Gawd yer won't!'

On the verge of blacking out Amanda realised someone had come up behind her assailant and was beginning to belabour him with a stick. She could hear the blows falling on the man's shoulders.

'Take that! Take that! Take that, you brute, and let the lady go!' was being shouted, but by no familiar voice. 'Let her go! Let her go, you brute, and let her go!'

Birker loosened his grip upon Amanda and threw her back to the ground. Now berserk with a ferocious rage Birker turned upon his attacker to push aside the flailing cane and punch hard at its wielder with clenched fists. The would-be rescuer of Amanda was no match for the bully and in a moment collapsed on the pavement. Then followed two sickening thuds as Birker lashed out with his heavily booted foot at his victim's head. 'I'll kill yer! Kill yer I will!'

But other help was now at hand. First out of the grey darkness came a man calling in a voice Amanda knew well, 'Amanda! Amanda! Where are you? Are you all right?'

'I'm here, Peter! I'm here! Here on the ground. But look out, he's mad!' Amanda's warning to Peter Bonnamy could only be croaked out but he heard sufficient to halt in his tracks. Simultaneously with her warning, the tavern door opened and the landlord rushed out, followed by three burly customers. Seeing the odds were so much against him Birker staggered away into the fog.

Whilst Peter Bonnamy went to Amanda's assistance the landlord gave his attention to the man stretched out on the pavement. 'By God!' he called out. 'This poor bugger's dead! The sod's done for 'im! 'E's bloody killed 'im!'

'Let's get this lady and him into the light,' said Peter, assisting Amanda to her feet. 'We can see better what to do!'

When Amanda was seated in a chair by the taproom fire and the stranger's body laid out on a long table at the opposite end of the room the landlord turned to Peter and said, 'We'd best get a doctor, 'adn't we, Mr Bonnamy. 'E'll be too late fer the gent 'ere but the lady needs lookin' at, don't she?'

'She does! Someone go for Mansell. He'll be the nearest and the quickest.'

'An' I knows where 'e is right now!' announced a pimply-faced youth who had been seated in a corner with mouth agape and staring first at Amanda and then at the body. ''E's only up at the White 'Art, 'e is. I saw 'im going in there as I were comin' 'ere!'

'Then go get him!' urged Peter. 'Tell him he's wanted here at once!'

The youth disappeared through the still open doorway and Peter turned to inspect Amanda more closely. Her right eye was swelling and blackening and she had a badly cut and bleeding lower lip. There were some ugly bruise marks on her throat and one ear was torn.

'I'm sorry, my dear,' he said. 'If I'd only been a few minutes earlier none of this would have happened. Mother sent me to get you as soon as I got home from the office but I was late tonight.'

'It wasn't your fault, Peter, it was my own foolishness. I should have waited for Mark to come back from London and not attempted to return by myself. If you can lend me your handkerchief to stop this bleeding I shall be all right until the doctor comes. Please see what you can do for the gentleman who tried to help me. From what I can see from here he doesn't look at all well.'

'Nobody'll do much fer 'im, Miss,' said the landlord. ''E's as dead as bleedin' mutton, beggin' your pardin.'

'Who is he?' asked Peter.

'Dunno, Mr Bonnamy. I dunno! Never seen 'im before to me knowledge but 'e's a gent from the cut of 'is clothes.'

'Look in his pockets,' suggested Peter. 'He may have some means of identification on him.'

''Ere, Mr Bonnamy, 'ang on like. You'd best do that, seeing yer a lawyer now and a gent yerself what can be trusted.'

Peter's search yielded little to help identify the body. There was a kerchief, a small purse containing eleven sovereigns and some small change, and a gold fob watch of considerable value.

'Nothing to help us,' said Peter, setting out the few items by the corpse. 'Nothing at all.'

As he said this Mansell hurried into the room. 'What have we here, Peter?' he asked, putting down his carpet-bag.

'A murder, I'm afraid, Doctor. One dead man and Amanda here who has been rather badly hurt.'

'Ah, Amanda! It's you, is it, behind that handkerchief?'

'I'm afraid it is, Doctor.'

'Hm! I'll just confirm this man is really dead and then I'll look at you, my dear, and see what I can do.'

Mansell's examination of the body on the table took only moments, but after staring down into the bloodied face with some intensity he looked across wonderingly at Amanda.

'This man came to help you?' he asked.

'Yes, Doctor. He did. Do you know who it is? He was very brave.'

'Brave? Him brave? Well, perhaps he was, for once in his life, but little could he have guessed who it was he was trying to save!'

'Who is it?'

'Who is it, Amanda? It's Simeon Radcliffe!'

Amanda's one good eye opened wide in astonishment. 'Him? The man who did that awful thing to my mother?' She rose from her chair and walked unsteadily across the room to look down into the weak-chinned face with its now lifeless but staring pale blue eyes. So this was the man who had so brutally fathered her? She had hated the thought of him ever since the day her guardian aunt in London had lost her temper with her over some naughtiness and called her a 'Radcliffe bastard', so revealing her origins.

'Cover him up, someone,' she commanded after a few seconds. 'Cover him up, please.' Then she burst into tears. 'God!' she sobbed. 'He's dead, but I still can't forgive him.'

'I don't suppose you can,' said Mansell, 'but don't forget this, Amanda, if you do ever think of him in the future, although he was a weak and sometimes even a wicked man he at least tried to do one good thing. He did make an effort to save you from Birker and lost his life in doing so.'

Amanda nodded acceptance of this and then insisted on helping the landlord's wife to drape a sheet over the body.

Mansell then asked for hot water and a towel so that, as he put it, 'I can patch up the lady'. But before starting on Amanda he turned to the pimply youth who had fetched him from the White Hart and said, 'And you, Billy, can go to the Police Station and ask the constables to come here at once. The sooner Birker is put under lock and key the safer it will be for everyone. And it had best be one of the constables that goes to the Priory to tell Mr Delme-Radcliffe about this matter, and to ask him what he would like done with this body.

*   *   *

Not long after the grandfather clock on the landing at Mrs Bonnamy's had struck nine that evening the much patched-up Amanda put herself to bed.

As she lay in the bed's warm depths, clutching a comforting hot-water bottle and watching the shadows cast by the fire dancing on the ceiling, her thoughts went back, over and over again, to the many events of what had been an eventful day. Uppermost in her mind was not the recollection of her encounter with Birker and the death of Simeon Radcliffe but the warm memory of a much more recent occurrence. Only twenty minutes or so before, she had met Peter Bonnamy at the foot of the stairs, and he had asked her to marry him. Despite the discomfort of her twice stitched lip she had laughed, but it was not an unkind or scornful laugh. She had said, 'You do choose the most peculiar time and the oddest of places to propose, Peter, you really do.'

He had replied with a smile and taken up her left hand to press a kiss upon it. Retaining her hand he had said, 'You must know that I love you, Amanda, and that I have loved you for a long, long time.'

'And I, Peter,' she had countered, 'have waited a long, long time for you to tell me so!'

Then had come an eager, 'But you will marry me, won't you?'

Amanda remembered laughing again before snatching away her hand and racing up the stairs. From the safety of the landing she had called down, 'Heaven help you but of course I will.' Then she had blown him a kiss and gone to her room.

As she drifted into a happy sleep she could see in her mind's eye the pleasantly dazed look which had spread across his face.

*   *   *

No attempt was made by the constables to apprehend Birker that night but at daybreak the following morning, when it was deemed safer to enter the Back Street area, Inspector Albyn and his men raided the hovel where he lived with his mother and found him curled up, still in a drunken stupor, on the kitchen floor. He was in no state to resist arrest or even walk, and he had to be carted off in a wheelbarrow to the Bridewell, at the far end of the town.

7. A Sentence of Death

A pensive Mansell sat alone in the great family pew he still continued to rent in St Mary's Church and stared with unseeing eyes at the nearby, exquisitely carved Angel Screen separating the South Aisle from the so-called Radcliffe Chapel. He was very early for Morning Service on that last Sunday in Advent. Intentionally so. He wanted time and some semblance of solitude, in which to bring his thoughts to order before the church began to fill and any members of his family came to join him.

On the previous day he had sought out Doctor Frederick Hawkins at the Town Infirmary, and his old friend and colleague had confirmed, after a rather painful examination, what he had self-diagnosed some weeks earlier.

'I am afraid you were right,' Hawkins had said, as he washed his hands whilst Mansell was pulling on his breeches. 'It is a cancer and one already fairly well advanced. I'll not mince matters, I know you too well for that. I strongly advise you if you've affairs to set in order to do so soon.'

Mansell had left him to go straightaway to Lawyer Hawkins's office in the Portmill Lane. The doctor's brother, after expressing sorrow at the news, had set about drawing up a simple will in accordance with Mansell's instructions.

The cottage in the London Road, together with its contents, was to go to his daughter, Mary Timmins and the great silver watch which had been presented to him by the captain and crew of the last whaling ship in which he had served as doctor was to go to Daniel Timmins, his eldest grandchild. Each of the other grandchildren was to receive five golden sovereigns and after these monetary bequests had been met and his funeral expenses paid the remaining balance at the bank, which wouldn't be much, was to be shared equally by his two sons. The will, in Hawkins's own fair round hand, had been duly signed by Mansell in the presence of Hawkins and his partner, Peter Bonnamy, and left for safekeeping at the lawyer's office. Although that

211

matter had been settled to his satisfaction Mansell still had to make up his mind on when he should make his demise. He was determined not to subject himself to the pain and distress of a long illness, in which he would become increasingly dependent upon his beloved Mary, when he could do for himself what he had done, on occasions, for others. He was, he was sure, going to be able for a while yet to continue to subdue the present pain, and he had no intention of bringing gloom to the family at Christmas. 'No, we will enjoy our last Christmas together', he said to himself. 'I am sure we shall be able to do that once again.'

Having made up his mind, he jerked himself out of his despondent reverie. No, he would take no action yet. When the right time came he would know it, and then he would resort to the small phial which he carried in his bag.

Having come back to the present moment, he consulted the silver watch he had willed to Daniel and saw that it still wanted sixteen minutes to eleven and the commencement of the service. The church was filling rapidly. Across the nave to his left Mrs Bonnamy, assisted by Amanda and a deferential sidesman, was ushering twenty or so of the Academy's young ladies into the reserved pews. Hovering in the background was a pleased-looking Peter Bonnamy, waiting for the fluttering girls to settle so that he could join Amanda at the end of the pew. She, as far as Mansell could see at the distance, now bore little trace of her nasty encounter with the brutal Birker. The blackened eye, having been through a range of rainbow hues, was back to normal colour again and her lip, thanks to his careful stitching, was only slightly scarred. She looked radiantly happy and, noticing Mansell's scrutiny, she smiled at him and raised her left hand so that he could see the glittering diamond ring on her third finger. He smiled in return, thinking to himself that she and Peter made a handsome couple and, God willing, he might even see them married.

Next to attract his attention was the arrival of the Squire, his family and some of his house servants making their way to the special pews in the Radcliffe Chapel. Delme-Radcliffe, in passing, nodded in Mansell's direction, and the doctor acknowledged the greeting with a slight inclination of his own head. He had called on Delme-Radcliffe the day after Simeon had been killed and told him of Amanda's involvement in the matter. In return, the Squire had enlightened him on the reason for Simeon's reappearance in the town, saying, 'It was money again, of course. The fool had gambled away not only his own inheritance but most of his wife's fortune as well. He wanted me to find him a well paid post with one of the companies I chair and I had promised him that I would see what could be done for him. He would have been disappointed had he reached me. I had found nothing!' There had been a grudgingly added, 'At least he died trying – for once in his nasty little life – to do something worthwhile. That it should have been his own daughter he went to help is strangely ironic. There was some good in him after all.'

As the Squire and his retinue settled down in their seats, the church bells resolved the touch of Stedman's Triples they had been ringing and went into harmonious rounds. Next came the urgent clangour of their being rung down to rest. With the beginning of the tolling of the five-minute-bell, Mary, Mansell's daughter, joined him in his pew with the remainder of the Timmins family. She was, he could see, regarding him with a look of reproach. He knew why. Twice in the preceding week he had, of dire necessity, been helped to her home from the Swan Inn. On the second occasion she had scolded him thoroughly. 'You mustn't do it, Father!' she had commanded. 'Pining for Mother in the way you are doing won't bring her back and you can't drown your sorrows in strong ale. You must know what she would be thinking if she could see you now in this condition. Perhaps she can. Sometimes I think she is still watching over us. No! You must stop this heavy drinking. You owe it not only to the family but to her memory!'

Mansell had promised her that in future he would not over-indulge but the promise had nearly been broken the night before, and she was, he was sure, aware that he had spent most of the evening with two of his drinking cronies at the Swan. 'Sorry!' he murmured, 'But I did get myself home on my own two feet!'

She had touched his arm sympathetically and then they and the remainder of the congregation rose to their feet to receive the procession of choir and clergy led by Mansell's youngest grandson proudly carrying the silver cross. As usual the boy glanced sideways and winked as he drew level with his grandfather's pew and the doctor winked back at him.

The vicar, then fairly new to the parish, was bringing up the rear of the procession; he observed this exchange and frowned. It was not proper and he would have to have a word with the choirmaster about it and to speak to the so-called doctor.

But the young and very earnest Reverend Lewis Hensley had another matter more to mind, and to the surprise of the congregation he did not make for his stall but climbed the stairs to the pulpit.

Once there, he stood in stern and forbidding silence until the choir and the two assisting curates had taken their places. When he did speak there was an undertone of anger in his voice.

'Listen, and listen carefully, to what I have to say!' he said sternly. 'Some of you here this morning, perhaps nearly all of you, will have heard of the strange rumours coming out of the village of Ickleford. A few of you, and I hope it is only a few, may have come to believe that history is about to repeat itself.

'It is not! I assure you it is not! There will be no second coming of Jesus Christ in that village on Christmas Day!

'Both the local vicar and I have questioned the young woman concerned in these rumours. She has convinced both of us that the child which she is bearing was not conceived in any supernatural manner but has come about in the normal course of wedlock.

'She has also sworn on the Bible that she has had no strange visitations, nor has she had any curious visions.

'She believes the child will be a normal one in every way and hopes, as I do, that this nonsense will cease at once.

'That is all I have to say and I hope that it will suffice!'

The vicar then glared around the church before beginning his descent of the pulpit steps. The watching Mansell was smiling inwardly. It was certainly going to be no virgin birth. The examination he had made of Mary before she had married Joseph Fostring had revealed that but he had not told Joseph what he had discovered. He had deemed it unnecessary to do so. Mary could keep her own little secret!

Later in the service that morning the banns of marriage were called for the first time in respect of Peter Solomon Bonnamy and Amanda Radcliffe-Fostring.

8. No Angels Sang

Mid-afternoon of that cold but clear Christmas Eve Amanda drove up to Mansell's house in her dog-cart to request that the doctor return with her immediately to Ickleford to attend upon Mary.

'And you don't think it is a false alarm this time?' enquired Mansell, as he clambered up into the small vehicle and seated himself beside her.

'I think not. The pains, when I left, were coming fairly regularly.'

'Then you are probably right in calling me. I'm not sorry she has started. The sooner the child is born and seen to be normal the happier I shall be.' Mansell paused, and then asked hopefully as Amanda touched her pony's flank with her whip and they moved off, 'You'll be staying with me and seeing it through, I hope?'

'I shall.'

'Good!' Mansell sounded relieved. 'I don't think Isaiah's wife is likely to be of much help if I need it. She's far too old and–'

'Not only that,' said Amanda, 'Minnie has taken up her husband's silly notions, and for the past few days while I have been staying at Uncle Joseph's she had been treating Mary in a most ridiculous manner. She even refers to her as the "Blessed Mary" at times.'

'You left her looking after Mary?'

'I did.'

'Where was Isaiah? Was he about?'

'Isaiah? He was out on the village green in front of the cottage, standing on a box, and ranting on about the Day of the Second Coming being at hand and all sinners should repent without delay! There were about twenty other fools gathered around him and some of them were wailing and down on their knees on the damp grass!'

'They'll repent of that soon enough when the rheumatics come along!' said Mansell with a grim smile.

With their journey nearly completed they rounded the corner by the squat-towered church to take the path across the green. The twenty had become nearer a hundred and the numbers were swelling rapidly as the walkers they had passed on the road from Hitchin hurried in to join the excited throng.

'How on earth did all these people know that something was about to happen?' asked Amanda. 'I told no one anything on my way in to see you.'

'God alone knows!' said Mansell. 'Somehow they've got wind of it and they're turning up in their dozens. See that curious staring look on most of their faces? Damn it, why don't they take notice of what the clergy have told them? It's like some madness which taken hold of them. I dread to think what will happen if Mary has a girl and not a boy!'

Amanda skilfully guided the dog-cart through the crowd, many of whom turned to gape open-mouthed at the doctor and her. As they fetched up by the gateway to Joseph's cottage a youngish man with a friendly grin ran out of the next-door house and took the pony's head whilst Mansell and Amanda alighted.

'Thanks, Harry,' said Amanda, 'please put the pony away for me and see she's snug for the night in your stable.'

'Aye, 'Manda, I will that. It's likely there'll be a real sharpish frost by the way the sun's setting and it'll be proper cold soon.' Harry nodded in the direction of the gathering crowd, 'And that lot'll notice it if they're goin' ter 'ang about 'ere all bloody night. They ain't gonner like it, they ain't.'

There was a loud shout, clear above the clamour of voices, of 'Doctor Mansell! I wants yer!' and Isaiah pushed his way to the front of the assemblage. 'You wait a minute, Doctor!' he called, 'I wants a word with yer!' The old man's face was frenzied and there was a bubble of froth on his lips. 'Minnie's bin out and she's told me. Mary's need'n yer. She's bleedin' an yer should 'ave bin 'ere afore!'

'Well, I'm here now, you old fool, and the sooner I get to my patient the better. Get back to your ranting and let me get on with what needs doing!'

'Old fool, am I? Ranting, is it? It's you and yer like what's fools. Them as don't believe! That babbie on its way is special!

Most special what ever was! It's 'Im agin! Come agin like 'E said
'E would–'

'Nonsense, Isaiah! Stuff and bloody nonsense!' The exasperated Mansell turned on his heel and followed Amanda into the
cottage to find a worried-looking Joseph at the foot of the stairs.

'How is she?' asked Mansell.

'There's been a little blood, William, according to Minnie, and
I can't say she looks too good. I'm glad you're here, old friend.
I'm sure she'll be safe with you.'

'Hm! Then I'll go up straight away,' Mansell turned from
Joseph to Amanda, 'And you, my dear, had best bring me a
bowl of hot water, soap and a towel, as soon as you can.'

*   *   *

It was, as Mansell feared it would be, a breech birth, with the
buttocks presenting first.

By nine in the evening, and only by careful probing, he
managed to deliver the baby's legs and part of its torso. The
arms were extended, making it difficult to free the shoulders.
After further probing, and amid Mary's screaming, he was able
to release first the left and then the right arm.

'God!' he murmured to Amanda, breathing a sigh of relief and
wiping the sweat from his forehead, 'Now for the head, but I'll
give her and myself a brief respite before I try it.'

Taking the towel being held out to him by Amanda he wiped
the blood from his hands and went to the window. Pulling aside
the curtains he could see that a huge bonfire had been lit in the
centre of the Green and many people were huddling around
the blaze to warm themselves. One large group were gathered
around a wheezing harmonium and were singing a carol. It was
'Hark the Herald Angels Sing' and he smiled wryly before closing
the curtains and saying in a low voice to Amanda, 'There'll be
precious few angels singing tonight, I'm afraid.'

'No? You mean?'

'The chances are I shan't save both of them! One possibly,
two, no.'

Isaiah's wife, entering the room at that moment with another bowl of hot water, must have overhead his words. She looked at him fiercely before placing the bowl on the bedside table and hissed, 'Then, Doctor, it's the child what must be saved or God will never forgive you. Nor will Isaiah! Nor me! Nor will all them what waits outside. If you don't save 'Im, 'E can't save us an' we shall all be took by the flames 'cos we're all of us sinners!'

Mansell returned to his task, saying nothing to the old woman. His mind had already been made up and it was Mary, but a terribly weakened Mary, who survived the next horrifying twenty minutes. When she was safe, and had gone into a heavily sedated sleep, he took up the woefully mutilated corpse of the tiny boy child and wrapped it completely in a towel before laying it in the carved cradle at the foot of the bed. Amanda was weeping but Minnie was glowering at Mansell with crazy, hate-filled eyes.

'You killed 'Im!' she suddenly screeched. 'You killed 'Im yer did!'

'No, he didn't!' said Amanda fiercely. 'The doctor did everything he could to save both of them and you mustn't say such things!'

'I shall! I shall! I shall tell 'em what he did! I saw it! Saw it with my own eyes!' Minnie's voice rose to a shrill screaming and, crossing to where the sadly dejected and silent Mansell stood, she spat in his face before scuttling out of the bedroom.

Her haste was her undoing. She tripped and fell headlong down the stairs. There was a high-pitched cry of terror as she tumbled, followed by a thud and an ominous silence.

Mansell and Amanda looking down from the top of the stairs saw Joseph bending over the huddled form below. The carpenter turned his concerned face upwards and called, 'She's hurt, William, but she's still breathing, so she ain't broke her neck, I reckon.'

'Then she's been lucky,' said Mansell as he clattered down the stairs with Amanda in his wake. Minnie, as he gently turned her so that her face was uppermost, suddenly began to breathe stertorously and opened one eye, momentarily revealing a rolling eyeball. Mansell, after feeling each of her limbs, announced, 'She's got nothing broken as far as I can tell, Joseph, She's just knocked herself out. She'll be bruised but no real damage has been done. Give me a hand, man, and you, Amanda, and we'll move her to the settle in the kitchen and wait for her to come round.'

After Minnie had been laid on the high-backed bench with her head on a pillow, and she had been draped with a blanket, Joseph said, 'I heard what she was shouting, William. You've no need to tell me. The child was stillborn, wasn't he?'

'He was. I did what I could but–'

'Mary? Is she-?'

'As well as can be expected. She's had a bad time. A very bad time. But she's young and she's strong and she'll recover very quickly. And, let me tell you, Joseph, she'll be none the worse for what she's been through tonight.'

'Can I see her?'

'You can but she's asleep now and will be for the next twelve hours. I've given her something, something quite strong.'

'The child? Where's the child?'

'I've laid the body in the cradle.'

'Tomorrow I'll make a box for him, poor mite.'

'Yes. But give Mary a chance to hold him in her arms and love him before laying him to rest. It will be better for her if she does.'

Joseph wiped the tears from his eyes with the back of his hand and then said, 'There's something I'd better do now. Them outside, they'll have to know, won't they?'

'Shall I tell them?' asked Mansell.

'No, William! It had best be me. I'll tell 'em.'

Joseph lit a lantern and opened his front door to stand with the light held high above his head to shine on his face. He was an impressive sight and almost immediately a silence fell upon those who were nearest to the cottage garden gate. The silence spread rapidly across the Green and the singing and shouting died away as the crowd awaited Joseph's announcement.

Joseph's voice, when he eventually spoke, was resonant and clear and carried well on the night's cold air.

'Listen!' he said. 'Listen! You wait tidings of the birth of a child! I bring you these tidings but they are not good! The child was stillborn-!'

A great sad groan swelled and rose from the assemblage and some began to weep and cry out hysterically. Sobbing could still be heard when, after a minute or so, Joseph went on to say, 'It was a boy but it was not the Jesus child you have been waiting for. It was just my son and Mary's son and not divine. Now go away and leave us in peace to bury our dead child!'

The carpenter did not turn at once to enter his cottage but stood and watched, as the people, scarcely murmuring, seemed to drift away into the darkness of the night, leaving the flickering flames from the fast dying bonfire to light the place where so many had been. In what was nothing more than a few moments none except an old, bent-backed man remained.

'Come here, Isaiah!' commanded Joseph. 'Come here!'

Isaiah shuffled forward. When he was close enough Joseph's lantern reveal a deeply lined face ravaged by glistening tears. When Isaiah spoke his voice was choked.

'So I weren't right, Master?'

'No you weren't right, Isaiah. You were wrong. Very wrong.'

'Aye, I were. I reckons if it had been The Child it wouldn't 'ave died. It couldn't 'ave, could it?'

'No. It couldn't have.'

'I've been a fool, Master. A fool, but I just longed for it to be 'Im, Master. 'Im comin' again like 'E primised 'E would.'

'But it wasn't, Isaiah. It never was, and now it's all over it's best forgotten. Tomorrow you must help me make a small coffin for my son that is dead.'

''Elp yer, Master? Yes, I'll 'elp yer willin'-like. There's a nice piece of oak, just about right, on the rack near my bench an' we can do 'im proud.' Isaiah paused and then asked, 'What about Mary? Is she all right, poor girl?'

'She's sleeping, Isaiah. Sleeping soundly.'

'Is Minnie with her?'

'No. She's not and you'd best come into the house. We shall want you to help get her to your place.'

'Why, Master? Ain't she well?'

'She's had a bad fall on the stairs and hurt herself. As soon as the Doctor says we can move her we'll get her home.'

Isaiah followed Joseph into the cottage and through to the kitchen where they found Mansell and Amanda with the already conscious Minnie. But it was a Minnie who no longer glared at Mansell with hostile eyes but one who regarded him with a somewhat puzzled expression. She was saying, 'So what you're a-tellin' me is that 'ad 'e lived 'e wouldn't 'ave been right in the 'ead?'

Mansell was nodding. 'I'm afraid not, Minnie.'

'Then what 'appened is for the best then?'

'Yes.'

Minnie looked past Mansell to Joseph and Isaiah standing in the doorway. 'You know what Doctor's been telling me?'

'Yes, Minnie, we do.' replied Joseph sadly. 'So it was for the best and now it's best not mentioned again. So let's hear no more of it and if you feel up to it we'll get you home to your bed.'

'And,' said Mansell, 'you'd better keep to it for a few days and be thankful its only bruises you'll be nursing and not broken bones!'

When Amanda, Joseph and Isaiah had departed with Minnie, half-carrying her across the Green to the Birds' cottage beyond the church, Mansell went upstairs with the intention of repacking his carpetbag. He felt tired, very tired, and as he entered the bedroom where Mary lay peacefully sleeping he yawned prodigiously. Shrugging off his weariness as best he could, he washed, dried and wrapped the ugly implement he had been forced to use to free the child, and packed it in the bottom of the bag. Then, feeling completely exhausted, he sat down in the armchair, close to the crib, and closed his eyes.

Fifteen minutes later, when Amanda entered the room, she discovered him fast asleep. Smiling to herself she fetched a blanket and carefully covered him with it.

1858

Postscript

Buff Birker was hanged at Hertford Gaol on Wednesday the twenty-fourth day of March 1858 for the murder of Simeon Radcliffe. Only his mother mourned his passing. On that same morning, it was a cold and blustery one, Mary Timmins went to Mansell's house and found her father dead in his bed. There was a small, empty phial on the floor close to his bed at which she sniffed and then sadly shook her head. Doctor Hawkins, when she called him in, also sniffed at the phial and he too shook his head.

'Best say nothing, Mary,' he said. 'Say nothing to anyone and let him be buried with your mother in consecrated ground. You knew he had cancer?'

'I did, Doctor. He told me so just after Christmas.'

'Then,' said Hawkins, 'so far as we and the rest of the world are concerned he had died of it and there will be no need for a coroner's inquest. Your father was a good man, Mary, and if he chose to die without pain or distress we'll not have him condemned.'

The funeral took place a week later and, despite the bitterness of the day, it was well attended. The Mansell family in full was by the graveside, so too were many of the town's notables and even more of those less notable. Among the latter was a group of white-aproned, black-shawled women from the Back Street slums, shepherded there by Lil Bongers. To Big Lil and them, Mansell had never been a quack but their own friendly, family doctor. Someone who had cured and eased their ills where he could at little cost. Someone who, for a few shillings, had been with them, and helped them with caring skill, through the pangs of bringing their babies into the grey world of poverty, dirt, disease and even depravity which was likely to be their lot in

223

life. Hardened though they were, many of the women were weeping.

Squire Radcliffe was there, with Amanda and her new husband, Peter Bonnamy, by her side. At the short service in St Mary's Church before the committal Delme-Radcliffe read a passage of his own choosing from the *Aprocrypha*'s Book of Ecclesiasticus. It was the passage beginning, 'Honour a physician with the honour due to him for the uses you may have of him: for the Lord has created him', and Amanda, who had never heard it before had listened entranced. Later had come the verse, 'The Lord has created medicines out of the earth; and he that is wise will not abhor them,' and she had remembered the occasion when she had found Mansell gathering wild herbs in a lane near Charlton hamlet; he had told her then that he was convinced every illness mankind suffered could be cured or alleviated by herbal means if we could only unlock more of Nature's secrets.

She was recalled from her reverie by her husband's light touch on her arm and she lifted her tear-filled eyes to see the coffin being gently lowered into the grave.

Bibliography

HINE Reginald L. *The History of Hitchin* (Vol.I 1927, Vol II 1929) *Hitchin Worthies* (1932)
Confessions of an Uncommon Attorney (1945)

LUCAS William *A Quaker Diary* (1934 2 Vols)

GADD Pat and PIGRAM Ron *Hitchin Inns and Incidents* (1978)

PIGRAM Ron *Strange Happenings in Hitchin and North   Hertfordshire* (1978)

FOSTER Anthony M. *The Book of Hitchin* (1981)